DEN OF THIEVES

Julia Golding

First published in Great Britain in 2007 by
Egmont UK Ltd
This Large Print edition published 2012
by AudioGO Ltd
by arrangement with
Egmont UK Ltd

ISBN: 978 1445 826264

www.juliagolding.co.uk

British Library Cataloguing in Publication Data available

Printed and bound in Great Britain by
MPG Books Group Limited

❧ The Critics ❧

'Not tonight, Josephine: I'm too busy reading Cat Royal'—NAPOLEON BONAPARTE

'Publish her and be damned—it's revolutionary hogwash!'—THE DUKE OF WELLINGTON

'It is the Right of every man to read her books'—TOM PAINE

'Cat Royal? She provides the oxygen of wit for the brain'—ANTOINE LAURENT LAVOISIER, SCIENTIST

'I was very disappointed: there's not a moment of Germanic obscurity or sublimity in it. I understood every word'—IMMANUEL KANT, PHILOSOPHER

'Cat Royal's life is like a fairytale, full of light and darkness'—THE BROTHERS GRIMM

'Who? I have no time for such frivolities while there is a wagon of aristocrats to behead'—MAXIMILIEN ROBESPIERRE

'Her wit has a cutting edge'—DR GUILLOTINE

'Like me, she sounds mad, bad and dangerous to know—just my type'—LORD BYRON

'She takes the dead corpse of history and breathes new life into it'—MARY SHELLEY

'Not a moment of drowsy numbness when reading her—she's all dance and Provençal song, and sunburnt mirth!'—JOHN KEATS

'What! She's not still writing, is she? I thought I asked someone to arrest her!'—RT HON WILLIAM PITT, THE PRIME MINISTER

🖎 A Note to the Reader 🖎

Considering the high tide of feelings running against our French neighbours at present, I should warn my reader that you will find no such prejudices in these pages. I, Cat Royal, late of Drury Lane Theatre, am a declared friend of the revolution (most of the time). If you only like to dine with absolute monarchs on good old English roast beef, suet pudding and beer, perhaps you should look elsewhere for satisfaction. In these pages you'll eat with the people on a meal of highly-spiced French adventure, washed down with a sparkling draught of dance.
Will you take a seat at my table, *mes amis*?

Cat Royal

Principal Characters

LONDON

MISS CATHERINE 'CAT' ROYAL—ward of the Theatre Royal, Drury Lane, your guide

MR PEDRO AMAKYE (FORMERLY MR PEDRO HAWKINS)—ex-slave, talented violinist

LORD FRANCIS (FRANK)—sartorially challenged heir to a dukedom

LADY ELIZABETH (LIZZIE)—his sister, in love with a rebel lord

THE DUKE OF AVON—peer of the realm

THE DUCHESS OF AVON—formerly the singer known as The Bristol Nightingale

MR JOSEPH—loyal footman to Lord Francis

MR RICHARD BRINSLEY SHERIDAN—man of many talents, theatre owner

MRS REID—wardrobe mistress

MADAME BEAUFORT—mistress of the ballet troupe bound for her native land

MR TWEADLE—devious bookseller

MR NOKES—his assistant with personal hygiene issues

MR SYD FLETCHER—Covent Garden gang leader

MR BILLY SHEPHERD—lowlife thug who unfortunately is on the up and up

MR JONATHAN (JOHNNY) FITZROY (AKA CAPTAIN SPARKLER)—British peer turned American citizen, cartoonist

M. JEAN-FRANÇOIS (J-F) THILAND—King of Thieves of the Palais Royal and a fine dancer to boot

MARIE and ANNETTE—ladies of the King of Thieves' Court

M. IBRAHIM—the charming but perilous Bishop of the Notre Dame Thieves

M. SCARFACE LUC—right-hand man to the Bishop, who has a powerful squeeze

M. MARIA-AUGUSTE VESTRIS—principal dancer at the Opera, popular idol of the people

M. RENARD THILAND—retired thief lord, concierge and grandfather to J-F

M. JEAN-SYLVAIN BAILLY—Mayor of Paris, astronomer

Ballerinas, *sans-culottes*, national guardsmen, French royal family, etc., etc.

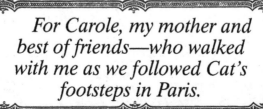

For Carole, my mother and best of friends—who walked with me as we followed Cat's footsteps in Paris.

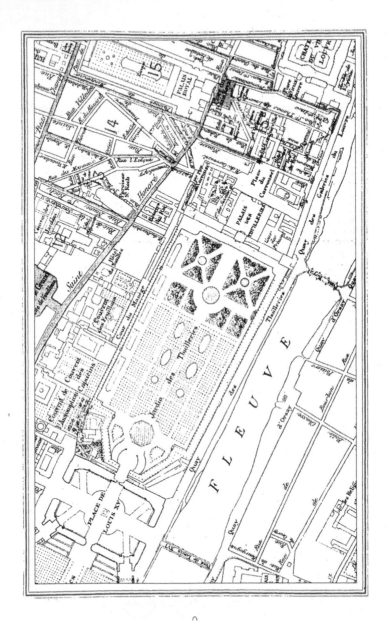

London and Paris, 1791

Curtain rises.

PROLOGUE

MOVING ON

In the theatre, there comes a moment when we bid goodbye to a play. The scripts are put back on the shelf, the scenery dismantled, the actors move on to new roles. Yesterday, my life at the Theatre Royal, Drury Lane, came to the end of its run.

What can I say to you, Reader? For me, everything is over.

I admit that I'm scared. I don't know what I shall do. I wasn't prepared for such a sudden termination to the life I thought I was going to lead. And so strange to think that the curtain was brought down with such a simple question.

Mr Sheridan caught me in the corridor backstage as I carried the actresses' wigs out of the powder room. 'Cat, come here. Tell me what you think.'

From the stage came the sounds of the orchestra tuning up. My friend Pedro would already be in his place, sitting with the other violinists. Counting the audience we were expecting a full house. Backstage was abuzz with excitement as the moment of performance approached. I really didn't have time to linger but my patron, Mr Sheridan, could not be denied. He hauled me into his office, snatched the tray, and dumped it unceremoniously on the floor.

'Watch it, sir! I'll get skinned if anything happens to those!' I protested as I tried to prevent many guineas' worth of powdered curls tumbling on to the hearth.

'No, no, forget about those,' he said, heedless in his enthusiasm. 'I want you to be one of the first to see the plans,' and he hooked me by the elbow and propelled me to the desk.

'Fifteen minutes!' called the stage manager outside. Three actors rushed by, not yet in costume. They'd obviously lingered too long in the Players' Tavern.

On the scuffed leather surface of the desk lay a sheaf of crackling white parchment scored with lines and tiny numbers.

'So?' Mr Sheridan asked, rubbing his hands eagerly, looking across at me, his brown eyes sparkling.

He evidently wanted my opinion—a fact that I would have found flattering if I hadn't been in such a rush to deliver the wigs; the actresses would not thank me if I made them late for their first entrance. I had better get this over with. I turned my mind to the papers in front of me. It was clearly a design for a grand building of some sort—a palace perhaps. Maybe Mr Sheridan's extravagant friend the Prince of Wales had yet another construction project in his sights?

'Er . . . what is it?' I asked.

'It's Drury Lane, of course.' My patron's flushed face beamed happily. Was he drunk already?

I took a closer look. I could now see the vast stage and auditorium, but this wasn't my theatre. None of my familiar landmarks were here; he must be joking. 'No, it's not, sir. Where's the Sparrow's Nest? Where's the scenery store?'

'You don't understand, Cat. Not *this* worn-out pile of bricks and cracked plaster,' he waved dismissively at the ceiling. 'These are the plans for the *new* Theatre Royal—one fit for our modern age that will rise from the ashes of the old.'

Mr Sheridan had often talked about sprucing up the theatre when he had the money—he never did, so I had always let these ramblings wash over me.

'Very nice, sir,' I said non-committally, wondering if I could get on my way. In fact, I thought the plans looked terrible—they represented a vast, soulless place where actors would seem like objects viewed the wrong way down a telescope, if I had understood the drawings correctly. It would kill the theatre—and probably quite a few of our leading actors as they tried to make themselves heard in that space. It was a good job that it would never be built.

'Ten minutes!' called the stage manager. 'Light the stage candles.'

'I'm glad you like it, Cat,' said Mr Sheridan, caressing the papers, 'because this evening I'm going to announce to the cast that the last performance within these walls will be on 4th June. When we close, the demolition crew will move in to knock the old place down.'

'What!' I felt as if he had just tipped a kettle of scalding water on me.

'I know that is very soon, but I didn't want to make a premature announcement. I couldn't get a builder for the job until I'd put the money on the table. Apparently, my reputation for not being prompt about settling my account had preceded

3

me.' He chuckled and smoothed his white silk cravat fixed in place with a diamond-headed pin.

This was serious.

'What, Cat? You don't look pleased.'

'How long will the theatre be closed?'

'Oh, I don't know—a couple of seasons perhaps. We're not talking about a refit here—this is a complete rebuild.'

'A couple of seasons! But that's years!'

He darted a look at me out of the corner of his eye. 'I know it's going to mean a lot of changes for everyone. We'll have to camp out at the King's Theatre for a while, but I'm sure the company will all pull together when they understand what we stand to gain.'

'I see.' I said no more. My home was about to be destroyed: the Sparrow's Nest, my foothold in the world for as long as I could remember was to be turned into rubble; the playground backstage that I'd shared with Pedro was about to be reduced to dust. Where would we go? At least Pedro had his master, the musical director—as an apprentice, he would be looked after. But I, as an orphan under the protection of the theatre, I'd been allowed a corner no one else wanted. In a new theatre, where no one knew me, would I be so fortunate again?

Mr Sheridan must have been following some of my thoughts from the expressions on my face.

'When this is all over, Cat, I think you'll recognize it was for the best. You can't bed down in the costume store any more like some stray kitten. You're a young lady now. You need to find proper lodgings for yourself—start to make your own way.'

With what? I wondered. I worked in exchange for

4

bed and board. I'd never had any money to call my own.

'I have every confidence that you'll fall on your feet as normal. You're not called Cat for nothing,' he continued cheerfully, ruffling my ginger hair and dislodging my cap.

I knew that for my own good I had to be practical. I couldn't indulge myself and let out the wail of grief that welled up inside me. 'Can I move with the company?' I asked. 'Will you start paying me wages?'

Mr Sheridan began tidying away the plans. 'We'll see. Money's a bit tight at the moment, what with the cost of the new building and the removal. Have a word with Mrs Reid—she might be able to squeeze something out of the wardrobe budget for you. Though I must admit I rather thought that you were going to make your fortune by your pen. I understood that the Duke of Avon was helping you find a publisher.'

He'd hit upon a sore spot.

'His grace has tried, but the booksellers find my stuff too shocking. They've told me to write about love and female duty—not boxing and battles.'

Mr Sheridan laughed. 'Don't you listen to them, Cat. You have to put up with your fair share of rejection as a writer if you want to succeed. Keep trying—you'll find your audience one day.'

'Yes, when I'm six feet under and women are equals to men—that means never,' I muttered sullenly.

'I wouldn't be so sure of that,' said Mr Sheridan, toying with the watch chain that looped across his broad expanse of waistcoat. 'It may happen sooner than you think. Events in France are transforming

5

things that, when I was your age, were thought to be untouchable. Maybe your sex will be the next to share in the benefits of the wind of change that is sweeping across Europe.'

Mr Sheridan was talking politics now. The theatre was only really a hobby to him: his real career lay in parliament so it didn't take much to jog him on to this track. I'd be getting a full-blown speech about progress and revolution if I didn't watch out.

'We'll see, sir,' I said humbly, bobbing a curtsey. 'May I go now?'

'Yes, yes, off you go, child. And don't worry: we'll make sure you are all right one way or another,' he said, leafing through the plans once more.

I picked up the tray of wigs and retreated from the office, full of doom. I knew my patron better than to trust to his vague promises. Many a shopkeeper had spent hours besieging him for payment only to be fobbed off with hints of money in the future.

'Cat, where's my wig?' screeched Miss Stageldoir as I pushed my way into the bustling dressing room. Half-clothed dancers clustered around the mirrors, elbowing each other out of the way to plaster their faces with make-up, gossiping to each other in quick-fire French.

Well, if I was going to persuade everyone I was an indispensable part of the backstage crew, I could afford to make no enemies by rudeness—even Miss Stageldoir, a middling order actress of indifferent talent.

'Sorry, miss. I was delayed by Mr Sheridan,' I replied meekly, battling through the ballerinas to reach her.

Miss Stageldoir curled her pretty lips sceptically. She had a patch on her cheek like a squashed fly, hiding a pox mark that spoiled her alabaster skin (this too came out of a bottle—she was really as red-faced as a laundry woman when seen in daylight). 'Put it on me then, girl.'

I lifted the wig from the tray, trying to blow off some of the soot before she noticed, and lowered it on to her head like the Archbishop of Canterbury crowning the king. She stared at her reflection.

'What have you done, you slattern!' She wheeled round and slapped my face hard. 'You've ruined it!'

Mrs Reid bustled forward to break up the commotion. 'What's the matter, Miss Stageldoir?' she said soothingly. I rubbed my cheek, boiling with resentment, but bit my tongue.

'The dirty little beggar's spoiled my wig! How can I go on stage looking like a chimney sweep?'

'I can mend that in a trice with some powder. Just sit tight.' Mrs Reid clucked and fussed over Miss Stageldoir's head. She enveloped the actress in a cloud of white dust as she repaired the damage. 'Look! As good as new.'

'Hmm.' Miss Stageldoir turned her face this way and that. 'I suppose it'll do, but make sure you punish the girl: it could have ruined my performance.'

As if it needed me to spoil it—she did that well enough herself.

'I will, you can be certain of that.' Mrs Reid glared at me.

This was so unfair!

'But it wasn't me, Mrs Reid. Mr Sheridan dropped the tray when he took me into his office.'

Mrs Reid raised her eyebrows, taking in my

7

crooked cap. 'What was he doing with you in his office on your own?'

Two of the dancers giggled as they brushed past. I blushed and tugged my cap back into place. 'He wanted to show me his plans.'

'Oh yes?'

'Yes, plans for the new theatre,' I continued loudly, savouring the moment when I would fire my broadside. 'He's closing Drury Lane and knocking it down. On 4th June to be precise. We've all got to move.'

You could have heard a pin drop. In fact, several did tumble from Miss Stageldoir's head as she jerked back in her chair to stare at me in disbelief.

'What did you say?' she hissed.

'It's the end. Drury Lane is doomed. The curtain falls. Can I put it any clearer for you . . . miss?'

She missed my rudeness in her surprise. 'But where are we going? Will we lose our positions?' she exclaimed.

An excited babble broke out in all quarters as the cast began to discuss their fate. Sooty wigs forgotten, the news spread as dancers darted off to whisper it to their boyfriends among the stage-hands. Soon there was no corner of the theatre that did not know what was afoot, no doubt as Mr Sheridan had intended when he chose to tell me first.

'Five minutes to curtain up! Beginners, please,' called the stage manager as he tried to hush the hubbub behind the scenes.

Miss Stageldoir swept past me without a word, her velvet train leaving a trail in the powder. With a sigh, I picked up a broom to sweep the floor.

The orchestra began the overture as I made my

exit from an empty dressing room. There was no one to see me go as all eyes were now on the stage.

With leaden feet, I climbed the stairs to my lonely corner of the Sparrow's Nest, and huddled on my couch counting the days until I had to fly away.

Only twelve left.

Act I - In which our principal characters take flight with varying degrees of success . . .

Act I

SCENE 1—THE PROMISE

The following morning, Syd Fletcher, leader of Covent Garden's Butcher's Boys gang, spotted me passing the door of his father's shop.

'Oi, Cat!' he called, striding out on to the sun-drenched pavement and wiping his bloodied hands on his apron like Hercules returning from the slaughter of the lion. His hair shone gold in the dazzling light.

'Oh, hello, Syd,' I said, pausing to rub my brow with a handkerchief. I was wearing my best clothes and already sweltering in the heat. 'I can't stop: I've been invited to Frank and Lizzie's this morning. They're expecting me. Why don't you come too?'

'What, like this?' laughed Syd, spreading his arms wide to display his stained working clothes. 'Nah, Kitten. You look swell, all togged up in that white dress of yours; I'd lower the tone if I came with you.'

'But Frank and Lizzie would love to see you.'

He grinned and rubbed his yellow-bristled chin. 'Perhaps, but not like this. I'll see Frank happily enough down 'ere any day, but 'e won't want me sippin' tea and eatin' off china plates any more than I'd like to be there. Nah, dook's children 'ave their world and I 'ave mine: that's 'ow it is and 'ow it's meant to be.'

'So what about me? Are you saying I shouldn't be mixing with the likes of them?' I suddenly felt very inadequate in my cheap muslin dress, knowing that Lizzie would doubtless be beautifully decked out

11

and there might even be other visitors quick to notice my humble origins.

Syd beckoned me to take a seat in the shade, first wiping the top of a barrel with his apron. The whole street had a tired, languid feel, like an old dog stretched out panting in the sun. Carriers' carts rumbled wearily by, raising clouds of choking dust. The gutters smelt foul. 'Course not, Cat. You're an exception to the rule, you are.'

That made me feel a bit better. I was, after all, going to visit my friends, not take part in a fashion parade. Lizzie and Frank wouldn't care what I turned up in. Their mother had been an opera singer before her marriage to the Duke of Avon so her children had not inherited the usual prejudices of people of their rank. They did not regard me as beneath their notice.

'So, what did you want me for, Syd? Was it about the theatre?' I wondered how far the rumour about its closure had spread since last night.

'What about the theatre?'

Not very far yet then.

'Mr Sheridan's knocking it down to build a bigger one.'

'What 'e want to go and do that for?' asked Syd in amazement.

'The march of progress, Syd, the winds of change,' I said ironically.

'The march of what? What you goin' on about?'

'Put it another way, some fool's lent him the money and my patron wants to make his mark on London—leave something for him to be remembered by.' I was feeling ungenerous to Mr Sheridan today. 'Oh yes, and I s'pose there might be the little matter of making a bigger profit by selling

12

more tickets.'

Syd whistled and shook his head. 'That's a rum do—spending a fortune to make one.'

'I couldn't have put it better myself.'

'But what about you, Cat? Where are you goin' to live now, eh, when they knock your theatre down?'

I shrugged, not wanting him to think I couldn't look after myself. Pedro had asked me the very same question when I'd broken the news to him the night before. But I couldn't bear to confess my worries to two of my best friends. Pedro was in no position to help me and as for Syd, he'd never let me in his gang if I appeared incapable of sorting out even this simple matter. I have my pride.

'I don't know yet, but I'll find somewhere,' I said more cheerfully than I felt.

Syd nodded. 'Mr Sheridan won't let you down, not after all you've done for 'im in the past.'

I didn't want to tell him that this was exactly the kind of matter over which my patron was entirely unreliable. I just gave Syd a non-committal smile and got up to go.

' 'Ere, Cat, wait 'alf a tick. I 'aven't told you my news yet.'

'What's that?'

A country girl walked past with a tray of strawberries and gave Syd the eye. He winked back then blushed when he remembered who he was with.

'I . . . er . . . I'm leavin' London for a bit.'

'No!' I was astounded. Neither Syd nor I ever left town. Our bones were made from the dust of its streets and our blood from the water of the Thames. I couldn't have been more surprised if he'd announced he was going to the moon.

13

Syd was pleased to see that I was shocked by his announcement. 'Just for a bit like, Kitten. Just for the summer. I'm goin' on tour with me manager. We're goin' to take on all-comers at the fairs up and down the country. 'E says there's a mint of money to be made in boxin'. 'E promises it'll set me up for me own place in the autumn if all goes well. I'll be able to think about settlin' down.'

I made a sceptical snort. Syd's face fell. 'What? You don't like the idea of settlin' down? Me startin' a boxin' academy?'

'No, Syd, not that. It's just that I don't like your manager. I don't trust him as far as I could throw him—which, as it's my muscles we're talking about, isn't very far at all.'

Syd turned away and ran his hands through his hair in exasperation. 'Don't start that again, Cat. What you got against Mick Bailey but his bad taste in jackets, eh? I know 'e looks a sharp one, but 'as 'e ever let me down, I ask you?'

'He hasn't had the chance. You've been on a winning streak.'

'It's more than a streak, Cat,' said Syd, bobbing on his toes and making a jab at his shadow. 'I'm good, bleedin' marvellous, 'e tells me.'

'For once, I agree with him. Just be careful.'

'Course I will, you daft Kitten,' he said, making a playful punch in the direction of my ribs. 'I'm a big lad. I can look after meself, you know.'

'I know.'

We'd been friends for so many years, but I couldn't see the grown-up Syd without remembering the boy who'd taken me under his wing when I was an infant. My earliest memories consisted of me trailing after him, pulling the little

14

wooden horse he'd made me, or sitting unnoticed at his side when he played marbles with the boys. Later, I climbed the apple trees with him when we went scrumping in the Reverend James's orchard and fled on his heels when we were spotted. Even then, he'd taken the punishment for me, saying it was his fault for leading me astray. I knew that he'd always been able to take care of himself and the others under his protection. It was only recently that I had come to appreciate that he was also sharper than he looked: a gentle, slow manner disguised an astute grasp of street politics. I was going to miss him.

'So, when are you leaving?'

'Monday. I'm puttin' Nick in charge of the boys. I won't let Billy Shepherd get on to my patch while I'm out of the way, don't you worry.' He stopped bouncing about and gave me a stern look. 'You not 'eard from 'im again, 'ave you, Cat?'

I shook my head, shivering as if the day had suddenly turned cold. Billy 'Boil' Shepherd, gang leader of the Rookeries mob, had both tried to kill me and saved my life in the last eighteen months. I wasn't eager to find out what else he had in store for me on our next encounter. But still hanging over me was the little matter of my promise to Billy, made when trying to stop Pedro being kidnapped by his old slave master. I hadn't heard anything more about this since that cold winter night on the Thames when I had given my word that I'd repay the debt I owed Billy. I had started to hope that he'd forgotten.

'No, I think he must've lost interest in me.'

'Good.' Syd gave me a hand up from my seat. 'Glad to 'ear it, Cat. 'E's not stopped 'is nasty 'abit

15

of dumpin' his enemies in the river with rocks tied to their ankles. Very best thing a girl like you can do with a lad like that is keep well out of 'is way.' The clock of a nearby church struck the hour. 'You'd better be off. I've made you late, 'aven't I?'

'Don't worry about that. I'm pleased you let me know your plans yourself.' I waved farewell as I walked briskly off towards the market.

I hardly noticed the streets separating Covent Garden from St James as I pondered the news. Syd leaving home? That didn't feel right—how would he manage away from his friends? And—a selfish thought slid into my mind—why did he have to go now? Just when I needed him more than ever.

*　　*　　*

A cool breeze found its way across Hyde Park to Grosvenor Square, fluttering the gold tassels of the canopy stretched over our heads. Lady Elizabeth and I were reclining in chairs, raspberry sherbets in hand, enjoying the shade of the oriental booth erected in the garden in the middle of the square. Her chestnut hair was plaited in a fashionable Grecian style, caught high off her neck, and she was dressed in a beautiful lightweight pale blue gown. Tiny navy slippers decorated with seed pearls peeped out from under the hem. If I'd met Hercules outside the Butcher's shop earlier, it wasn't hard to imagine that I was now lying beside Helen of Troy. Out in the noonday sunshine, Lord Francis and Pedro were playing a very competitive game of Pall Mall. Lulled by the regular 'clock-clock' of mallet striking balls, I had begun to doze off when a row erupted.

16

'That ball went through!' protested Lord Francis.

'Didn't,' challenged Pedro. My African friend tilted his head defiantly up at his lordship. Frank had sprouted several inches during the spring and, unless you knew him well, struck an imposing figure with his shock of curly dark hair.

'Did!'

'Did not . . . my lord,' said Pedro archly, bowing low.

'Did, you . . . you musical dandy!'

Pedro grinned, brushing off his impeccable yellow and blue livery. 'Did not, you sartorial disgrace to the name of Avon.' Frank's shirt was hanging out and his cravat untied. He never liked conforming to the high standards expected of the heir to a dukedom.

'Lizzie, Cat, tell Pedro that it went through!' Frank appealed to us.

'I'm not getting involved,' said Lizzie wisely, waving her fan at her brother. 'Both of you need your heads examining, if you ask me, for standing out there in that heat for so long.'

'Cat! You tell him.'

I laughed. 'You are an outrageous cheat, Frank. It missed by inches. Just because you were blocking the hoop from Pedro's view, doesn't mean we don't know what you were up to.'

Frank threw his mallet on to the ground in a huff. 'I tell you, it went through as sweet as a nut. If you were a boy again, Cat, I'd beat you for calling me a cheat.'

'Frank!' exclaimed Lizzie. 'When are you going to start treating Cat properly?' Frank shrugged and helped himself to a glass of sherbet. 'I'm serious,' Lizzie continued. 'You've set the tone with the

17

servants, you know—they all treat her like an honorary boy in the house, taking all sorts of liberties with her.'

Frank gave me a quick look then turned away to watch Pedro who was collecting up the balls with his mallet. 'What sort of liberties?' he asked stiffly.

'Lizzie, it's nothing—,' I tried to interrupt. I knew what she was going to say and blushed to be reminded of my latest indiscretion. There was something about being in the splendid surroundings of the Duke of Avon's residence that made me incapable of behaving as I knew I should.

'No, he should hear what he's done,' said Lizzie firmly. 'Only last week, Joseph jumped out on her in the library and pushed her along on one of the ladders so she fell off and broke Father's bust of Voltaire.'

Frank laughed. 'Oh, that's all right then. I thought you meant something far more scandalous.'

'Well, to some people that would be, Frank. And do you know what Joseph told me when I challenged him about it?'

Frank shrugged.

'He said, in his best Joseph manner, that he "couldn't resist it, my lady" and that he "knew Miss Catherine liked it". In his defence, I should say he offered to pay for the breakage out of his wages. I refused, of course—the bust was an ugly thing that none of us really liked. Now don't tell me that you haven't encouraged your footman to behave like that?'

'Lizzie, I—' I began.

'No, Cat, this is between me and Frank. It's not that I want to spoil your fun but you're both growing up fast. My brother needs to treat you with respect

18

or, well, you might find it very difficult in the future.'

I didn't want to listen to her. So many things were changing; I couldn't keep pace. Behaviour that I had got away with just six months ago was now thought immodest for a young lady of my age. Everyone seemed to expect me to grow up, make my own way.

'I'm sorry, Lizzie, I'll try to behave better when I'm at your house,' I said, unsuccessfully trying to hide my frustration.

'Oh Cat, I'm not scolding you,' said Lizzie with a smile. 'We all like you as you are. I'm just trying to drum some manners into my incorrigible brother.'

'I stand corriged,' said Frank with a bow. 'Miss Royal, if you would be so kind as to move your delicate toes from the end of the seat so that my sitting apparatus can place itself in the shade, I would be most obliged.'

Even I had to laugh at that. Lizzie poured two more glasses of sherbet and the four of us sat at our ease, sipping them appreciatively.

'So, you're both leaving Drury Lane and Syd's off on tour, is he?' asked Frank. 'I wish I could go with him.'

'We all seem to be on the move,' said Lizzie.

'Oh? Are you going to the country soon?' I enquired. The Avons usually spent the summer on their estate near Bath.

'No, it's better than that,' Lizzie replied, her blue eyes shining with a light I hadn't seen since a certain gentleman of her acquaintance had left England. 'Our cousin, the Comtesse de Plessis, has invited us to Paris. She thought that Father, as a friend of the revolution, might enjoy the 14th July celebrations.'

19

'What do they get up to?'

'Since the people of Paris stormed the Bastille prison on that day two years ago, they have begun to hold an annual holiday. They have music and processions—it all sounds wonderful.'

'Lizzie wouldn't think it was so wonderful if a certain foreign dignitary wasn't going to be there,' added Frank in an undertone. 'I fear Cousin Rebecca is playing cupid.'

'Oh?' asked Pedro.

'Don't tell me, Johnny's going to be in Paris!' I exclaimed.

Lizzie nodded shyly, her face wreathed in smiles. 'He's been sent by an American newspaper to record the proceedings.'

'Lizzie and Lord Johnny have been plotting this between them for some time,' Frank continued.

'Not exactly plotting, Frank,' corrected Lizzie. 'Just taking advantage of a happy coincidence.'

As pleased as I was to hear that the two young lovers were to be reunited, I couldn't help but feel disappointed that my friend Johnny was going to be so near and yet I wouldn't have a chance to see him. Johnny still had the little matter of an arrest warrant hanging over his head for treasonous cartoons—he would be unable to return to England for many years.

'Are you going too, Frank?' I asked enviously.

'Lord no, Cat. I'd be quite the wallflower. Mama and Lizzie will be shopping all day, Father talking to the political chaps. In the evening, Lizzie will be billing and cooing with Johnny and my honoured parents going to dinner parties—I'd be in everyone's way. No, I've been exiled to the family pile.' He gave me a sour smile.

20

'What nonsense, Frank! You know that's not why you've got to go to Boxton. You need to prepare for your college examination,' said Lizzie, prodding her brother with her fan. 'Father doesn't want you to get by on your rank but on your merit.'

'And unfortunately, according to my tutors at Westminster School, my merit is not sufficient,' Frank added sorrowfully. 'I wish I had your feel for Latin, Cat: it would make my life much easier and the summer much shorter.'

'And I wish we could swap places,' I replied, thinking that I wouldn't mind spending the summer on a country estate improving my language skills— it would certainly be better than the uncertain future I was facing in London.

'Unfortunately, I think my tutor might notice this time.' Frank nodded at my hair which now reached my shoulders after being cut short six months ago so I could masquerade as a Westminster schoolboy. 'What about you, Pedro? What are you going to do when the theatre closes?'

Pedro stretched out on his back on the grass, hands behind his head. 'I'll be with the maestro. He did say something about going to Paris and then on to Italy.' He'd evidently been saving up that little gem of information, just waiting for us to ask for it. That's Pedro's way: to appear quite collected about the most exciting things. I guessed he was really enthusiastic underneath his cool demeanour.

'What! You lucky thing!' Frank exploded. 'So I'm the only one stuck in old England, am I?'

'Apart from me,' I said quietly.

'Of course, you. That's a given. You leaving Covent Garden is as about as unthinkable as the ravens leaving the Tower of London.' Frank turned

21

back to Pedro. 'Will you see the Colosseum? Venice?'

I refilled my glass, not entirely pleased with this speech. Why did Frank think it inconceivable that I would leave London? Why did my privileged friends think I couldn't move beyond the world I knew? Did they consider me so limited that I wouldn't be able to cope? Another voice whispered, perhaps they were right? Perhaps I couldn't survive outside the Sparrow's Nest? My hand shook and I splashed raspberry sherbet on my white gown.

'Oh, b*****!' I swore.

'Cat!' exclaimed Lizzie as Frank and Pedro howled with laughter at my obscenity.

'What was that about behaving at our house?' crowed Frank. 'Treating her like a lady?'

I got up. 'Sorry, Lizzie. I'd better go.'

'No, no, I'll summon someone to bring a cloth to wipe off your skirt. Raspberry leaves terrible stains.' She reached for a bell.

'No, I clean my own clothes, thanks.' Pride dented, I took off across the grass before they could stop me. Larking about in the library was one thing, but swearing in front of Lizzie another. I'd let myself down. I knew that my anxious state of mind about the future was some excuse for the bad language. What did Lizzie and Frank know about worrying where your next meal was coming from or where you could shelter for the night? Their reaction to my bad language only served to emphasize the gulf that I had always known stretched between us. What had Syd said? Duke's children had one world, he another. The problem was I didn't seem to have any world at all any more.

I heard soft footsteps running up behind me and

Pedro appeared at my elbow.

'Frank and Lizzie sent me to accompany you home,' he explained. 'Frank's sorry if he offended you and Lizzie said not to worry about your lapse in ...er...taste.'

I turned. The duke's children were standing watching us from the shade of the pavilion, Frank at his sister's shoulder. He gave me a salute when he saw I was looking in their direction. I waved back, having a strange sensation that they were on board a ship sailing away from me, separating us for ever.

'What's the matter?' asked Pedro, noticing my uncharacteristic silence.

'I don't think I'll be coming back to Grosvenor Square,' I said, giving voice to my intuition.

'Don't be silly, Cat,' he laughed. 'You didn't swear that badly. You didn't say...' He proceeded to reel off a list of the saltiest words in my vocabulary that he had picked up in my company.

It was my turn to laugh. 'True. No, I just meant that I feel as though these separations are bringing something to an end. All of you are going in different directions. It's never going to be the same again.'

Pedro kept silent for a moment but I could feel his eyes were on me. 'Will you be all right, Cat? Lizzie and Frank were wondering if they—'

'I'll be fine,' I said, cutting him off. I wasn't going to spoil my friendship with the Avons by becoming a hanger-on, living off their charity. 'The theatre will look after me, I expect.' At least, I hoped so. From the angry voices I heard last night, I wasn't the only one to have worked out that with a full staff at the King's Theatre already, not all of us would have jobs when the company moved.

23

We walked on, and turned into Piccadilly, a smart district of gentlemen's clubs, wine merchants and tobacconists. It was quieter than normal as the season was ending and noble families were departing daily for their country residences. A brace of two-wheeled curricles raced down the street as the young bloods on the driving seats put their horses through their paces.

'More money than sense,' I grumbled to Pedro as we waited for the dust to settle. He sneezed.

As the cloud thrown up by the passage of the carriages cleared, I noticed two heavily-built men in sharp cut brown jackets watching us from the opposite side of the street. They had the unmistakeable air of hired hands paid to execute their master's orders, be it to collect debts or break limbs.

'Let's go,' I whispered to Pedro, giving him the merest hint of a nod towards the danger I had spotted. My first thought was that they had been sent by his old master to rough us up in revenge for squeezing Pedro's manumission from him in the winter. Quick to reach a similar conclusion, Pedro's eyes widened in alarm and we picked up our pace. The men started to walk briskly in the same direction, but parallel to us. I looked about for a shop to retreat into, but we were in the stretch of Piccadilly that ran in front of several clubs—we'd not gain admission in there even if we had a mad axeman on our tail.

'What shall we do?' hissed Pedro as one of the men crossed the road behind us.

I took a quick look around; the heat had driven most customers off the street but there were still a respectable number of people in sight. 'Carry on walking and keep to the centre of the pavement.' I had now noticed a hackney cab travelling suspiciously slowly near the curb a few yards behind. Was it an attempt to snatch Pedro?

The second man sped up and strode over the road to reach the pavement in front of us. We stopped. With lazy confidence he walked towards us, swinging a cane in his hand. I grabbed Pedro's arm, determined not to let go. I had a piercing scream, plus a few unladylike moves taught me by Syd if necessary.

The man stopped a few feet from us and bowed.

'Miss, I think you dropped something.' He held out a black silk pouch.

What dodge was he up to? Did he think I'd fall for a magsman's trick like that?

'You are mistaken, sir,' I said coolly. 'That does not belong to me.'

'Are you sure, miss?' said the man. His voice was harsh as if he had gargled with iron filings and forgotten to spit them out. He thrust his hand into the bag and drew out a long piece of red hair. 'My master said you were certain to remember it. 'E swore you'd come along like a little lamb.'

I gripped Pedro's arm, trying not to show the panic inside. My own hair—cut from my head by a razor eighteen months ago—Billy Shepherd's calling card.

'But 'e said, in case your memory was not too sharp today, that we should bring the means to . . . 'ow shall I put it? . . . to ensure that you keep your appointment with 'im.' He nodded to his friend standing at my back. I heard knuckles crack as the bully flexed his fists.

'You will not lay a finger on this young lady, you blackguard,' said Pedro fiercely, stepping in front of

25

me. He knew nothing about the promise I'd given Billy.

'It's all right, Pedro.' I had to get him out of here or we were both in deep trouble. I had to persuade him I wasn't scared. 'It's just the Boil. I . . . er . . . I owe him something.'

'You don't owe that sewer rat anything,' replied Pedro with a proud toss of his head. 'Look, it's broad daylight: they can't take you against your will before all these people.'

He had more faith in the decency of the London man on the street than me. I doubted very much that there were many who would risk taking on these two apes in our defence.

'If I don't go now, there'll be another day—or night—in a dark alley with no witnesses,' I argued, wishing to spare him a pointless beating.

'The young lady's no flat,' grinned the man, 'as Mr Shepherd told us. 'E said she'd come nice and easy.'

'Well, she's not going without me,' said Pedro, trapping my hand on his arm under his. 'You're not getting into a cab with them on your own, Cat,' he argued as I tried to pull away.

'I haven't got a choice. I'll have to see Billy if he wants to see me.'

'So it would seem. But not by yourself. I'm coming too.'

'Suit yourself, Blackie,' said the man. 'You can come for the ride if you like.'

'Can we have a moment?' I asked.

Billy's messenger shrugged and stood off a couple of paces.

'Pedro, you'd better stay out of this,' I urged. 'Remember what he did to you last year—kept you

26

chained up in a pit for days!'

Pedro's jaw was set. He shook his head.

'There's no point both of us disappearing into the Rookeries. If you leave now, you can let Syd know where I've gone. That means if I need help—though I doubt I will—you'll have alerted the gang. If you come with me, Billy will just use you against me—you know what he's like. He'll threaten to hurt you just to get at me. I couldn't bear that.'

Pedro unclenched his teeth.

'You know Billy and I are old sparring partners. He probably just wants his annual dose of insults from me.'

A pause followed this suggestion and then Pedro nodded. 'I'll run and tell Syd. If you're not back by dark, we'll come in after you. Agreed?'

'I'll be back long before then, don't you worry.'

'Agreed?' he repeated.

'Yes.'

'Right. And good luck.' He squeezed my hand and darted off down Piccadilly before my guard of honour could stop him.

'The young African gentleman not accompanying you after all, miss?' asked the messenger sardonically.

'He had another, more pressing engagement,' I said airily as if I had not a concern in the world. 'As do I. I hope your master is not going to keep me long?'

'No idea, miss,' he replied, helping me into the cab. ' 'E's a law unto 'imself, is Mr Shepherd.'

SCENE 2—THE CROWN JEWELS

I was wrong about the Rookeries. I should have remembered that Billy Shepherd's empire had grown overnight like a particularly poisonous species of toadstool. He had decided to let his fungus sprout in Bedford Square, Bloomsbury, surrounded by the elegance to which he now aspired; though his roots were still planted not far away in the stews of St Giles where he made his money and ruled his own criminal kingdom.

The cab drew up outside a brick house at the end of the terrace on the southern side, the first floor embellished with a cage-like iron balcony. The front door was framed by an archway of alternating black and white stone, reminiscent of a badger's snout. Billy had appropriately chosen a fox's head for his brass knocker. I suppose that made me the first chicken in history to walk voluntarily into the den.

A cool chequered-tile entrance hall stretched out before me. I was glad I happened to be appropriately dressed for my surroundings and could meet the servants' eyes without embarrassment. I folded my skirt in my fist to hide the pink sherbet stain and followed the butler upstairs, intrigued despite myself to see what Billy was doing with his newfound riches.

Was it my imagination or did all of Billy's household look like barmaids and cracksmen playing at dressing up? Having known a properly managed staff at Grosvenor Square, I couldn't help but notice that the maids' skirts were too flouncy and the stripes of the butler's breeches too broad.

28

I was brought up short when we reached the first floor landing. The neutral entrance hall had lulled me into a false impression; up here Billy had got to work, stripping out the previous tenant's decorations and bringing in his own objets d'art. It was as if King Midas had been invited to run riot. Everything—and I mean everything, Reader—was gold. A figurine of a crude-looking satyr leered at a shepherdess on the other side of the doorway. Fleshy goddesses lolled about on clouds in heavy gilt-framed pictures. The chairs were painted gold, the drapes made from golden silk. I had the impression if I stood still any longer I would find myself gilded to the spot. It was the most ostentatious display of wealth and poor taste I'd ever had the misfortune to see.

The butler opened the door in front of us with a flourish.

'Your guest has arrived, sir,' he said in sepulchral tones.

If the first floor landing was a study in gold, this drawing room was an exercise in white and glass by some unhinged set designer for the pantomime. It was like standing inside an ice sculpture. A huge cut-glass chandelier dripped from the ceiling; mirrors glittered from the walls, snowy painted floorboards stretched at my feet. Impractical white-covered furniture floated like icebergs on an Arctic sea.

'I'll disappear if I set foot in here,' I joked to the butler, looking down at my dress. 'All you'll see is a ginger head bobbing about.'

His face refused to crack. He ushered me forward.

'Suit yourself, shipmate,' I muttered as I

launched myself into the room. I shouldn't have expected Shepherd's employee to be friendly—or to have a sense of humour.

I didn't see Billy at first. That was because he was lounging on the chaise longue at the far end of the room in his shirt sleeves and white silk breeches, his dark hair caught back with a black ribbon. I snorted with ill-timed laughter. He'd obviously planned this white-thing to impress me.

'Cat!' Billy exclaimed, rising on his elbow as he helped himself to a fistful of cherries. 'A pleasure to see you as always.' His grey eyes sparkled with mischief—he must have something unpleasant planned for me then.

'The pleasure is all yours, Billy,' I said briskly. 'What's all this about? I haven't got time to waste playing games with you.'

He spat a cherry stone into a silver bucket. It rang like a bell and I could see he was pleased with the effect.

'Take a seat, make yourself at home,' he continued, waving me towards a chair opposite him.

'A gentleman would've risen when a lady entered the room.' I paused by the seat but did not sit down.

'Well, when one comes in I'll make sure I stir myself.'

Ouch! I walked into that one. A point to him.

'Sit down, sit down, Moggy. Our business might take some time. No need to stand on ceremony.'

True. Remaining standing in his presence was a bit too much like a courtier before a king. I sat down.

'Cherry?'

I shook my head. 'Very nice, Billy,' I commented, looking around the room. 'Very . . . er . . . tasteful.'

30

He missed the irony. 'Glad you like it. I'm havin' the place done over by London's top craftsmen. Every room has a theme.'

I noticed that he over-pronounced his haitches. So, he was taking elocution lessons too, was he?

'What's the subject of this one then? Bedlam? All you need are a few lunatics in white gowns and the picture would be complete.'

He grinned. His teeth were as bad as ever. 'Nah, I've got you for that, Cat, ain't I?' he quipped, slipping back into his old manner of speaking.

'You're right, Billy. I was mad to come.'

'You 'ad no choice.' His manner stiffened; he sat up, scattering cherry stones on the white rug at his feet. We were getting down to business at last.

'What was it to be if I hadn't come? A knife in the ribs or a trip down the Thames?'

'Would I do that to you, Cat?' he asked with feigned innocence, hands spread wide. 'Me, a respectable man of property?'

'Respectable, my a**e. You're about as honest as Molly Everymans from the Jolly Boatman.'

'Watch it, Cat. My patience with you 'as its limits.'

He was riled: a point to me then.

I put the black silk bag containing my lock of hair on the table. 'As I infuriate you so badly, Billy, why not finish it between us? Tell me what you want. I'll do it if I can, then we'll call it quits. You leave me alone and I promise never to lay my eyes on your ugly mug again.'

'I'm glad to see you're a girl that keeps 'er word, Cat. I 'alf expected you to make some excuse about promises extorted unfairly. I 'ad you in a bind that night, didn't I?' He chuckled at the memory.

'When you've stopped congratulating yourself on

31

your low cunning, Billy, perhaps you'll get to the point?' I scratched at the upholstery, feeling the stuff split under my nails. He'd been cheated by his supplier if he thought he was getting the finest.

'All right, Kitten—'

'Don't call me Kitten.'

'Kitten, I want you to get me something.'

'What exactly?' I didn't like this—I didn't like this at all.

'I've got everything a man could want, but I've found that recently I've developed the tastes of a con-a-sewer.'

How appropriate. He meant connoisseur, of course.

He rose from the couch and beckoned me to follow him. 'Come and see my collection.' Seeing him on his feet for the first time, I noticed that he loomed over me these days. Leading me to a door in the wall beside the over-large mantelpiece, he took out a key and unlocked it. I hesitated: the room he had revealed was dark; I suspected a trap.

'Don't worry, Cat, it's not what you think,' he laughed.

'What do I think?' I tried to keep my voice steady.

He leant over a candelabra standing ready on a table and lit it with a taper. 'You think I'm like some wicked Italian count in one of Mrs Radcliffe's books, waiting to lock up the heroine in a dungeon.'

'Congratulations, Billy! You've learnt to read at long last. I hadn't realized you had such feminine tastes.'

'I was just pitchin' my conversation to your level, as a gentleman should.'

His repartee had improved. I wouldn't be

32

surprised if he was taking lessons in that too, to pass himself off as a gent in any society stupid enough to give him houseroom.

'*Generosus nascitur non fit*,'* I quipped, knowing full well he wouldn't understand.

'Don't come over all clever with me, Cat. Just because you spent a couple of weeks in breeches learnin' fancy languages, don't mean you can outwit me.'

'Course not, Billy,' I said with a great show of humility. 'What, I, a poor little ignorant maid, dare to rival the great, the learned William Shepherd?'

'You know wot, Cat?' he retorted, his accent on the slide. 'I wish I'd 'ad the beatin' of you when you were at that school. I 'ear you were quite the favourite punchbag for a while there. 'Ad I known, I'd've enrolled and whipped some of that cheek out of you.'

'You're a true gentleman, Billy, do you know that? One would never guess you were raised in the gutter and made your way through thieving and thuggery.'

I truly was insane. Here I was in his house, with his servants waiting on his call, and I was insulting him as freely as ever. But Billy had had enough. 'Shut yer mouth and get in there.' He gave me a shove in the small of the back.

I gasped. I had stumbled into Aladdin's cave. It wasn't a dungeon but a display cabinet for Billy's collection of—

'Jools, Cat, that's wot I like. See a bit of work that catches me eye and I 'as to 'ave it.'

The shelves were laden with cameos set with pearls, ruby-encrusted snuffboxes, diamond tie-pins. A sapphire necklace was spreadeagled on a

33

red velvet cushion, just begging for a fine white neck to wear it. An emerald ring glistened in an ebony box like a winking eye.

'Where did you pinch all these from?' I asked, aghast.

'Pinch? You think I stole these, do you, Cat?' He leant against the door, blocking my exit.

'Course I do.'

'I won't deny that some came to me strangely cheap from irregular sources, but I buy them above board, all fair and square.'

I raised an eyebrow.

He grinned. 'Well, perhaps I don't ask enough questions, but I never stole none of these, I swear, your worship.' He saw where my eyes were resting. 'Try it on.'

Before I could refuse, he put the sapphire necklace around my throat and held up a mirror so I could inspect it. It was the most beautiful thing I had ever seen, though the stones felt cold against my skin. I shivered.

'Look, it suits you, Cat. You were born to wear fine stuff, anyone can see that. Your father must 'ave 'ad blue blood, even if your mother was a harlot.'

I pulled it off my neck, feeling sullied that I'd half fallen for the lure of all these garish treasures.

'Easy with that!' Billy chided, taking the necklace from me and laying it reverently back on its pillow.

'So, you've got a lot of rocks, Billy. What's that to do with me?'

He rubbed his chin, gazing around him like a painter trying to decide where next to place his brush. 'It's a fine collection, I grant you, but I feel it lacks something.'

34

'What?'

'I want the Crown jewels.'

'Oh yeah, pull the other one, it's got bells on,' I laughed hollowly.

'Nah, I'm deadly serious, Cat. I want you to get me the Crown jewels. I'm a reasonable man—I don't ask for all of 'em, just something to put in that space . . . there!' He pointed to a gap in the middle shelf occupied by an empty cushion.

'You are joking?'

He shook his head. 'You gave your word, Cat. You said you'd do anything to 'elp your African friend.'

I gulped. He was purposely setting me an impossible task. He had to have a reason.

'Isn't there something else I could do?'

'I like collectin', Cat: jewels, money, people . . .'

'You really should get out more, Billy—'

'If you don't get me wot I want, you'll 'ave to take its place.' He placed the lock of hair on the cushion.

'You're a sick man, Billy, very sick.' My knees were trembling. I wasn't sure if he meant he wanted a bit of me carved off and put up there like a fetish belonging to some savage tribe of Captain Cook's, or whether he meant he wanted me as a permanent guest in his house. A possession. Knowing Billy, both were possible and I didn't want to find out the answer.

He just smiled.

I looked down at my skirts. I'd forgotten to keep the raspberry stain hidden—the blot taunted me, reminding me of my failings. 'All right, damn you! I'll get you your Crown jewel even if I have to rob the king myself. How long do I have?'

Billy picked up the candelabra. ' 'Ow long do you

35

think you'll need before you decide?'

He meant before I decided if I was going to join his little collection.

'Oh, I don't know,' I said irritably, hating him for this. He loved humiliating me. 'Till the end of the summer, I s'pose.'

'Fair enough. Your cushion will be waitin' by my fireside for the autumn then, Kitten.'

'Don't call me Kitten.'

He ushered me out and pulled the bell cord. 'You know, I always wanted a pet,' he said in a conversational tone. 'Somethink to come 'ome to.'

'Something to kick when you get angry, you mean.'

'That too.' His hand darted out and stroked my hair before I had time to duck. 'Looks better now it's grown again. You're turnin' out all right after all.'

'Shame the same can't be said for you,' I said quickly, batting his hand away.

He gave me a superior smile. 'Well, I don't need looks, do I? Not when I've got power. But you, what else 'ave you got to fall back on now they're closin' the theatre?'

'Brains, Billy, brains, as you once told me. Keep the cushion; I'm taking no place at yours or anyone's fireside any time soon.'

The butler appeared at the door to show me out. I paused on the threshold.

'Oh, and Billy?'

He was locking the door to his strongroom again. 'Yeah, cherub?'

'I'd sack the elocution teacher if I were you. It's pissing in the wind to think you can learn to speak properly.'

With that, I made a fast exit and showed myself out on to the street.

*   *   *

I set off in a mad dash across town to prevent Syd and Pedro bringing the rest of the Butcher's Boys to my rescue. Having started the day with a relatively creditable appearance, I was ending it in a crumpled mess, stained with raspberry and besmirched with dust. But the deepest soil on me was the feeling I had carried away from Billy's white room—that wouldn't wash off. He had an unhealthy obsession about me. I had the impression that getting me as part of his kingdom had come to represent the final proof that he had conquered the world. While I still existed, rude and irreverent, he would always feel his lowly origins dragging him down. If I failed to fulfil my part of the bargain, as seemed all too likely, I would have been proved as fallible as all his other minions, someone he could control. To him I'd be part of his menagerie of tame bullies and thieves.

'Never,' I swore to myself as I turned into the alley leading to the back of the shop. 'I'll leave London before I let that happen to me. Exile must be better than being enslaved to Billy.'

'Bloody 'ell, Cat, you 'ad us that worried!' shouted Syd as I burst into the yard.

Pedro threw aside the cudgel he had been holding and gave me a hug. 'Are you all right?' he asked. 'He didn't harm you?'

'No. It was like I told you—he just wanted to swap insults.'

The boys relaxed their warlike stances. Syd

37

grinned. 'I bet you gave 'im what for, eh, Cat?'

'Yeah, I think I came out on top.' For now, at any rate.

I proceeded to entertain them with an edited version of my call on Billy, leaving out all reference to our deal. They were highly amused to hear about his attempts to pass himself off as a gentleman.

'I don't know who 'e thinks 'e's foolin',' marvelled Nick, Syd's second-in-command. 'Billy's as refined as horse-dung.'

Jo the Card bowed before me and produced a posy of flowers from up his sleeve. 'To our Cat, Insulter Extraordinaire to the Prince of Darkness.'

I smiled, though this felt too near the knuckle to be truly funny. 'Thanks, Jo, but I'll relinquish the position to anyone who wants it. It's not my idea of fun to spend the day with the Boil.'

'I'll take it over,' growled Syd. 'And before 'e 'as a chance to open 'is gob, I'll shove 'is teeth down the back of 'is throat.'

'Well, you'd be doing him a favour—it's either you or the tooth-puller from what I saw. Gilded dung, that's what he is. Rotten to the core.'

'Right then,' said Syd, pushing up his sleeves. 'As there's no call now to rescue Cat, I think we all deserve a pint. Let's go to the Jolly Boatman.'

His boys all rose eagerly and filed out into the alley, laughing and whistling in anticipation of a good night out. Hoping no one had noticed, I started to follow.

'Nah, not you, Cat,' said Syd gently, hooking me by the arm as he spotted me trying to blend in with the crowd. 'You know the Boatman is no place for a respectable girl. I'll walk you 'ome.'

I too was feeling thirsty after a long hot day.

Surely just a very little drink of something would do no harm? Why did I always have to miss out on the fun? 'But Syd, if I stick with you, I'd be all right,' I protested.

'Nah, Kitten.'

'Why not? Have you got a girlfriend waiting for you or something? Are you too embarrassed to be seen with me in your company?'

He shook his head. 'Leave it. Let's not argue now. I'm off soon—I don't want to part from you with a quarrel.'

I subsided. Perhaps Nick wouldn't be so strict about not letting girls join the gang while Syd was away? Maybe I'd only have to wait a few days?

Syd patted my wrist. 'I've asked Nick to keep an eye on you while I'm gone—to make sure you don't do anythink stupid.'

What was Syd now? A mind-reader?

'No, Syd, I won't.'

'Stay out of trouble, won't you?'

'I'll try.'

'And when trouble finds you out—' I laughed: he knew me too well to think I'd have a problem-free summer '—don't forget that any of me boys are sworn to protect you. You can call on any of 'em, night or day.'

'Stop fussing, you old woman, you,' I chided.

We had arrived at the back door to the theatre. Syd squeezed my hand once and let it go.

'Goodbye, Cat.'

'Goodbye, Syd.' I felt strangely bereft, realizing that the straw-haired giant before me, my most faithful friend, was leaving me for the first time ever. So much was changing. Unbidden, a tear broke free and escaped down my cheek.

'Sorry,' I sniffed, embarrassed to show my weakness. I didn't want anyone to know how scared I was, least of all Syd who had never been afraid of anything.

'Don't be sorry, Cat, never be sorry.' He reached out to wipe the tear away. There was a strange look in his blue eyes. Suddenly, he bent forward, gave me a quick kiss on the lips, turned tail and left.

SCENE 3—EXEUNT OMNES

The next time I saw Syd was on the morning of his departure. Both of us avoided each other's eye as we mingled with the crowd that had gathered to see him off. My lips felt as if they were still burning— my cheeks certainly were—though I tried to behave as normal. Syd moved among his friends, shaking hands, cracking jokes, but something about the set of his shoulders told me that he was acutely aware of my presence wherever I was standing. We knew each other too well, having been together for as long as I could remember: both of us realized that everything had changed with that kiss. Today was the first time more than a square mile would come between us. His decision to leave London had stripped off the cosy covers of our relationship, leaving me shivering in the cold light of day as I took stock of where we had reached.

'All right, Cat? Look after yourself,' Syd said, reaching me last.

'I will.'

'I hope the move to the new theatre goes well.'

'Thanks.'

I risked raising my gaze to his face. His eyes were saying much more than his words, but he gave me a perfunctory shake of the hand before climbing up on the carriage beside Mick Bailey, his manager. Part of me ached for a hug; part of me was glad he'd left it at that.

With a flick of the whip, Syd bowled off west in Bailey's high two-wheeler to the cheers of the people of Covent Garden.

'Punch 'em to kingdom come, lad!' yelled his father as his termagant of a mother wept into a white handkerchief.

I stood among Syd's boys. They gave three cheers as the carriage turned the corner. Their leader rose in his seat, waved his cap to us and was gone. Sad though I was to see him leave, I was in some ways relieved. His brief kiss had forced me to see what I had, I now realized, purposely been closing my eyes to: Syd loved me. I could never just be one of the boys to him. He didn't want me in his gang because he thought he might have other plans for us when we both came of age.

I found the thought terrifying. I didn't feel old enough to consider marriage and family seriously. Though never exactly sure of the year of my birth, I guessed I was about thirteen or fourteen. Many girls from Covent Garden of my age had paired up by now; some poor souls already had babies hanging on their skirts, despite being barely out of childhood themselves. We all know we don't get long on this earth—death a daily occurrence where I come from. Most of us will be dead by twenty-five, probably in the course of bringing into the world another orphan like me to shift for herself, but even so, I wasn't in a hurry. I knew Syd would want to

41

wait until we could get properly married and do the decent thing, but that wasn't far off now. A couple of years and I could be Mrs Fletcher. Help. I didn't want that. I didn't want a life of babies and washing and shopping and cooking and cleaning. I wanted to stay in the theatre. I wanted to write. I wanted to be free. I wanted to marry for love.

Don't get me wrong, Reader: I do love Syd. He is the best, the most honourable boy I know. But marry him!

Stop the pen right there. I'm getting carried away, jumping from a kiss to wedding vows. Let us return to business before I get any more foolish ideas.

*　　　*　　　*

I arrived back at the theatre to find the place humming with excitement.

'What's going on, Caleb?' I asked the doorman.

He shifted along and patted the bench beside him. 'It's the list, Cat. Mr Kemble said it'd go up today.'

'What list?'

'The master . . .' (he meant Mr Sheridan) 'asked Mr Kemble to work out who the company could take with them to the new theatre. There's going to be blood spilt later, or my name's not Caleb Braithwaite.'

I felt as if I had just stumbled into a pothole in the dark. I hadn't known about this, though I should have guessed.

'What about you, Caleb? Do you know if you're going to be on it?' I felt very afraid for him: the King's Theatre was certain to have a doorman in

42

residence. What would an old sailor like Caleb do? He had no family I'd ever heard of and I had known him all my life.

'Nay, lass, I won't be on that list. Drury Lane is my home. I ain't going nowhere.'

'But Caleb, don't you know what's going to happen to this place?'

He gave me a sad smile. 'Aye, Cat. Don't you fret about me: Mr Kemble and his sister have said they'll see that I'm all right and they've been as good as their word. The old widow who keeps the cookshop in Gerrard Street said she could do with a man to watch the place.' He leant closer and whispered conspiratorially, 'That means Mr Kemble has paid her to give me a post at the fireside but doesn't want to hurt me pride by telling me so.' Caleb chuckled. 'Old age is a terrible thing, Cat. I'm proud, but not that proud. I'll sit and guard Widow King's pastries for her.'

'I'm pleased to hear it.' I breathed a sigh of relief.

'Old age is bad, but being a young maid with no family ain't that much fun either, Cat. What will you do with yourself? I don't want our Cat to fall into bad company like so many wenches do.' His cloudy blue eyes were full of concern.

'Oh, I'll be fine, Caleb,' I said brightly. 'I'm hoping my name will be on that list—and if not, well, I'll cross that bridge when . . . if it comes.' I was not encouraged to see that he looked doubtful. There was no immediate riposte of 'Of course you'll be on it, Cat.' He for one thought I was not indispensable to the company.

'It's here. The list's here!' Long Tom, a stagehand, bellowed from the Green Room. There was a stampede of feet from all directions, screams

43

and cries as actors, dancers, stage crew, labourers, scene painters, carpenters and front of house staff all converged backstage. I sat for a moment—too terrified to look, yet knowing I had to.

'Do you want me to find out for you?' asked Caleb gently. He must think me a coward for hesitating so long.

'No, no, I'll do it, thanks.' I patted his gnarled hand and stood up. Feeling as if time had slowed down to crawling pace, I made my way to the Green Room.

'I'm in!' shouted Long Tom, slapping me on the back as I passed.

'What about me?' I asked huskily.

He frowned. 'Sorry, Cat, I didn't notice,' and he went off to celebrate the good news with the others who had also been chosen.

I couldn't get to see the list at first: the crowd was so thick. Two dancers were weeping on each other's shoulders. Mr Salter, the prompt and box office manager, looked self-righteously pleased with himself. I overheard Mrs Reid talking to her assistant, Sarah Bowers.

'I'm sorry, Sarah, the only way I could manage it was to make a cut in your wages. We're going to be so hard-pressed. The budget's been slashed; we've got to transport the costumes, put others in store. I did my best.'

Sarah nodded miserably. 'I understand, Mrs Reid. At least I've still got me job. I appreciate all you've done for me.' Her eyes fell on me and she flushed scarlet. 'I'm not complainin', really I'm not.'

By now my heart was pounding, my throat dry. Had Mrs Reid cut Sarah's wages so that she could do something for me? Was that what Sarah's look meant? I wormed my way to the front of the crowd and scanned the list pinned to the wall. All the names were familiar, people I'd known since I was a baby. It took a moment to work out who hadn't made it into the lifeboat. Two-thirds of the stagehands were going, most of the set painters, half the front of house staff. No carpenters—they'd been transferred to building the new theatre. No doorman as Caleb had predicted. And no Cat.

It couldn't be! I started at the top again. Catherine Royal. I had to be there. I looked under Wardrobe—just Mrs Reid and Sarah. I searched under Messengers—no one was being taken. I even checked under Actors as I had once appeared briefly on the stage. Nothing. I turned to ask Mrs Reid if there was some mistake but her expression told me everything.

'I'm sorry, Cat, but I couldn't squeeze you in. I've already had to reduce Sarah's wages, poor girl, and she's got a sick mother to support.' Mrs Reid led me out of the Green Room and into the corridor. She lowered her voice. 'I had to choose between you and Sarah—it's been a very difficult decision. But, as I told myself last night, now you've got those fine friends of yours in Grosvenor Square, I feel sure you'll get by. They'll see you all right, won't they?'

I nodded dumbly. I didn't know what else to do. My strongest desire just then was to be on my own.

'Cheer up, Cat. When we get back here, I'm sure I'll find something for you to do if you still need the work.'

In two years' time she meant.

'But you'll have to do something about that sewing of yours,' she said with a smile. 'I couldn't really afford you, you know, at the moment as I'd

45

have to do the work twice over, wouldn't I?'

She was right. I was useless at sewing. Sarah had the makings of a fine seamstress. There had been no competition.

'Excuse me, Mrs Reid, I'd better go and . . .' And what, I wondered? 'And pack.'

She patted me on the shoulder. 'No need to leave until Saturday, child. That gives you plenty of time.'

I bobbed a curtsey and left, not wanting to see or be seen by anyone, particularly not by those lucky ones who were moving with the company.

The Sparrow's Nest is a good place to hide. I tucked myself between a trunk of Roman robes and a pile of musty furs, pulling my favourite moth-eaten bearskin over me. I wasn't sure what I was feeling. Empty was the closest I could come to describing it. I couldn't believe that they could do this to me after all these years—and yet I perfectly understood the decision. They had called me their cat, Mr Sheridan had once dubbed me his diamond, but all that counted for nothing in the cold light of day. I was nothing to them. I had no skills to speak of; I'd outgrown my time as theatre pet; as of Saturday night, I was on the street. Through pride, I'd turned down offers of help and now had to survive on my own. I couldn't even tell the Avons I'd changed my mind; Lizzie and Frank were gone— Lizzie on the boat to Paris, Frank in his carriage to Bath. He'd be learning irregular verbs and she sampling the latest fashions while I was left to sample the irregular life of the homeless.

Anger welled up inside me. Didn't I mean more to everyone than this? Hadn't I rescued Johnny for Mr Sheridan? Didn't I save Drury Lane's favourite boy star when I'd thrown myself between Pedro and

46

Mr Hawkins' blade? Despite all this, everyone thought someone else was looking after me and all were quite happy to be shot of the responsibility.

Even in my foul mood, I knew I was being unjust. I had many friends. The problem was that those with the means to help had gone away; those that remained were in as precarious a position as me.

'Pull yourself together, Cat,' I hissed at myself. 'You're not the first girl to be expected to earn her own living. Look at it this way: you've been incredibly lucky for ten or more years: now that luck has run out.'

'All the same,' a miserable voice piped up, 'at least the management had the decency to let Caleb know in advance and arranged a soft landing for him with Widow King. After all these years, no one thought to let me know; they made me go through the humiliation of seeing the list.'

'They're treating you just like everyone else.'

'But I thought I was special. I thought I was Drury Lane's Cat.'

'Well, if that's your attitude, go and curl up at Billy Shepherd's fireside. Become his Cat. He'd have you quick enough.'

'Never.'

'Well then, pull yourself together. Pack and make the best of it.'

This bitter dialogue with myself ended, I started to gather up my possessions. It didn't take long. Apart from a few hand-me-down clothes, I had little I could call my own. My notebooks and papers—all gifts from Mr Sheridan—were my most treasured belongings. I stowed them in a canvas bag. Frank had passed on to me his old Latin primer—this also was given a respectful burial in the sack. Lizzie's

47

gifts were mostly of the practical sort: silk stockings and gloves, much finer than the stuff I usually wore. I kept them for special occasions but right now there seemed no call for them. Folding them into a ball, I tucked them away, mentally noting that I could sell them if the worst came to the worst. Then there were a few mementoes that only had value for me: the playbill for Pedro's first appearance as Ariel, a cartoon by Captain Sparkler, a note from Mr Kemble, a pressed flower once worn by the great actress Mrs Siddons. My entire life fitted into that bag—and still it was far from full.

*   *   *

Saturday 4th June came round all too quickly and I had yet to sort out new lodgings. Lack of funds was some excuse. When I counted the contents of my purse, they were alarmingly light. But I knew what I was doing: part of me was still pretending the day would never come when I'd have to leave. I was like King Canute, stubbornly sitting on his throne as the waters rose to his neck. The crisis was upon me and yet I still waited.

Pedro couldn't fail to notice that something was seriously wrong. He had commiserated with me when he had learned of my fate, but he had more confidence in me that I did. He thought I would soon be on my feet again.

'Why don't you write a short story, Cat? Something that'll sell,' he suggested as we watched the audience assembling for the last night. There was a carnival atmosphere in the room. I noticed several people breaking off bits of the decorative rail as souvenirs.

'Oh, you mean some silly love story where a poor girl wins a rich man with just her wit and vivacity? Ple-ease!'

Pedro shrugged. 'Why not? It could be good if told well.'

'Ah, but to sell to a bookseller it'd have to go on about female duty and polite manners—I'd feel sick writing such stuff.'

'Can you afford to be so squeamish?' he asked wisely.

'Would you play any old tune on your fiddle for the drunks who chucked you a penny, Pedro, or would you prefer to play Handel and Mozart?'

'You know the answer to that, Cat. But it's not about what I prefer—I'd play "Black-eyed Susan" all night for any bunch of sailors if it made the difference between a bed under a roof and under the stars. You have to find somewhere to go and you'll need money to pay for it.'

He was right, of course, but that only made me feel angry with him. What did he have to worry about? He'd be off to Italy Monday morning, travelling through France. He would see Johnny and Lizzie in Paris in a couple of days.

'I'll be fine, Pedro,' I lied, wondering why I was telling everyone this when it was so patently untrue. 'I've got some money to tide me over. I'll manage.'

'Hmm,' said Pedro sceptically. He dug into his pocket. 'Look, I don't have much but—'

'No!' I pushed his hand away, taken aback by the strength of my feelings on this. 'I don't want anything from anyone—not unless I earn it. I don't want anyone's charity.'

'But you're my friend, Cat.'

'Exactly, so I'm not taking from you. I know you

49

need it yourself. Do you think I'm so pathetic that I can't find myself a place to go?'

Put like that, he had to say that of course I was quite capable but I could see he was suspicious that I was hiding something from him.

'Look, I've got to go now,' said Pedro. The orchestra were taking their seats and it would not do for him to miss the final chance to perform in the old Drury Lane. 'I'll be busy afterwards as Signor Angelini is giving us all a farewell supper and then we have to pack, but promise me you'll come and tell me your new address? I have to see you before I go to Italy. I really, really don't want to leave you.' He squeezed my hand urgently as I was pretending to inspect the audience.

'Of course I'll come to say goodbye. I wouldn't miss seeing you off for the world,' I said gaily. 'It's a new adventure for all of us, isn't it?'

'Hmm.' My false tone had not fooled him. 'Come and see me, Cat, understood? Or I'll send the Butcher's Boys to find you.'

I was dismayed at the thought that my incompetence would be exposed to all of Syd's gang. I couldn't bear that. 'I'll come, don't worry about me. Hadn't you better go?'

Pedro nodded, patted my shoulder and left the box.

Watching the final performance was a bitter pleasure. I mouthed along to every speech, the words ingrained in my memory by long acquaintance. Each move, each song, each laugh: I anticipated them all. I stood apart from the audience that night, watching how it behaved like a beast tamed by the skill of the actors: a witticism thrown to the mob causing a growl of laughter, a poignant deathbed scene provoking it to roll over and sob helplessly. The play ended with a magnificent epilogue by Mr Kemble predicting the phoenix-like rebirth of Drury Lane. The audience cheered, clapped and whistled, before making off with any movables that we had not already thought to pack away. How I envied the crowd's light-heartedness as the auditorium emptied for the last time. They seemed to be taking my soul with them. I was drained of all feeling except sorrow.

Backstage the atmosphere was subdued. Too many had lost their livelihoods to allow for celebration; if anything it felt more like a wake in progress as Mr Sheridan toasted the demise of the old theatre in champagne in the Green Room. The orchestra left for their supper party, Pedro in their midst. Then, at around eleven-thirty, those of us remaining shuffled off and went our separate ways. I said farewell to Mrs Reid and Sarah Bowers in the now empty Sparrow's Nest. The costumes were boxed and waiting downstairs for the carrier tomorrow. All that remained was my bundle and the old sofa, judged too far gone to be worth anything.

'You've got somewhere to go, haven't you, Cat?' Mrs Reid asked as she locked the door behind us for the last time.

'Oh yes,' I lied. The waters were well over my chin by now and still I was not budging.

'There'll always be a welcome for you wherever I am,' said Sarah. 'When you've found your feet, come and 'ave a nice cup of tea and a natter.'

'I'll do that.' My voice sounded false to my ears—overly cheerful.

'It's the end of an era,' said Mrs Reid, looking

51

about her as we descended the stairs. 'Mr Garrick's theatre gone. It's a special place this, full of memories.'

It's the only place, I thought.

We were among the last to leave by the stage door. Mr Sheridan and Mr Kemble were standing there to shake hands with everyone—and to check no one carried off something they shouldn't.

'See you at the Haymarket, ladies,' Mr Kemble bowed to my companions. 'You all right, Cat? Got somewhere to go?'

The thought streaked across my mind that I should scream that 'no, I bleeding well didn't have somewhere to go, for his employer was knocking down my home', but the impulse had fizzled out before I opened my mouth to speak.

'Yes, sir. Goodnight, sir.'

I must have sounded so unlike myself that Mr Kemble was suspicious.

'So where are you going?'

His concern almost did for me. I could have wept there and then, melted away in tears so that nothing was left behind.

'I'm staying with friends,' I lied, too ashamed to tell the truth. 'Goodnight.'

'Goodnight. Come and see us very soon,' said Mr Kemble, waving me off.

'Let me know where you are,' called Mr Sheridan. 'Send a note to my house. I want to be sure you have found a good home.'

No thanks to you.

'Of course, sir.'

And that was that. I watched from the shadows opposite as Mr Kemble turned the key in the lock and handed it to Mr Sheridan. They shook hands and parted to return to their comfortable houses.

As the darkness swallowed them up, I considered my position. I had exactly one shilling and sixpence in my purse. Next to nothing. Just enough for the next day's meal. If I spent it on shelter I'd go hungry. Just a few yards away, the streets were still bustling with people going in and out of the taverns and gaming houses, but I couldn't afford to join them, nor would it be safe to do so. I slipped back across the road and into the alleyway to the stage door. I knew it was locked but it was the nearest I could get to home. I stowed my bundle against the doorpost and curled down with my back to the comforting solidity of the oak. I wasn't ready to leave—not yet.

SCENE 4—MR TWEADLE

'Cat, you look terrible.'

Pedro was hanging out of the window of the Dover mail coach biding his friends farewell as I slid to the front of the queue. I'd purposely left it to the last moment, mingling with the crowds until the coachman took his seat and picked up the reins. I couldn't cope with answering too many questions from Pedro today. After two nights of sleeping rough, I knew I must look a sight. To tell the truth, I was less worried about my begrimed state than the gnawing hunger. I'd only had a penny roll yesterday and nothing so far this morning. I wasn't managing well and I was too humiliated to let anyone know. They all thought of me as the girl who always landed on her feet, good for a laugh, guaranteed to look on the bright side when others were moaning. I wasn't finding anything funny at the moment.

'Have a safe trip, Pedro,' I said huskily.

'Cat! Where have you been? Why didn't you come earlier? I've been frantic with worry. Look, I'll write to you—where shall I send it?'

I was about to say 'Drury Lane' but pulled up short before I made so obvious a mistake. 'Um, send it to . . . to Syd's parents. I'm sure they won't mind.'

'But why can't I send it directly to you? Where are you staying?' Pedro asked shrewdly.

The coachman cracked his whip.

'Oh, look: you're off.' I gave Signor Angelini, Pedro's master, a smile. *'Buon viaggio!'*

'Grazie, Caterina,' the maestro replied. 'I look after your little friend for you!'

Pedro was not satisfied. 'But Cat, tell me where . . .' The coach surged forward in a clatter of hooves and jingle of harness. 'I'll write to Frank if you—' The rest of his words were lost as the mail pulled out of the stable yard. I kept up my smile, and waving, until he was out of sight, then I let it slide off my face like greasepaint under hot lights. I had to do something today. It was Monday. I couldn't spend any longer mourning for the home that was now barred to me. Even though it was early summer, the nights were chilly. Sleeping rough was exactly how it sounded. If I carried on I'd lose all claim to a respectable appearance and would find it even harder to get serious attention anywhere.

Struggling with my despondency, I sat down on the milestone in the inn yard. Dover 70 miles. All being well, Pedro would be on the high seas by nightfall, off on his grand tour like a proper gentleman. I knew I had another tour to make: a round of the booksellers. With my ducal patron abroad, I would have to see what a direct approach would do for me. It was all I had to offer. Picking up my bundle of stories, I set off towards St Paul's.

Noon passed. The sun beat down on the stones, bleaching them a blinding grey-white like an expert washerwoman. My eyes were watering—but that was only the glare, of course. I assure you, Reader, I was becoming hardened to rejection. First the ingratiating, though slightly doubting, smile from the assistant as I stepped into the shop. Then the sneer that began as soon as I opened my bundle. A hurried 'No, thank you, miss' and ejection on to the pavement with the door snapped shut behind me. One or two were gentler with their refusals, making a pretence at glancing over my work, even offering a word or two of advice, but it still ended up at the same point with me outside, shut out from the world of books within.

I had started with the larger premises, the shops owned by names I recognized. By late afternoon, I had started to explore the little stores in the side-streets, producers of radical pamphlets and scandal sheets. After my twentieth rejection, I was on the point of giving up.

'Just one more,' I promised myself.

Chance had brought me outside a dingy shop in a passageway off St Paul's Churchyard, belonging to one Mr Tweadle, *purveyor of fine literature to the respectable classes*, according to the sign on the door. I wasn't convinced by this, nor by the creepy-looking customer who sloped out as I entered, but then again, beggars can't be choosers.

The shop was dark by contrast to the sunny street and it took my eyes several moments to adjust. It appeared deserted: rows of dusty books lined the walls as though untouched for many years.

'Yes, miss?' A thin man with a limp cravat and lank white hair popped up from behind the counter, making me start.

'Um, sorry to bother you, Mr . . . ?' I began.

'Tweadle, miss, *the* Mr Tweadle.' He rubbed his hands together and smiled at me without showing his teeth.

'Mr Tweadle, I have some stories that I wondered if you might be interested in publishing.' I pushed them over the counter towards him, anticipating his 'no' before it came. He pawed at the manuscripts with his broken nails but said nothing, looking at me curiously from under his sparse white eyebrows.

'They're not the usual thing one expects from the female pen, I know, but they have been read and enjoyed by some of this country's noblest families. I have a character reference here.'

I placed my final card on the table: a letter from Mr Sheridan vouching for my years of faithful service at Drury Lane.

Mr Tweadle flicked at the letter with a paper-knife. 'Sheridan,' he read out. 'You know him?'

What was this? A chink of light? Some interest at last?

'Yes, sir. He was my patron—until a few days ago.'

Mr Tweadle's eyes were running over the first page of my story. An eyebrow shot up.

'*You* wrote this?'

'Yes, sir.' I wasn't sure how to take that question:

56

was he shocked, surprised, disgusted? I looked down at my shoes.

He picked up the letter again. 'This says you served as a maid-of-all-work backstage. It says nothing about writing.'

'I know. But I did write them, I swear.'

'Hmm.' Mr Tweadle was now tapping his teeth with the paperknife. 'Out of work, are you?'

'Yes, sir.'

'Not got a place to stay by the looks of you.'

I blushed. Was it that obvious?

'No, sir.'

'Any family to speak of?'

'No, sir.'

'Who's looking after you then.'

'Me, sir.'

'Hmm.'

There was a pause in which I heard the bells of St Paul's toll the hour with funereal solemnity.

'I don't think these will do,' Mr Tweadle pronounced at last.

'Oh, of course.' I reached out to take them but he snatched them from me.

'But I'll give the matter more consideration. There may be something I could use.'

I was reluctant to be parted from my manuscripts: they were all I had now. 'But I must—'

He cut me off. 'I do however need a maid. The last one left at short notice and things have been rather neglected since then with just me and my assistant to manage on our own.'

'You want me to be your maid?'

'Of course. I'm hardly going to ask you to serve at the counter while I cook the supper, am I?' He gave me a strangely humourless smile.

'I see.' My mind was whirring. It wasn't what I was expecting, but it was better than nothing. And there was his promise to give my work more thought. 'Thank you, I accept.'

'There are conditions, of course.'

'Yes?' I wasn't in a situation to demand much.

'If I take you into my household, you'll work in exchange for bed and board.'

I'd been here before, but I suppose I could look on it as a start. Maybe I'd get some money if he published something of mine?

'I wish to take proper care of you so you are not to leave home without my express permission. Nokes—that's my assistant—will continue to go to the market so there should be no need for you to wander.'

I must have looked doubtful for he added, 'I don't want a gadabout maid, miss. I have my good name to consider—and yours. I stand *in loco parentis* to my household, so I expect you to behave as a daughter to a father.' He smirked. 'I don't suppose you know what that means, do you, miss?'

I was liking this Mr Tweadle less and less. 'Oh, but I do. In place of the parent, sir.'

This took him by surprise. 'My word, you are a clever girl! Where did you learn Latin?'

'It's a long story.'

He waved this aside. 'What other languages do you speak?'

'French—a bit of Italian.'

'Hmm.'

That 'hmm' again. I was learning to recognize it as a sign of him scheming.

'Perhaps when you've done your duties as maid, I may be able to make use of you with cataloguing the

58

foreign books.'

'I'd like that.'

'Good. That brings me to the last condition. If you work here, you are not to set foot in the shop, do you understand? If you wish to speak to me, you knock on the door between here and the rest of the house and wait for me to answer.'

This seemed so unreasonable. What was wrong with me? I didn't have two heads, did I?

'But why?'

'I will not have my kitchen maid, even a clever one, interfering with my customers. You stay out of sight, do you understand?'

Bed and board versus the pleasure of telling him to get stuffed. Guess which won out.

'Yes, sir.'

He gave me another of his insincere smiles. 'Then you can start right away. What's your name?'

'Catherine Royal.'

'Well then, Cathy. Come this side of the counter and I'll show you where you are to live.'

Stepping through the gap, I shed my status as 'Miss' and became just 'Cathy'. I thought to say that my friends called me 'Cat' but realized at once that I didn't want Mr Tweadle addressing me on those terms. Cathy was a stranger I was sharing my life with for a few weeks until I could get myself out of here. She wasn't me—not really.

*   *   *

Mr Tweadle led me down a dark passage to the back of the house. It didn't take long to work out why the last maid had left. Mr Tweadle and his assistant had the eating and sleeping habits of

59

pigs—though perhaps, Reader, I am slandering those worthy porkers whose only fault is that they like to roll in a little mud. The kitchen was filthy—not a clean utensil anywhere, rotting food in the cupboards and an inch of muck on the floor. Even a rat would have turned his nose up at dining here. Mr Tweadle thrust a cap and apron in my hand, pointed to the pump in the yard and turned to go.

'Where am I to sleep, sir?' I asked, thinking that I'd like to get that clean before I bedded down for the night.

'Here of course. This is your kingdom now, Cathy. You'll find your bedchamber behind that door.' He crunched his way out over the grit that had accumulated on the flagstones. 'I'll have my dinner at five, supper at ten. I'll send Nokes in with the necessaries when he gets back. I've an urgent errand for him.'

He left, roaring the name of his assistant. I heard the thunder of feet down the stairs and a hurried conversation in whispers before a door slammed.

How had I come to this? I wondered, looking at my sordid surroundings. It was only a week ago that I had been sipping sherbet in Grosvenor Square; now I was to scrape every foul thing known to mankind off the floor of a windowless kitchen. My bedroom was no more than a cupboard with a straw mattress. I propped the door open to let in some fresh air. The backyard went nowhere—just a square of bricks barricaded by high walls. You could look up to the heavens to see some colour and movement, but everything else was sooty and barren. It felt like a prison exercise ground with me as the only inmate.

Well, I was here by choice. I could walk out if I

60

wished. My job was to make the best of it as so many had had to do before me. I rolled up my sleeves and started working the pump handle.

After several hours of work I felt quite pleased by the impact I had made on the kitchen. You could now at least see the flagstones on the floor and the table was scrubbed clean. I had lit a fire in the old stove and was just contemplating making myself a cup of tea when the door from the passageway burst open and a young man with a crop of greasy mud-brown hair clattered into the room carrying a basket.

' 'Ere you go, skivvy,' he said, dumping it on to the floor. I could tell at a glance that he was a poor shopper: the vegetables were old, the meat scraggy and tough. He then parked his bony bottom on my clean table and stared at me.

'What you looking at?' I asked sharply, quelling the urge to poke him off with a toasting fork applied to his rear.

'Pleased to meet you too, Copperknob.' He put his big dusty boots on the chair, elbows on his knees, and continued to gaze at me. ' 'Ope you're a better cook than the last one. She nearly poisoned us, she did, buying off-meat so she could keep the change.'

'I'll try not to.' Little chance of that if I wasn't allowed out to market.

'I'm Nokes.'

'I would never have guessed.' I began sorting through his purchases.

'Friendly soul, ain't you?'

I said nothing.

'Well, wise up, Copperknob, I'm either yer best friend in this 'ouse, or yer worst enemy. Treat me nice and I'll be nice to you; go all superior on me and you'll regret it. Just 'cause you can read and write don't mean you're better than me.'

So he knew about my writing, did he?

'I don't think I'm better than you,' I said quietly, wishing he would leave me in peace.

Nokes picked his nose and ate the contents with relish. 'Too right, girl. You're not better than anyone now, are yer? Old Tweadie said your "patron" was Mr La-di-dah Sheridan—we all know what that means, don't we? 'Ad flash friends once, 'e says.'

His thin face was lit up by a malicious smile. In my anger, I snapped a carrot in two—but at least it wasn't his neck—you should give me some credit for that, Reader.

'But you're 'ere now—and don't you forget it. At our beck an' call.'

I didn't think this speech deserved an answer so I took out a knife and began vigorously chopping vegetables for a stew.

'You know what?' he said loudly.

I shook my head.

'I don't think I like you.'

'I'm so sorry,' I said sardonically, throwing some meat in the pot. 'See, your cruel words have made me weep.' Tears caused by chopping onions were trickling down my face. 'I am devastated by your penetrating character assessment and will forever be labouring under the burden of your displeasure.'

Nokes scratched the back of his head, confused by this last speech. 'You talk funny, you know that?'

I shrugged. It was his problem if he didn't understand the king's English.

'See you at dinner then—make sure it's good or I'll box your ears.' And with that parting endearment, Nokes clumped out of the kitchen.

My 'kingdom', as Mr Tweadle had called it, returned to my sole charge, I took cook's privilege and tested the stew frequently while it was on the stove. It was as well that I did for my new master and his assistant ate it all without leaving any for me, scraping the pot clean. I gathered they had not eaten properly for weeks either.

'Not bad,' commented Mr Tweadle. 'Bit more salt next time, Cathy.'

Nokes belched and patted his stomach. 'I take back wot I said earlier, skivvy. You might turn out all right after all.'

Mr Tweadle took a keen look at his assistant and then at me. 'You,' he said to Nokes, emphasizing each word with a wave of his knife, 'are not to touch her, you understand?'

'Me? Touch a skinny little bag of bones like 'er? As if I would!'

'Hmm. Remember, I stand *in loco parentis* to you both.' This was obviously a favourite phrase with him—possibly his only Latin. 'She has proved very useful and I don't want that spoiled.'

Nokes scowled but dared not say anything before his master. Mr Tweadle got up to go. 'Leave a tray of supper in the passage for me before you go to bed, Cathy. You've made a good start. I think you and I will get along splendidly.'

'Goodnight, sir.' Still not liking him much, I recognized that Mr Tweadle was the closest thing I had to a protector in this house. He at least was trying to be welcoming.

'Come along, Nokes. I want you to fetch those . . . er . . . things from the printers for me.'

Nokes took a while to leave, making a great show

of tying a bootlace. When Mr Tweadle had disappeared back into the shop, the assistant pounced on me, backing me up against the stove. 'Listen, Copperknob, you may've made a friend of the old man, but you don't tell 'im nothink about me, all right? If I knock you about a bit, that's our business, all right?'

I wasn't standing for this.

'Shove off!' I was used to dealing with bullies like him and kicked at his shins. My shoe made a satisfyingly complete connection with the bone.

'Ouch!' He hopped away, cursing me, obviously not accustomed to maids who hit back. 'You'll regret that, you little witch!'

'Listen carefully, Mr Nokes. I will do my job, cook and clean, but that's it. If you want to punch someone, go pick a fight with a man your own size. I know a few that'd be delighted to give you a good pasting. Now get out of my kitchen, you flea on a rat's bum, before I turn nasty.' I picked up the toasting fork and gave a significant look at the area of his body in which I was contemplating planting it. He took the hint and left hurriedly, his tail between his legs.

I saw little of Nokes and Mr Tweadle after that. They would turn up at mealtimes, say a few words, then leave. Mr Tweadle always made an effort to be complimentary; Nokes just scowled. The shop appeared to be keeping them very occupied. Business had picked up and the bell was forever jingling as customers came and went. That first Monday must not have been typical, I decided. Mr Tweadle must be a bookseller of some repute if he was this busy. It might not be a bad place to launch my literary career if I could persuade him to put me

64

in print.

After a week of being kept indoors I began to go a little crazy with the imprisonment. Though I took my vegetables outside to peel in the yard and spent as much time as I could excuse sweeping the bricks, I still had not been allowed into the shop or out on to the street. Mr Tweadle was taking his desire to keep a respectable household too much to the extreme.

I tackled him about it after seven days of this treatment. I had cooked what I hoped was a passable dinner. Mr Tweadle was in a very good mood: he had ordered in a jug of wine and was treating Nokes and himself to a glass or two.

'To our customers!' he crowed, raising his vintage in the direction of the shop. 'To those who keep us in this delightful style.' His eyes flicked over to me, standing by the stove. 'Do you want some, Cathy?'

'No thank you, sir. But I was wondering if I might go out tomorrow—just for a half hour or so. I know a good butcher's where I can get much better meat than the poor stuff Mr Nokes has been buying. That last bit of mutton was surely from a sheep that died of old age—you must have noticed how tough it was?'

Mr Tweadle frowned and put down his glass. 'No, I'm afraid you can't go wandering.'

'I promise to go there and come straight back. I won't talk to anyone.'

'I said no, Cathy. My word is final.'

I'd had enough of being his slave. I took off my cap and began to untie my apron.

'What are you doing?' he asked sharply, all pretence at being friendly abandoned.

'I'm sorry, sir. I can't continue like this. I'll go

mad if I can't get out and about.'

'You hear that?' he appealed to Nokes. 'The ungrateful girl frets over her freedom to roam the streets like some common hussy. You see how right I was to insist she stayed inside?'

'Very wise, sir,' Nokes intoned. 'She's got to be kept close, this one, or your name will be mud.'

'I don't think a walk to a butcher's shop would place Mr Tweadle's name in peril, but as you both do, I had better take my leave. If I could have my manuscripts back, please?' I held out my hand.

My employer and Nokes exchanged looks.

'What manuscripts?' asked Mr Tweadle coldly.

'My manuscripts—the ones I showed you last week!' I felt a rising sense of panic. I had to get them back—I had to!

'There were no manuscripts.'

'There were! In a canvas bag. You looked at them in the shop.'

'Oh, those bits of old paper. I think I put them down somewhere—can't for the life of me remember what I did with them.'

'Kindling for the fire, sir?' suggested Nokes with a malevolent grin at me.

'Very possibly. If you're so worried about it, you'd better write some more, girl. I'll give you pen and paper so you can keep up your little hobby. I like to encourage innocent pursuits. If you're good, I might be able to remember what I did with them in a few days.'

'A few days!' I exclaimed. The slimy cheat was holding my manuscripts hostage to keep a cheap maid about the place.

Mr Tweadle got up. 'I'll send Nokes back with the paper for you. I do so want you to be happy

66

while you are staying here, Cathy. You'll feel so much better if you let your mind rather than your person wander and write a few more stories to pass the time. You won't mind if I lock you in now, will you? You have to understand it's for your own good.'

Of course I minded, but they were gone and the bolt clunked into place.

*   *   *

That night, I considered my options. Mr Tweadle couldn't keep an eye on me forever—I had no fears about that locked door. If the worst came to the worst, I'd simply climb over the back wall and make my escape that way. But he needed no real shackles—my manuscripts were like a ball and chain keeping me here. They were irreplaceable. No one else might have any use for them, but they were everything to me. I'd have to find them, then flee—that was all there was to it.

To lull Mr Tweadle into a false sense of security, I scribbled down a little story that night—something about star-crossed lovers and dutiful daughters. It was poor stuff—but better than many a tale that made it into print. I left it on the table so that Mr Tweadle would see it when he came down for breakfast.

'Ah, I see you've passed your time profitably, Cathy,' he said, stirring his porridge and smiling at me as if for all the world our quarrel of yestereve had not happened.

'Yes, sir.'

I went out the back to escape his presence. I wasn't sure how long I could keep up the pretence of obedience when I hated every wispy hair on his head. I'd only swept the yard twice over when he came to the door holding my new story.

'What's all this?' he asked me. 'Where are the boxers and the villains? The musicians and actors?'

So he had read my stuff then.

'I wrote what I thought you, standing *in loco parentis*, would approve of, sir,' I said with a passable imitation of meekness.

'Well, no, no, I do not approve, Cathy. I want the other kind of story from you—something with guts and excitement, not this curds-and-whey stuff.'

'Why? I thought I was supposed to be just amusing myself—a hobby you called it.' A suspicion was forming in my mind that perhaps after all his delays he might, just might, be considering putting out a collection of my work. This might all be a test to see if I really was the author.

'Hmm.' He looked up at the sky and then down at me. 'If you are ever going to make it into print, Cathy, you have to be true to yourself. This . . . this is cheap imitation. I want the genuine article.'

I nodded. 'I understand. I'll write something for you—to show you I can do it.'

'That's it. You do that. Take the morning to see what you can knock out for me.'

Heartened by this exchange, even partially reconciled to my position in the household if I was allowed time to write, I cleared the kitchen table and set down to work. I was soon lost in an account of a visit to a crime lord's flashy household and forgot the time. I was amused to find that even Billy made good copy when turned into a story—the repellent reality becoming quite amusing when looked at from a distance.

68

I was so pleased by the end product that I was determined to take it to Mr Tweadle directly. I tried the kitchen door: it wasn't locked this morning. Running along the corridor, I paused outside the shop entrance, wondering if it was safe to knock. Mr Tweadle would not want me to interrupt him with a customer. I could hear voices. I put my head close to the door to listen.

'I asked you, sir, if you knew where I could find Catherine Royal.' It was Mr Sheridan. Thank goodness I hadn't burst in dressed in my dirty scullery maid's apron—I would have died of embarrassment.

'As I told you, I have no idea where the young person can be found,' Mr Tweadle said airily.

'He's lying, he must be.' Frank! What was he doing here? 'It's her stuff, I know it is.'

Mr Sheridan spoke again. 'Look, Mr . . . er . . . Mr Tweadle, the young lady has disappeared and her friends are most anxious to locate her. I'm not asking you to betray any confidences—we're not fortune hunters trying to muscle in on her success or anything of that kind—but we know that you must be in contact with her or you wouldn't have all this.'

All what? What were they talking about?

'I repeat, sir, I have no knowledge of the lady. You are mistaken if you think this belongs to anyone but my talented young assistant, George Nokes. He's a prodigy.'

'He's a fraud and a thief!' interrupted Frank, outraged. 'If he's told you those stories are his then he's lying through his teeth.'

'Am not!' protested Nokes. 'I've sweated over those, I 'ave. I'd swear it in court, I would. No girl

69

could write that stuff.'

I went cold and leant against the door.

'Well, you are wrong,' countered Mr Sheridan. 'I know the only girl in London who could write "that stuff" as you call it and I'm prepared to say so in court. Produce her or I'll fetch the constable.'

'There's no young lady on the premises. There's just me, Nokes and the maid, as I am more than happy to prove to anyone who comes with a warrant.'

The dirty double-crossing liar! Roused by my fury, I pushed the door open, pulling the cap from my head as I entered the shop.

'I suppose it's not exactly a lie, is it, Mr Tweadle?' I said flatly. 'That's all there is—but you've a maid no longer. I resign.'

'Cat!' Frank vaulted the counter and gave me a hug. He then held me out at arm's length. 'You look terrible.'

'Thanks.'

Despite having demanded that I be produced, Mr Sheridan was shocked to see me. I suppose I did not cut a very good figure in my shoddy clothes and I'd been living off scraps, thanks to the large appetites of my employers.

'Cat, you're not staying another moment under this man's roof. I've a carriage outside,' Mr Sheridan said. 'Come along.'

'Not without my manuscripts.'

'I think you'll find he no longer has them,' he said, casting a disgusted look at Mr Tweadle. 'They'll be locked in the printer's safe. That is now a matter for my lawyer. I'll be instructing him immediately to take action on your behalf.'

He put a small magazine in my hand, the kind

you can buy unbound on any street corner at a penny a time. *London Life—Tales of Cat of Drury Lane, the mischievous orphan girl.*

'I'm afraid he's made you quite sensational, Cat. I was surprised that you'd allowed it when I first heard of the success of the series– but now I see you had no say in the matter.'

So Mr Tweadle had not only stolen my stories— but my character too! The magazine trembled in my fist. This wasn't at all how I had imagined my print debut: a cheap pamphlet with crude woodcuts. How I wished I was a big man like Syd and could punch his nasty face. But I wasn't—I was a stupid fool of a girl who had fallen for so simple a trick. I'd even cooked the meals that my own work had bought him—he and Nokes must have been laughing themselves silly over me. I should have taken a leaf out of the last maid's book and tried poisoning them.

'I don't know what to say,' I said faintly.

'Let's get you out of here, Cat. We'll leave this to Mr Sheridan's lawyers,' said Frank, steering me gently towards the door.

And shaking the dust of that foul place off my feet, I let myself be led out of Mr Tweadle's shop.

Interlude—A Comic Dance

LONDON LIFE

Tales of Cat of Drury Lane, the mischievous orphan girl

READ THE NEXT EPISODE FROM THE PEN OF THIS REAL-LIFE MOLL,

Queen of the London Underworld

PRICE 1D, FROM TWEADLE'S BOOK EMPORIUM, ST PAUL'S CHURCHYARD

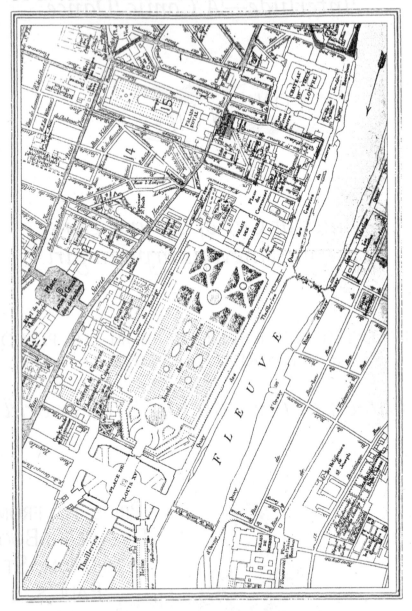

*Act II - In which Frank and Cat
discover the significance of the
cockade . . .*

Act II

SCENE 1—CORRESPONDENT

You may guess my feelings, Reader, as I sat in a corner of Mr Sheridan's carriage watching St Paul's Cathedral disappear behind me. I was heartily ashamed of myself. I had taken pride in being wise to the ways of the street but, once truly thrown on my own resources, I had fallen at the first hurdle. How could I have let a lowlife like Mr Tweadle get the better of me? He must have thought I was quite the Christmas goose, turning up on his doorstep and offering to pluck, stuff and cook myself for his dinner.

'The first thing we need to do is get a square meal inside you, Cat,' said Mr Sheridan in a fatherly tone. 'There never was much of you but you seem to have diminished dangerously over the past few weeks.'

'And a change of clothes wouldn't go amiss,' added Frank, smiling at me from the seat opposite.

I looked out of the window as we rattled down Fleet Street, gazing at the piles of books displayed on the booksellers' stalls—stacks of respectable volumes bound in leather, produced by highly-regarded authors.

Mr Sheridan gave an awkward cough, finding my silence difficult after years of me speaking out of place. 'Cheer up, Cat, it's over now.'

But it wasn't over for me—not till I had my manuscripts back. I felt like I'd left a part of me behind.

'It was good luck that Lord Francis turned up this

morning demanding to know where you were. I had thought of finding you myself as I wanted to ask you a favour, but I assumed that you would be too busy to see me in the bloom of your success.'

'What success?' I asked in a dull tone of voice.

'The stories, of course. That man may have changed a few things here and there, but they were essentially yours. The public love them. I've heard of nothing else all week—you are quite the fashion. The Prince of Wales told me his favourite was the incident where you rampaged through Brook's; mine was the boxing match, as I've always had a soft spot for the Fancy.'

I felt a glimmer of pride that my tales had made it into the hands of the most illustrious personages in the land. 'How did Tweadle change them?' I asked, feeling a flicker of curiosity. 'You said he had made them sensational.'

Frank suddenly became very interested in his nails. Mr Sheridan avoided my eye and looked out the window.

'Aside from massacring the language with a hurried print job, he . . . er . . . made you out to be rather less respectable than you are.'

'What did he say about me?' If my reputation was in tatters, I wanted to know the worst.

'Well, the language was rather stiff for one—and you appear to spend your time in the company of some rather bad characters, criminals and the like.'

Perhaps Mr Tweadle hadn't had time to change very much then, I thought sourly.

'But it is not so much what was in the stories as the way he presented them.' Mr Sheridan placed on my knee the pamphlet he had briefly shown me in the shop. I turned to the smaller print. *'Read the next*

76

episode from the pen of this real-life moll, Queen of the London Underworld.'

'I'm nobody's moll!' I said indignantly. 'I'm not a thief, neither do I live among them!'

'We know you're not, Cat,' interjected Frank, 'but I'm afraid the damage is done.'

Mr Sheridan looked out of the window—we were approaching his house. You could always tell which one it was because it had a perpetual queue of creditors waiting outside in the hope of catching a few moments of the great man's time.

'You may find it best to lie low until the furore about your print alter ego dies down,' Mr Sheridan said, patting me on the knee as the carriage came to a stop. 'We writers can't let the booksellers get away with this kind of sharp dealing, can we?'

I shook my head miserably.

'Come on, Cat, cheer up! I'll get my man to take Tweadle to court to get your manuscripts back. I haven't yet decided if exposing his cheat would do you more harm than good, but if we decide to go public, we'll seek damages too.'

Mr Sheridan's display of writerly solidarity did hearten me a little but I still felt as if my life had been taken out of my hands. I let him conduct me through the noisy crowd of petitioners and pass me over to his wife's maid. In half an hour, I was bathed and dressed in fresh clothes, ready for dinner.

Mrs Sheridan was dining out. It was well known in theatre circles that husband and wife were no longer on good terms with each other so I was not surprised to find myself alone with Frank and the master of the house in the dining room. Even in my despondency, it registered somewhere in my brain that this was the first time I had ever sat at a table with my patron. Perhaps if Frank had not been there I would have been invited to eat in the kitchen. Whatever the reason, I found myself being waited on by footmen and served a fine meal that I had not had to cook. I thought of all those involved in preparing this food, knowing all too well exactly how long it took to wash, peel and boil the vegetables on my plate. It was a pity I couldn't summon the appetite to do justice to their hard work.

We ate in silence for some minutes before Mr Sheridan put down his knife and fork. I looked up; he hadn't finished but he was gazing at me thoughtfully as he topped up his wine from the decanter in front of him.

'I'm surprised at you, Cat.'

Was this the scolding I had long been expecting?

'Yes, sir?'

'Surprised that you haven't shown any curiosity at all as to what favour I wanted to ask you.'

I remembered dimly that he had said something about this in the carriage.

'I'm sorry to disappoint you, sir.'

'The old Cat would have pounced on this the instant I mentioned it.'

'Perhaps.'

'There's no perhaps about it! You would have plagued me until I revealed all. What's got into you?'

I shrugged, biting my lip to stop the embarrassing display of tears that were close to falling, and pushed the peas around on my plate.

'I think, sir,' said Frank boldly, 'you are to blame for this new Cat. It was you, after all, who forced her out of Drury Lane so she fell prey to the likes of

78

Tweadle. I—we thought the theatre was going to look after her.' He had obviously been saving this speech up, resentful that I had been so casually abandoned.

Mr Sheridan splashed some wine into Frank's glass.

'Well said, young Avon. I'm glad Cat has such an able supporter. But if she would rouse herself to show the merest glimmer of interest, I'll tell her how I wish to make amends.'

I looked up. 'Sir?'

'Over the past few weeks, I've been feeling at a bit of a loss.'

Not as much as me, he hadn't.

'Events are happening so fast in France—things that will decide the fate of Europe—and I only get to hear about them long after, when some newspaper gets round to printing an inaccurate story or two. Even then, they rarely cover the really important matters, such as how the French are reacting to the changes.'

He was right of course: I'd often thought that newspaper editors saw it as their national duty to send us to sleep with their accounts of debates and legislation. I rarely picked up a paper and then only to read the scandal column.

Mr Sheridan refilled his glass. 'I was thinking that I need a correspondent in Paris, someone who can keep me up to date. A couriered letter would take only a few days to reach me—I could be among the best informed in parliament. This person could find out for me what the common people are thinking without alerting the governments of either France or Britain to my interest. This revolution is not going to be decided in the debating chambers or

79

palaces of Europe, but on the streets. Only last week, I was asking myself who I know who understands both worlds—that of the poor as well as the rich—and could move between them without being noticed.'

Very interesting, but what was it to do with me?

'I'm sorry, sir,' I ventured. 'I don't know anyone who could help—unless you count Johnny—Lord Jonathan Fitzroy. Perhaps if you—'

'No, no, you halfwit. Not Johnny. In any case, he's transferred his allegiance from us to his adopted country. I thought the answer was obvious. Don't you, Lord Francis?'

Frank was now grinning at me. 'As clear as daylight, sir.'

Surely he didn't mean what I thought he meant?

'I'm talking about you, Cat.'

'Me? But I couldn't even look after myself in London and you expect me to do so in Paris?'

Mr Sheridan waved this objection away with the decanter. 'You mustn't take one mistake as the last word on your abilities. Chalk it up to experience. Learn from it.'

'I've learnt that I'm useless.'

'Never say that—you are not to say that.' Mr Sheridan exchanged a worried look with Frank. 'It's not like my Cat to let a scoundrel like that bookseller put her down—not the Cat who saved my diamond, the Cat who rescued Pedro, the Cat who wrote those stories.'

His words reignited a glimmer of pride in my achievements. He was right. I was wallowing in my own misery—not an attractive sight. It was time I struggled back into the mêlée as others had done before me. Syd never gave up if he was floored in a

80

fight. He pulled himself up to the scratch and continued to slog it out. Mr Sheridan himself had not conceded defeat when his debut play, *The Rivals*, failed dismally on its first night: he revised it and continued on to a triumph.

'Tell me what you want me to do,' I demanded, pushing my plate aside.

'That's my girl,' replied Mr Sheridan, raising his glass to me. 'As I told you, I need to place a confidential agent in Paris and I have been keeping you in mind. You have shown yourself to be resourceful and loyal—important qualities for the job.'

His praise was like water on parched earth. I felt relieved to hear that someone did not consider me entirely worthless. He was giving me a chance to travel like all my friends; I could prove to them that I was not limited to Covent Garden as they thought.

'I have a few ideas as to how it can be done,' he continued. 'First, we must get you there without anyone being any the wiser. I'm glad to say that fate has handed us the perfect opportunity.'

'How so?'

'Our ballerinas have to return to their native land after the closure of Drury Lane. I have sounded out Madame Beaufort as to the possibility of smuggling you in with them.'

'You want me to pretend to be a ballet dancer?' The idea was so absurd as to be laughable.

'Exactly,' he continued, not seeing the joke. 'Madame Beaufort will tell the girls that she has decided to give you a trial.'

'It's going to be a very short one—I don't know the first thing about dancing.'

'Nonsense, Cat,' interjected Frank. 'You're light

on your feet and quick to learn—you might turn out to be perfect.'

'A perfect disaster like enough,' I muttered.

'Lord Francis here will escort you to Paris on the pretext of visiting his family,' Mr Sheridan explained. 'He will be on hand to sort out any . . . er . . . diplomatic problems you might encounter at the border.'

Frank winked. 'Cat, I have you to thank for getting me out of studying for a month. Mama and Papa will understand that I had a higher duty to perform.'

Once again, I had the sensation that my life had been taken completely out of my control, but this time the feeling was exhilarating, like sledging down a steep hill not knowing exactly what was at the bottom.

'Once in Paris at Madame Beaufort's I will expect you to write regular letters to me,' continued Mr Sheridan. 'To keep the arrangement private, you'd best write them with an eye to the fact that they may be opened in transit. I suggest you sign them as "Diamond".'

'Why the need for a secret name? Does that mean my role will be dangerous?' I wasn't afraid of a bit of risk but I wanted to enter into this with my eyes open.

'No, no,' said Mr Sheridan, with not entirely convincing ease. 'It's just that it could be embarrassing for me if my interest in foreign political affairs came out.'

'Do you think my French will be up to the task? Do you think they'll tell me anything?' He seemed to have every confidence that I would be able to keep him informed of events in Paris but I wasn't so sure. My own experience on the streets of London had taught me that you could still be a stranger even in your own country when you moved beyond your circle.

My patron smiled, playing with the stem of his glass so that it caught the candlelight, casting diamond-shaped patterns on to his face. 'Put it this way: I expect you to come back with a much increased vocabulary—the sort they don't teach in the classroom—but I am convinced that you, if anyone, will get by with the people of Paris and earn their confidence.'

'And payment?'

A familiar evasive look passed over Mr Sheridan's face. 'Well, we'll see about that on your return, shall we?'

That was no good. 'I think, sir, we'd better see about it now.'

He sighed. 'It is a sad day when even my own protégée does not trust me.'

'Of course I don't.'

'You're very wise, Cat. All right, you'll get your expenses and a guinea a letter—if it is informative.'

'And what sort of things do you want to know?'

'What the people are thinking and feeling. I don't want summaries of political speeches; I want an insight into what is really going on.'

'You mean, which way the wind of change is blowing?'

'Exactly.'

*   *   *

The first stage of my transformation into a confidential correspondent was to disguise myself

83

as an aspiring dancer. The following day I was ordered to report to Madame Beaufort at her lodgings just off the Strand where a dressmaker was also in attendance.

'*Eh bien*, Cat, we are to turn you into a little ballerina, yes?' said Madame Beaufort, making me stand in the centre of the room while she looked me over with a professional eye. She was an odd looking woman—like an owl in an ivy bush with her thin face peeping out of masses of blonde, frizzy hair. The rest of her was so tall and slender that she reminded me of a dandelion clock and I half expected the wind to start blowing her away. 'We speak French from now, agreed?'

'Agreed, Madame,' I said, switching into French. Though I had gained a tolerable fluency mingling with the dancers backstage, I knew I was badly in need of practice if I was to do a proper job in Paris.

Madame Beaufort turned to the dressmaker, a compatriot she had introduced as Madame Chenier.

'What do you think?' she asked.

Madame Chenier was as fat as the ballet mistress was thin. She rose from her seat like a cow from clover and trotted over to me with a determined expression on her round, rosy face. She then proceeded to prod and measure me so enthusiastically that I was sure I would be covered in bruises.

'This will be no problem—the child has the bearing of a dancer already, though a little on the short side. I have a few things with me that will do,' declared Madame Chenier, giving my chin a playful—but painful—tweak. Clearly, she was a woman who didn't know her own strength.

'What kind of things, madame?' I asked with a feeling of trepidation.

'You must look like my other girls, *ma chérie*,' said Madame Beaufort.

'Oh yes, and what does that mean?'

'Pretty—very pretty. We will have a little thing going here with the hair, no? And a few lace trims around there?' She directed her remarks to Madame Chenier and they were soon clucking together, dragging my arms out of one set of garments and draping new clothes over me.

'I have been looking at this little one for years, madame, and simply longing to get a hold of her,' continued Madame Beaufort, turning to her friend. 'She has no style; she hides her pretty person behind dirt and such clothes as you would not believe! But Madame Reid . . .' she wrinkled her nose in disgust, '. . . she has no sense of what is chic, *n'est-ce pas*? But today we can strip away the layers of that English pudding and reveal the soufflé within!'

I snorted but they were oblivious to my derision. My fashion advisers were getting quite beside themselves. With Mr Sheridan footing the bill for my outfit they were thoroughly enjoying dressing me up like some doll.

'Ta-dah!' trilled Madame Beaufort, pushing me to arm's length. 'What do you think, madame?'

'Beautiful, very beautiful! I'll just pin up that hem and she will be finished.'

I looked down at myself; I was in a dress the colour of pink sugared almonds—not a good shade for a redhead. 'May I see?' I asked fearfully.

'Of course, and I think . . . *oui*, I think you will be very surprised, *ma cherie*.' Madame Beaufort clapped her hands together, holding them on her breast. 'Now I will not be ashamed to have you as part of my ensemble.'

Madame Chenier pulled me over to the mirror. 'Close your eyes!' she said playfully. 'And now—open them.'

Surprise is one word for it. Another is horror. I looked like an over-decorated cake, frills and ribbons everywhere. If any of Syd's boys saw me like this, I'd be a laughing stock.

'Is that really it?' I croaked.

'Oh?' said Madame Beaufort, coming to stand behind me, resting her hands on my shoulders. 'You think we've forgotten something? Perhaps you are right.' She seized a large pink bow from Madame Chenier's work basket and plonked it on top of my curls. 'Oh, you look so sweet.'

I scowled, speechless at the horrendous apparition in the mirror.

'Enough fun,' continued Madame Beaufort, tossing one of my locks playfully . . .

Fun!

'Now we dance!'

The next hour was agony. She took me through the basic steps like a sergeant major drilling a new recruit. Never again will I mock a ballerina. I'd been fooled by the fluffy skirts: underneath they must be made of sprung steel. Madame's favourite method of correcting an erroneous posture was to rap the offending limb with a thin birch rod. As most of my limbs were more often in the wrong than the right, I felt as if I'd spent the afternoon being lashed by a tree in a gale.

Every muscle aching, I staggered out at four to find Frank waiting to escort me home. His jaw dropped when he saw me then, most ungallantly, he howled with laughter. Doubled over on the pavement, he roared until he had tears streaming down his face.

'What's the matter with you?' I asked tersely—though I had a fair idea.

'You look—you look—'

'Lovely? Elegant? Feminine?' I asked sourly.

'Ridiculous.'

I heaved a sigh. 'And don't I know it. Stop it, Frank, you know why I'm doing this. You're not making it any easier acting like you've never seen a girl dressed up before.'

'But you!'

'Thank you, Frank, that's quite enough humiliation. I had a basinful yesterday; I don't need a second helping today.'

He took command of himself, gasping for air. 'Sorry, Cat. That was quite out of order. You look . . . you look very nice.' The last word turned into a snort and he gave up trying to speak as he conducted me back to Mr Sheridan's.

*   *   *

Madame Beaufort's company of nine ballerinas left London early on Saturday morning, escorted by Frank in his own carriage. He had handpicked the servants so it was no surprise to me to find Joseph, my special friend among the footmen, included in the party.

I hung out of the window as we trotted out of London on the Dover road. Only days ago I had sat on the milestone and lamented being left behind; now I too was on my way. What was the world beyond the city like? I couldn't wait to see. The familiar landmarks fell away surprisingly quickly as we crossed the Thames and travelled on into Kent. Except for one short stay in the village of Clapham, I had never spent so much time in the countryside. All that open space made me feel nervous.

Frank was watching me with an amused expression. We were alone in the carriage, as Madame Beaufort had elected to travel with her girls to seed in the story of my trial with the troupe. She hoped the tale would be in full flower by the time we reached Paris before any awkward questions were raised as to why a protégée of Mr Sheridan should take it into her head to travel at his expense. She was representing it as the pay-off for making me homeless—which in a way it was.

'Beautiful, isn't it, Cat?' Frank said teasingly as we passed through a field where the hay was entwined with splashes of red and blue wild flowers like paint spilled by a overenthusiastic set decorator. Butterflies danced above, tiny winged ballerinas in multicoloured gowns.

'It's . . . er . . . it's . . .' I couldn't find the words. I wanted to say that it was 'empty', 'strange', 'frightening', but I knew from my reading of poetry that I should be saying things like 'arcadian', 'pastoral' and 'peaceful'. For me, the silence was deafening.

'You don't like it, do you?'

I didn't want him to find me so unrefined as not to be able to appreciate nature. 'It's very . . . green.'

'True . . . honest and true, just like you,' he laughed. 'I'm so pleased you didn't come out with any of that tired old poetic stuff. Yes, the country-side is green, undeniably green.' He offered me a chicken leg from the hamper stowed under his seat. 'You must let me show you Boxton one day. It's very green too, but there's loads to do—riding, hunting, fishing, walking.'

'Frank, can you really see me on a horse?' I asked, wrinkling my nose.

'I can see you excelling at anything you turn your hand to, Cat, horse riding included,' he replied loyally.

'I didn't excel at looking after myself, did I?' The bleak mood settled on me again as I remembered the humiliation of my time at Mr Tweadle's.

Frank rubbed the bridge of his nose. 'Why didn't you tell us, Cat? I thought you knew you could ask us to do anything for you. Any of us would.'

'I thought I had to make my own way.' I stared at my hands, still coarse after weeks of scrubbing and peeling.

'But why? None of us do. Lizzie and I—we have our parents. Syd's got his family, his manager, and his boys around him. Pedro has Signor Angelini looking out for him. Why should you be on your own?'

How could he understand what it was like to be me?

'I always have been, Frank. On my own, I mean. Ever since I can remember, my place in the world has been precarious, bound up with Drury Lane. When that went, I felt as if I too no longer existed.'

'But you're far more than a theatre, Cat. Don't you see that?'

'Thank you, Frank. I'm trying to.'

'We all think highly of you—and not just your friends. Lord, Cat, even Billy Shepherd compliments you by thinking you worth his attention.'

89

His comment took me back to Billy's collection and the empty cushion. I wondered if I should tell Frank about the deal I had made. It would be good to share the burden with someone—and he was as good as inviting me to rely on him.

'There's something you should know about me and Billy Shepherd, Frank,' I began awkwardly.

Frank threw his chicken bone out of the window. 'Oh, yes? Don't tell me you're engaged?' he joked.

'Not exactly . . .' I then told him about the promise I had given and how Billy wished me to repay him. When he heard that Billy had asked for the Crown jewels, Frank gave a bark of laughter which turned abruptly into a growl when he learned of the alternative I had been offered.

'You don't think you have to do anything that that cockroach asks, do you?'

I should have realized that he wouldn't understand. If I'd told the same story to Syd, Jo or Nick they would have got it at once. 'It's street honour, Frank.'

'Street honour!'

His aristocratic assumption that the people of the lower classes were less men and women of their word than the nobility rankled with me.

'If you gave your solemn promise to someone you'd keep, it wouldn't you, Frank, or expect to be shamed in your circle?'

'Of course, but . . .'

'If I don't keep my word, I can't go back. You wouldn't want me to take the second choice Billy gave me, would you?'

'Heavens no, Cat.' He looked shocked at the idea.

'Don't worry, Frank. I may have made a mess of

90

the last few weeks but I can handle Billy Shepherd. I'll come up with something—or I'll hitch a lift to America with Lizzie and Johnny. Exile is better than putting myself under Billy's tender loving care.'

Frank shook his head and looked out at a windmill revolving slowly on the horizon. 'I'm pleased Lizzie never gives me any cause for concern, Cat, for with you as my honorary sister, I have more than enough worries.'

I felt a lump in my throat. That he looked on me like a sister was the most wonderful thing I had ever heard. I had an adopted family of the very best. How could I have ever thought I was abandoned and let myself get into such a fix?

'Thank you, Frank. I'll try not to disgrace you.'

'Though I advise you to take some fashion tips from Lizzie,' he added with a significant look at my frills, 'I don't think I can cope with a younger sister who looks like she's wearing the entire contents of my maiden aunt's workbasket.'

My chicken bone sailed through the air and struck Frank on the forehead.

'Now I know the old Cat's back!' he said, rubbing the spot with a rueful smile.

Reader, if you have not yet had to endure a sea crossing, take advice from me and keep your feet firmly on dry ground. I have discovered that I am not what one would call a natural sailor.

The wind began to pick up as we descended into Dover at nightfall. Frank made light of it, telling me it was only a summer squall, and I, not yet knowing my own weakness, followed him innocently on board the little vessel that was to transport us across the water.

'Quickly, quickly, girls,' Madame Beaufort trilled to her troupe. 'Get below.' She cast a disapproving look at the sailors who were leering at her charges.

'Show us a bit of ankle, love,' shouted one tar to the prettiest of the chorus. 'Give us a twirl, will you?'

The ballerinas twittered with pleased outrage at this impertinence and scurried off to their cabins. I suddenly remembered that I should think of myself as one of them. With a sigh, wondering what I had let myself in for embarking on this adventure for Mr Sheridan so far from my natural habitat, I took one last look at the twinkling lights of Dover at the foot of the great white cliffs and dutifully followed Madame Beaufort.

It was then that my torment began. Leaving Frank with his footman, Joseph, up in the bracing fresh air of the deck, I found myself closeted with three dancers called Mimi, Colette and Belle. I'd never much liked them at Drury Lane and closer acquaintance did little to improve on this impression. They greeted my arrival in their cabin as an unwanted intrusion on their gang. The spare bunk had already been covered in clothes and they made no effort to move them.

'Why, girls, it's the little cat,' simpered Mimi, preening her blonde curls in a tiny hand-mirror. 'Mr Sheridan's *old* favourite.'

'Thought you were too good for us, did you, travelling with that young lord of yours?' asked Colette with a bitter twist to her lips.

'Pleased to meet you too, ladies,' I said, ignoring these slights. It was useless to explain to these creatures the idea of a friendship with someone so far above my social status. You can't live behind stage as long as I have without experiencing the petty jealousies and spite of some performers.

'I can't understand what that young gentleman sees in her, can you, girls?' asked Belle, as if I wasn't there. 'She's such a queer little thing and he so handsome. And as for thinking that she'll make it as a dancer! Madame Beaufort has gone quite mad.'

'No, it's not madness,' replied Mimi. 'Old Sheridan must have paid her to take his discarded pet out of the way. And who can blame him now she's made herself notorious with those stories she wrote? She's become an embarrassment.' Mimi pulled out a little magazine from her trunk. 'Queen of the London Underworld—I mean, who does she think she's fooling?'

'Queen of the chamberpots more like,' added Colette.

So I was to be punished for making myself famous, was I? I suppose I could look on it as the penalty for falling for Mr Tweadle's cheat. I only wished that I had as many piquant French words to

93

hand as I had English so I could answer back in style. Perhaps if I hadn't been feeling so green, I would have tried. But as it was, I saved my breath and attempted to quell my growing nausea.

There was a creaking overhead and the sound of feet running across the ceiling: we were getting under way. I contemplated returning to the deck for some fresh air and the diversion of watching the sailors hoist sail, but my assigned role required me to act as if I were part of the troupe. Instead I took revenge on my three companions by climbing into the bunk and spreading out regardless of the clothes.

'That's my best pelisse!' protested Mimi, pulling a violet cloak from under me.

The ship gave a lurch as she left the protection of the harbour and was hit broadside by the wind. The pelisse gave an ugly ripping sound.

'Look what you've done!' Mimi held up the torn sleeve, for all the world acting as if it were my fault that a storm was blowing.

I was about to reply but was prevented by a strange feeling in my stomach. Opening my mouth, it wasn't insults that poured out, but something far more offensive. Mimi screamed and jumped back. Belle and Colette fled to the other side of the tiny cabin.

'Clean it up, you disgusting thing!' screeched Mimi.

As if I could in my current state! I rolled over, not to repair the damage but to add to it.

'I want another cabin! I'm not staying in here with her!' Mimi stormed out, crying for Madame Beaufort, closely followed by her two friends.

I didn't care. They could call me all the names

94

under the sun, shout and scream at me. I just wanted to die as the ship bucked and reared like an unbroken horse. Why, oh why, had I thought Mr Sheridan's idea of sending me to France a good one? It was the stupidest thing ever! I was going to be useless! I couldn't even travel without collapsing in a helpless smelly heap! My dejection was so complete that I didn't notice Joseph enter ten minutes later, armed with bucket and mop to cleanse the cabin, nor Frank place a cool cloth on my head. He told me later he'd given up his berth to the fugitives from mine, though they were soon retching with the rest of the troupe as the storm worsened. They should have stayed with me for I had the best nurses in Frank and Joseph, neither of whom—curse their iron constitutions—showed the least discomfort in the heavy seas.

The crossing to France, which had appeared such a small thing in Mr Sheridan's study as I had examined a map, now took on an epic stature as our little ship battled its way to Calais. When my stomach was so empty I could be ill no more, I dozed, drifting in and out of nightmares in which our ship foundered on rocks or broke apart, casting us all on the waves.

'Kill me, Frank. I just want it to end,' I groaned some hours later.

'Don't be silly, Cat, you don't mean that,' he chided.

I looked across to find him reading by the light of the swinging lantern. Reading! How could he? It was the story Mimi had brandished at me earlier. I crumpled flat on my back.

'You know, this really is capital stuff. I hadn't realized what an attractive fellow I am till I read it in your own words!'

'Don't flatter yourself,' I muttered wretchedly. 'It's fiction, remember.'

'You must be feeling better,' declared Frank, 'if you are up to insulting me.'

He was right: I had begun to improve. The storm was still raging but as we drew into the more sheltered waters of the French coast, the terrible stomach cramps subsided. Feeling light-headed and weak, I propped myself up on Frank's cloak. Joseph was chuckling away to himself, deep in another of the magazines. I couldn't help but feel proud that my stories had the power to amuse my friends.

As our ship entered Calais harbour, it came back to me that I had a tricky time ahead. If Mr Sheridan's reason for sending me all this way was to remain a secret, I had to blend in with the troupe while our papers were examined. Would the officials buy the idea that this little redhead was a bona fide ballerina? If they looked closely, surely they would realize that I was like a duck among the swans? I wished I felt more up to the interview, but after all that retching, I was too washed out to do more than stagger on deck very sloppily dressed. Fortunately for me, the weather had taken its toll on my companions: none of the dancers looked their best. They neither noticed nor cared as I mingled with them in the early dawn.

'Good morning, citizens and citizenesses,' announced the port official as he came aboard. He had obviously had a good night's sleep and had not spent the night with his head in a bucket, as his brass buttons were well polished, his uniform crisp and neat. His upper lip was adorned with a splendid black moustache. 'Now, who do we have here?' The captain presented him with the passenger list. 'Where is this Lord Francis, son of the Duke of Avon?' he asked with a frown on his brow. The master of the vessel pointed to Frank, who had taken up his station alone at the far end of the ship from me, assuming an uncharacteristically aristocratic distance from the commoners he had been thrown among. 'I'll deal with him last,' the official said with relish. 'Ladies first, *n'est-ce pas*?'

As if to rub in his slight to the young noble, the Frenchman fawned over Madame Beaufort and her charges. 'I rejoice to see such pretty flowers of French maidenhood returning to our shores,' he said with overblown gallantry as he kissed her hand. 'Much has changed even in the few short years since your departure, madame. You left us slaves and return to a free France.'

'Indeed, sir,' the ballet mistress said with a grave nod of her head. 'You honour us with your welcome.'

He took the sheaf of papers from her hand and leafed through them, making the occasional remark to the French girls, flirting with each in turn. Mine were at the end—conspicuous for being the only English national among them. 'What is this?' he chuckled. 'You bring a little roast beef with you to turn her into a dancer? Where is she, this marvel?'

I stepped out from behind one of the tallest of the dancers. The chuckle turned into a full belly laugh.

'You have your work cut out for you, madame. Surely she is too small for the chorus line?'

Madame Beaufort gave me a nervous look. It had only now struck her what she was doing: smuggling a foreign agent into her native land. Some would

97

think her a traitor.

'Her appearance is deceptive, sir,' she said hurriedly. 'Catherine is very promising.'

Mimi snorted disdainfully. The official frowned. 'And you, madame, will you be responsible for her conduct while she is here?' he asked the ballet mistress.

'I . . . er . . .' Madame Beaufort hesitated, doubtless wondering what repercussions would fall on her if my true role was detected. I felt an unpleasant twist in the pit of my stomach that was nothing to do with seasickness. I could see Frank stirring restlessly as he kept a close eye on proceedings.

'I have agreed to give the girl a trial, sir—that is all.'

'And if she fails? We do not want English girls abandoned in Paris—we have enough vagrants of our own. I cannot grant her a passport unless I know she has the means to support herself. Who will pay for her return?'

'Her sponsor,' said Madame Beaufort awkwardly.

'Sponsor?' The official checked the papers again. 'Who is that?'

This was not going well. I hadn't even set foot on French soil and already my connection to Mr Sheridan, a name that would be well-known even this side of the Channel, seemed on the point of being blurted out.

'It's Mr—'

'My man!' A haughty voice rapped out from the far end of the deck. 'When you have quite finished dallying with the ladies, some of us have pressing business to attend to.' It was Frank. He strode purposefully across the planks to confront the

98

official. 'Shocking lack of efficiency!' he continued. 'I'll be having words with your superior.'

The official folded up my papers and absent-mindedly handed them back to Madame Beaufort. 'And just who do you think you are, citizen, talking to an officer like this?'

'I am Lord Francis of Boxton, the son of the Duke of Avon. I am used to being treated with more respect where I come from. I have had my fill of being made to wait behind a pack of women.'

The official gave a tight smile, relishing his opportunity to put down a popinjay of a noble. 'Well, citizen, you are in France now. You'll wait for as long as I say you should. Ladies, you may go.' And the Frenchman waved us commoners off.

I waited on the busy pier for Frank for over an hour. Grumbling at the English boy's rudeness, Madame Beaufort and her dancers disappeared into a quayside coaching inn to engage carriages for Paris and have breakfast, leaving me kicking my heels with mounting anxiety. Around me the fishwives were screeching in rapid, incomprehensible French. Buckets of forlorn fish gaped on the boards before being swiftly dispatched by efficient fingers, gutted and tossed into crates. Still feeling delicate from my night of sickness, I turned my eyes and sank against a wooden post.

'Cat?' It was Frank's voice.

'Thank goodness! I thought he was going to send you back to England.'

'He would have done if he could have found anything wrong with my papers,' laughed Frank. 'Instead, he had to content himself with holding me up as long as he could. Joseph here was quite

99

frothing at the mouth by the time he'd finished with the revenge of petty officialdom.'

Joseph did indeed look very cross. He was fiercely loyal to his master and any slight, real or imagined, was sure to meet with his severe displeasure.

'Thank you, Frank,' I said. 'I think you saved my bacon back there. I'm not sure Madame Beaufort is to be relied on any longer now she is out of the reach of Mr Sheridan's charm.'

Frank nodded his agreement. 'Where is she?'

'Over at the inn. She's seeing to the carriages. Apparently if we don't leave soon we will not be in Paris until after dark on Monday. I hadn't realized it was so far.' All these distances were confusing me. I was used to being able to get to places at a day's walk at the most. Two or three days at the rapid speed of a carriage suggested miles that I found hard to imagine.

'Well, what are we waiting for?' said Frank cheerfully. 'Let's grab some breakfast before those girls eat the lot.'

When we entered the dining room of the inn, we found the ballerinas had already finished. They were distinctly cool towards Frank and barely civil to me.

'I have engaged four carriages,' Madame Beaufort said in clarion tones as Frank and I sat down at the table. 'Not of the highest standard, unfortunately. The girls and I will wait for you outside. Please do not delay us any longer, my lord.' She said these last words in a sharp tone I had never heard her use before.

'I think Madame Beaufort is infected by the revolutionary air of her country,' I whispered. 'I

100

think she wants to be rid of us.'

Frank nodded and took a gulp of his coffee. 'But Mr Sheridan is a friend to the revolution, isn't he? He's not trying to undermine what's happening here: he just wants to find out what's happening.'

'I know. All the same, coming home has definitely changed her attitude.'

Not wishing to give further provocation to my new mistress, we hurried our breakfast and emerged into the yard. Three carriages were drawn up, already filled with dancers.

'Where is the fourth carriage, madame?' Frank asked.

'Over there,' Madame Beaufort said with a careless wave of her hand, pointing out a dilapidated four-wheeled fiacre. She saw our downcast faces. 'It was all I could get, my lord.' Mimi giggled; Belle looked smugly at me from the safe confines of their relatively comfortable carriage. Joseph marched up behind us, face like thunder.

'My lord,' he said in a brittle voice, 'you cannot travel in that deathtrap. The coachman is either drunk or a halfwit. I couldn't get a word of sense out of him.'

'Not good enough for his lordship, is it?' demanded Madame Beaufort shrilly. 'Surely you're not suggesting that some of my girls should travel in it so his lordship can have one of these?'

Frank bowed gallantly. 'Of course not, madame.'

'There really is no other carriage available—ask the hostler if you don't believe me.'

'I do not doubt you. It will have to do. Joseph, please see to my luggage. Miss Royal is to travel with you, I suppose?'

101

'You suppose wrong, sir. All these carriages are full.' Mimi and Belle spread their skirts on the seat, hiding any spare inch of upholstery. 'She was happy enough to journey with you to Dover; I assumed she would do so again.'

'But madame . . .!' Frank began to protest. This hadn't been the plan at all: I was supposed to be mingling with the troupe, not journeying conspicuously with a peer of the British realm.

'Leave it, Frank,' I muttered, pulling on his arm. There was no point making a scene about this. It would only risk attracting more attention. I tugged the stupid bow from my hair. At least I wouldn't have to continue to look like a doll if I was no longer travelling with the dancers.

We clambered into our evil-smelling carriage. The poor horses looked on their last legs, fitting steeds for the vehicle.

'Don't worry about them,' said Frank, noticing where I was staring. 'We'll change horses at the next staging post. The next pair must be an improvement.

But there was nothing to be done about the driver though I wished we could swap him too. He reeled out of the public bar, and tried and failed to climb to his seat, until Joseph seized him by the scruff of the neck and hoisted him up.

'I'll keep an eye on him, sir,' Joseph said from his post behind the fiacre.

The driver then made a meal of filling his pipe as all the other carriages jingled into life. With a clatter of hooves, they pulled out of the yard.

'Follow those carriages! Allez!' ordered Frank.

Our driver gave a shrug and continued to light his pipe. He obviously had no intention of setting off until he was quite comfortable. Joseph gave him a firm shove in the shoulder blades.

'You . . . trot-trot!' he said loudly in English, balling his fist to emphasize the point.

'Poof!' said the driver, but this time with a hint of anger. He glared at Joseph and picked up the reins.

Thinking we were now finally off, I retreated from the window and gingerly sat down on the ripped seat, composing myself for the long journey ahead. Nothing. Frank got up again. Our driver was now talking animatedly to the hostler.

'Monsieur, can we go, please!' Frank shouted.

Our man took a swig from a wine bottle he had stashed at his feet, clicked his tongue and the horses started to amble off. Every cobble and pothole made the carriage rattle alarmingly as if it were about to fall apart.

'Do you think we'll ever get there?' I asked as we turned out on to the post road to Paris.

'Poof!' said Frank with an acutely observed Gallic shrug.

*　　　*　　　*

Reader, as you might imagine, we soon fell far behind the other carriages, arriving at each staging post hours after them. This meant we always had the last choice of horses, delaying us further still. It was well past midnight when we clattered into Amiens and found our inn. Frank had to shake me awake. I made my way to a room and tumbled into bed beside one of the dancers. I was asleep before my head hit the pillow—which was as well for the sheets were none of the cleanest and the bed harboured other things beside two tired travellers.

The next day followed the same pattern except I had the added indignity of angry red bites all over my body. Frank couldn't help but notice me itching and shifting in my seat.

'Best not to scratch them,' he advised. 'It'll only make them worse.'

'How come you didn't get bitten?' I asked enviously.

'I took one look at my proposed bed next to a snoring merchant from Brussels and decided to sleep out in the stables. The hay was very comfortable.' He removed a strand of it from his hair.

'I've heard of people travelling for their health—they must need their heads examining,' I grumbled as we jolted against a kerb stone.

'Watch it! Regardez!' shouted Joseph from somewhere above.

'Admit it, Cat,' teased Frank, 'you're loving every moment. The excitement of never knowing what is going to happen next, your first taste of a foreign culture—think how your mind is expanding!'

'The only thing expanding right now are my ankles. They've been bitten so badly they are swelling up.'

'Poor little Cat. You should have stayed in your basket at home.'

'I don't have a basket or a home, thanks for reminding me, Lord Francis of Boxton.'

'No,' he said brightly, 'but you have an adventure ahead of you and a job to do. Many girls would love to have the freedom you have.'

This was very true. 'You're a good traveller, Frank,' I told him. 'I need to listen to you more often.'

He grinned. 'Look and learn, Cat; look and learn.'

*   *   *

The first thing Frank taught me was not to be too proud to ask directions. It was late as we passed the gates of Paris and headed into the centre of the town. Tall houses loomed up on either side of the road, chinks of light peeping through slatted shutters, striped awnings billowing, strings of washing swaying, fluttering like naval signals saying 'Welcome to Paris, Cat Royal'. Closer to the centre the finer the houses became with ornate carvings and smart shopfronts of shining plate glass. Majestic trees rustled in the night breeze. The air was ripe with the scent of cooking—strange smells, pungent and rich.

We were supposed to be meeting Madame Beaufort at her lodgings near the Opera but the driver was too drunk to understand the address Joseph was shouting at him.

'Why don't we ask someone the way?' I suggested.

'No, no, Cat,' said Frank, getting out a map of Paris from his coat pocket. He spread it out and studied it carefully in the poor light from the carriage lanterns.

'Do you know where we are?' I asked.

He shook his head. 'But it can't be that difficult to follow a map. We must have come in through this gate.' He muttered away to himself, consulted Joseph, stared out of the window for inspiration, did everything but humble himself to ask one of the

Parisians who were walking along the pavement only a few feet away.

'It's on the right. I'm sure it is,' Frank said determinedly over an hour later as we passed a great palace of a building. I was losing faith in his map-reading skills. We'd already ended up in a cemetery, in a blind alley and in the middle of some very bemused nuns in a convent as they filed in to vespers. The horses dutifully turned right, clip-clopped on the cobblestones and came wearily to a halt.

'We've stopped,' said Frank. 'We must be almost there.'

'Er, Frank,' I said, tapping his shoulder. 'Look out my side.'

It was a moonless night. A darker expanse like a bolt of black silk glinting with starlight marked the passage of the great river at the heart of the city, the Seine. Across the bridge in front of us, the buildings were dwarfed by two square towers rising behind the rooftops. It was a breathtaking sight: they were so tall they seemed to stretch to heaven like Jacob's ladder. All that was lacking were the angels climbing up and down.

'Now I know where we are!' exclaimed Frank. I resisted the temptation to point out that he had been confidently claiming this for the past hour. 'That must be Notre Dame, the cathedral of Paris.'

'I thought we were supposed to be at the Opera.'

He shook the map out with just a hint of petulance.

'Please, Frank, let us ask someone.' I was feeling exhausted. The thought of driving around in yet more circles held no attraction, not even to save Frank's pride.

'There's no one to ask.'

I had to agree that the streets were almost completely silent at this late hour as Monday night shaded into Tuesday morning. A carriage flanked by uniformed men rattled past our stranded vehicle, too fast for us to stop them. That was no good. It would have to be someone on foot.

Frank hopped out and approached a man huddled in a doorway. 'Excusez-moi, monsieur,' he began in his best schoolroom French.

'*Quoi?*' the man grunted.

'*Ou est l'Opera?*'

'*Quoi?*'

Frank was speaking louder and louder as if this would help the man understand him.

This was no good: we were getting nowhere. Frank would have to learn that, if you want directions, it was best not to pick on a halfwit beggar. I jumped down from the fiacre, determined to take matters into my own hands.

'Look!' I tugged Frank's sleeve as I'd spotted a woman standing with her face to the wall, shielding herself from the dust kicked up by a passing carriage. 'There's someone else. Let me ask her.' The woman was now moving swiftly, keeping to the shadows. We had to be quick if we were going to catch her.

'Excusez-moi, madame!' I called. The woman sped up, perhaps suspecting some assault as I too would have done in her situation. 'We mean you no harm. We're lost!' I called after her.

She turned, her face shadowed in a deep hood, but I saw the faint sparkle of eyes wide with alarm. She was of middle age and dressed in black, but smelling of expensive perfume and powder.

'Ssh!' she hissed, glancing over her shoulder as if fearful of pursuit. 'You are English, yes? Did Count Fersen send you for me? Speak softly now.' Her accent was strange: French laced with a hint of German.

None of this made sense to me. 'Sorry, madame, I don't know any Count Fersen. I was just saying that we were lost and wondered if you could direct us to the Opera?'

The woman's reaction was most strange. She sprang away from me without so much as a word and hurried off into the night.

'Friendly soul,' I commented sourly to Frank as we got back into the coach. 'French women are very odd. I mean, what is a lady of her quality doing wandering around the streets at this time of night on her own?'

'She probably had an assignation with this Fersen person,' said Frank with an air of worldly wisdom. 'No wonder she dashed off; she probably didn't want to be recognized and cause a scandal.'

'Well, that doesn't help us, does it? We're still lost.'

Frank gave me a wink and took out the map again. 'Nothing else for it, eh, Cat? Got to trust me now your plan has failed?'

'If you'd asked at the gate we would never have got ourselves into this mess.'

'Ah, but where's the adventure in that? You would never have seen Notre Dame by starlight.'

'That's right. I'd've been tucked up in bed, asleep. What a hardship!' I grumbled though I knew he was right. I would not have missed it for the world.

'Come on, let's try again. If Captain Cook found his way to Australia, surely we can find our way to the Opera,' Frank said happily, consulting his map.

SCENE 3—TO THE LAMP POST

To give Frank his due, we did eventually find our way to Madame Beaufort's lodgings. It was with no feeling of regret that we waved our driver off. I doubted very much if he would make it far without steering into a ditch. Only Joseph's careful watch had prevented a like accident for us. But mercifully that was no longer our concern—all we needed to do was find a bed and sleep.

The concierge of the apartment was waiting up for us and showed us through to where a cold supper had been laid out in the kitchen. I was almost asleep on my feet but Frank and Joseph managed to make a significant impact on the bread and meat between them.

'Go on up to bed. You look like you need your beauty sleep,' said Frank when he noticed me nodding over my plate.

'What are you going to do?' I asked, picking up my candle.

'Well, as my honoured parents know nothing of my arrival, I suppose I'd better wait until morning before I burst in upon them.'

'You can stay here,' said the concierge in a growl of a voice. He wore a red floppy cap on his sparse white hair and stooped as if perpetually searching for a pin on the floor. 'In exchange for a small consideration, of course.'

'That would be splendid.' Frank dug in his well-filled purse and threw the man a coin. The concierge's eyes twinkled with lively interest as he eyed my friend's riches. 'Two blankets and two chairs by the fire are all we need.'

Leaving Frank and Joseph to catch what rest they could, I went upstairs. Madame Beaufort had lodged her girls all under one roof. Expecting to find myself sharing with one of them, I discovered that I had been allocated a room right at the top of the house—a little cupboard of a place, but as it had a bed with clean sheets I was not complaining. On my bed was a note scrawled in black ink.

Daily routine for Madame Beaufort's dancers
Breakfast at six-thirty
Ballet rehearsal ten till two
Study two till three-thirty
Dinner at four
Performance six till ten
Supper
Lights out midnight

Performance—well, that was nothing to do with me. I could count on some free time in the evenings then. I would have to negotiate more if I was to do my job properly. Not even bothering to find my nightgown, I tumbled on to the mattress in my shift and instantly fell asleep, plunging into a dream where I was rooted to the spot, arms flailing like a windmill, while butterfly dancers floated elegantly across the stage.

*   *   *

A bell rang downstairs. Dragging myself out of bed, I rubbed my eyes. I could smell fresh coffee and bread. For the first time in two days, I felt hungry. Dragging a comb through my hair and dressing in my pink gown, I followed my nose down to the kitchen. Frank was sitting with Mimi, Belle and Colette at one end of the long table, while Joseph stood at his shoulder waiting to serve his master. I stood unseen in the doorway for a moment observing them. Frank was flirting outrageously— mussing up his hair and giving Mimi his most twinkling smile. I'd never seen Frank flirt before; it was highly entertaining, though I would have recommended he find a more worthy object for his attentions.

'Good morning, miss,' said Joseph solemnly when he spotted me. He pulled out a chair. 'Would you care for some coffee?'

'I'd prefer milk if they have it,' I replied, taking a seat opposite Frank and winking at him. He blushed.

'A saucer of milk for the cat: I should have guessed!' declared Mimi, none too pleased that I had come in to interrupt her attempt to hook herself a lord. 'One forgets that she's such a baby.'

Joseph presented me with a beaker of milk as if I were the queen herself.

'Miss Royal is no baby, mademoiselle,' said Frank loyally. 'I could tell you tales about her that would soon convince you of her wit and bravery.'

'No need, sir,' said Mimi primly. 'She has told the world herself.'

Mimi was beginning to really annoy me but there was nothing to be gained by exchanging insults with her.

111

'Shall we call on your parents and Lizzie, Frank?' I asked, ignoring her. 'I don't have to be at practice until ten.'

'Good idea, Cat. It's a lovely morning—let's walk.' Frank rose from the table and bowed to the company. 'Excuse me, ladies.'

Emerging into the summer sunshine, Frank got out his trusty map. Joseph appeared at his elbow and coughed.

'I took the liberty, my lord, of asking directions from the concierge; rue de Clichy lies a little to the north of us.'

Frank looked downcast to have this opportunity to navigate snatched from him but swallowed his disappointment.

'Lead on then, Joseph. Miss Royal and I will follow you.'

Paris was already awake. A baker's boy trotted by carrying a stack of long loaves in a basket. A woman swept her front step, humming to herself. Carts rumbled in from the countryside, heading to the markets. The buildings looked quite grand from the waist up, as it were: windows sparkling in the sunshine, pots of flowers blooming on the sills. However, Paris didn't bear too close an inspection lower down: the gutters were full of filth and the smell was ripe to say the least. Many of the people we passed had a bleary-eyed just-got-out-of-bed look. One pretty maid was plaiting her hair at a casement, enjoying the good-humoured compliments thrown her way by the messenger boys. As we walked, we caught the occasional whiff of fresh bread and pipe smoke from the street corner cafés.

'Well, this isn't so bad, is it?' announced Frank cheerfully, quite in the holiday mood. 'Certainly beats studying at Boxton.'

I yawned. 'You could do with brushing up on your French though. You talked to that beggar last night as if he were the king. No wonder he didn't understand you.'

'You're right.' Frank steered me round a pile of manure. 'I was never taught the equivalent of "Oi, you, how the hell do I get to that flash place where they sing and dance?"'

'Just as well, as I doubt he'd've directed us to any-where very respectable on the basis of that description.'

A dog trotted over and sniffed around our feet until called off by a whistle from its owner.

'What do you make of your first proper view of Paris?' Frank asked me.

'I like it. It seems more peaceful than London.'

No sooner had these words passed my lips than a rider galloped by, crying something at the top of his voice.

'What was that? I didn't catch what he said,' said Frank.

'I didn't hear him either. Something about the king. He's not ill, is he?'

Though we may have not understood, it was clear those around us had. Like a wind passing through a forest came the noise of voices repeating the news, shouting it from one house to the next. It swept passed Frank, Joseph and me.

'The king has fled! The royal family have disappeared!'

'To the palace!' the baker's boy shouted and took off at a run down the street, closely followed by the woman bearing a broom. They joined a tide of people all heading south. I grabbed Frank and

113

pulled him around.

'Come on—let's go and see for ourselves!' I urged him.

'But Cat!'

'It's my job to be inquisitive.' Frank had evidently not been brought up on the streets of a capital city as I had: when there's a free show, everyone goes.

Shielded by Joseph, we rushed along with the crowd. It was like being a stick carried by a flooded stream. It didn't matter that I had not the first clue where the palace was: the crowd were taking me there no matter what.

'It can't be true!' cried a woman on my left. She sported a red, white and blue ribbon pinned to her apron. 'He's the father of the nation: he won't have abandoned us!'

'He must have been abducted,' shouted a man beside her, clearly unable to imagine that the man they had all been taught to revere could leave them. 'He wouldn't betray his people!' He too wore the ribbon. Now I came to think of it, everyone was wearing one—everyone except Frank, Joseph and me. Was there something I was missing?

'It was the Austrians—that evil wife of his,' cursed another.

I glanced across at my companions. Frank had his lips pressed in a worried frown; Joseph was concentrating on protecting us from being trampled—neither appeared to be enjoying the experience. But I was. After weeks of feeling low, I felt buoyed up on the surge of people, exhilarated by the shouting, excited by being part of a momentous event. The king gone! When I reported this to Mr Sheridan, he could not deny that my first letter was worth a guinea.

Bells began to ring across the city. Drums rolled and men dressed in uniforms stumbled out of their houses, still pulling on their jackets.

'The National Guard have been called to arms!' cried the woman. 'It must be true then!'

The crowd slowed as we neared some big iron gates. As people were still pouring in from all directions, the press increased. Being a good head shorter than nearly everyone else, I was in danger of being crushed between a fat country woman and a sweep carrying a sack. Joseph grabbed me from behind.

'Excuse me, miss,' he said firmly, lifting me up on to his shoulders so that now I towered above the crowd, having a grand view of events.

'What's happening, Cat?' asked Frank.

'The gates are locked. I can see some people arguing with the guards. That's it: they've pushed them open.'

The bottleneck eased, the crowd started flowing again like wine decanting into the bowl-shaped gardens of the palace. We splashed and spread over every inch. I ducked as Joseph took me through the archway into a courtyard.

'Put me down, please,' I called to him.

He lowered me to the ground. 'Forgive the liberty, miss,' he said solemnly.

'Not at all. It was most necessary.' Taking Frank's hand, I pulled him towards the tide of people invading the palace building itself.

'You're not thinking of going in there, are you?' he asked nervously.

'Of course!'

'Cat, you are the most reckless, the most foolish—'

'I know—and don't you love me for it!' I called over my shoulder as I towed him after me.

Hot on the heels of angry Parisians, we entered the Royal Palace. For many of us, it was the first time we had seen such splendour with our own eyes. It felt almost as if we were desecrating a temple— the mystique of royalty trampled by our commoners' feet. We made our way through a grand entrance hall and into a set of interconnecting rooms lined with mirrors. Rich red and gilt flashed by as we rushed forward; priceless paintings, statues, and frescoes were for the first time on view for the masses. Fine chairs and tables were overturned, turkey rugs sullied by our boots. Servants fled before us like rabbits from a pack of hunting dogs, disappearing further into the building. But it wasn't the rich furnishings and paintings we had come to view—it was the king's bedchamber. And there it was: an empty bed, surrounded by heavy drapes, a pair of monographed slippers peeking out from underneath. The curtains had been pulled back to show that the sheets had not been slept in. A set of small clothes lay unused on a chair, abandoned by a valet when he discovered his master gone. A large mirrored dressing table stood under the window, covered in bottles and grooming implements. Among them lay an envelope weighed down by an ornate letter opener. A boy picked the knife up to inspect it, the diamonds in its handle glinting. A woman squinted at the letter but seemed unable to read the handwriting.

'What do you mean, you imbecile?' a rough-looking man was shouting into the face of a terrified servant who had not managed to escape. ' "He went to bed as normal"—how could he have done!'

'I swear, m-monsieur,' stammered the man, 'I knew nothing about it until I pulled back the curtains. It's like magic.'

'Black Austrian magic, you mean,' said the man, shaking the unfortunate valet by the lapels.

There was a crash over by the fireplace. Two members of the crowd had taken it upon themselves to smash the royal chamberpot.

'You can't do that!' squeaked the valet.

'With his high and mightiness gone, who's going to stop us?' shrieked a woman as she grabbed a bottle of cologne from the dressing table and threw it on the hearth, releasing a strong odour to mingle with that of the sweaty crowd. It seemed that not everyone was prepared to give the king the benefit of the doubt: some here were not sad to see him go.

'Let's get out,' Frank whispered in my ear.

More people were coming and the mood was turning ugly. I had to agree that it was time for us to leave. We elbowed a path back the way we had come and out into the courtyard. A detachment of guards was marching briskly towards the building with the look of men come to restore order.

'Citizens, this building is to be closed to preserve the evidence!' announced the man at the head of the column. He'd better hurry or there would be little left to preserve.

'Where's the king and his Austrian witch? Where's the dauphin and the princess royal?' shouted someone in the crowd at the palace entrance.

'You will learn more as soon as we establish the facts, citizens,' the guard said with admirable calm. 'For now, please return peacefully to your homes.

Rest assured, the National Assembly is doing all it can to return the king to Paris.'

With some grumbling, the crowd began to flow back the way it had come, massing outside the gates on a great square, not quite knowing what to do with itself. It did not feel right to be at a loose end on such an historic day.

'So the king really has left Paris,' said Frank, gazing back at the palace. 'I wonder why? I thought he had sworn to uphold the revolution.'

The rough-looking man we had seen in the king's bedchamber spun round on hearing foreign voices in the crowd. His red cap was pulled low on his brow and he had no breeches, just loose trousers such as all working-men wear.

'I saw you there, didn't I, citizens?' he challenged us. 'I remember you: the little redhead and the rich boy with the buckskin breeches. You were up in the king's bedchamber.'

There seemed no point in denying it. 'Like yourself, monsieur, we wanted to see for ourselves if it were true,' I replied politely.

'You speak funny.' He took a step towards me, a couple of burly mates in his wake. 'Austrian spies, are you?'

'Austrians! Austrians!' The cry was repeated on all sides.

Frank held up his hands in a placatory gesture. 'Not Austrians, monsieur, English.' This didn't appear to make things any better.

'But we are friends of France, not enemies,' I added hurriedly.

The man seized Frank by the arm and looked him over. Joseph stepped forward to intervene, only to find himself restrained by two men from behind. 'If

118

you are our friends, where are your cockades then?'

'Cockade?' Frank swallowed, darting a look at me but I was as clueless as him.

The man tapped his ribbon. 'Your cockade. Every citizen loyal to the revolution wears one.'

'I'm sorry, we only arrived last night. We haven't had time . . .' began Frank but he was pushed aside as the man turned his attention on me.

'And where's yours, citizeness? Among all those ribbons, surely you would have had time to put on the red, white and blue?'

I looked hopelessly down at the dress Madame Beaufort had chosen for me. It was covered in pink bows. I couldn't blame him for being offended; the dress upset me too.

'I apologize, monsieur, I didn't know . . .'

'A likely story. Everyone knows. What's your name?'

'Catherine, monsieur.'

'Catherine what?'

'Royal—I'm named after the theatre . . .'

But he didn't want to hear about that. 'Royal!' he roared, seizing me by the scruff of the neck. 'Messieurs, we have foreign royalists in our midst— enemies of the revolution. They have collaborated with the queen to poison the king against us—they persuaded him to leave.' An angry muttering rippled through the crowd surrounding us.

'They helped the king escape!' shouted a woman wildly. 'I saw them do it!'

'I did too,' shrieked another. The mood against the royal family was changing from bewilderment to indignation—and we were unfortunately about to suffer for it.

'But we didn't!' Frank protested. 'We had

119

nothing to do with it. We only arrived last night!'

'And the king fled last night!' bellowed the man triumphantly as if this was proof of our guilt. 'To the lamp post with them! Hang the foreign traitors as an example to our enemies!'

'No!' I shrieked as he dragged me with him to the edge of the square. 'We're innocent—we've done nothing!'

Joseph was struggling frantically with his captors; Frank had been wrestled to the ground by three men. A woman spat on him.

'Death to the foreign spies!' she jeered.

'Cat, run!' Frank yelled, but there was no chance of that: the man had a firm grip on me. Someone produced a length of rope and threw it over one of the arms of a lamp post, a noose tied on one end. I was now fighting for my life. I twisted round and kneed my captor where it would hurt most. He bent double, eyes watering, but still kept a hold of my hair.

'Hang the girl first,' he gasped. Two men stepped forward and took me by the arms, lifting me off the ground as I wriggled in their grasp.

'But she's only young,' one said doubtfully, looking for guidance to our self-appointed judge.

'Not too young to be a royalist traitor,' he firmly replied.

'I'm not a royalist. I'm a dancer!' I screamed. 'I'm from the streets like you.' I let out a string of expletives, calling them every name I could think of which, had they known English, would have convinced them of the truth of my claim.

'A little aristocratic firecracker, this one!' jeered a woman as the noose was put round my neck.

I couldn't believe it: this was the end. I didn't

120

want to die like this—not today, not dressed up like a pink sugar confection. These stupid halfwits were going to murder me because of a name they didn't understand! I was so angry that I forgot even my fear.

'You imbeciles!' I shouted. Someone tried to pull my hands behind me to bind them. I wrenched them free and employed them in a universally rude gesture. If I was going down, I was damn well going down fighting. 'That to you, citizen—and you—and you!' My escaped hands were caught and tied together with a handkerchief. 'You'll regret this, you will!'

'Not as much as you!' laughed my judge. 'Up, up and away with the royalist witch!'

'Not Cat, no!' yelled Frank. 'Let her go!'

'Not likely, mate. You're next so shut it!' The man gave a tug on the rope.

'Stop!' A new voice was unexpectedly raised in my defence. The boy I'd noticed in the king's bedchamber picking up the knife pushed his way to the front of the crowd and planted himself before me, poised on the balls of his feet like a dancer about to spring into action. He was barefoot and had a red cap pushed back on his head. A gaudy waistcoat edged with gold braid covered his tattered shirt.

'Who are you, citizen?' asked my judge, letting the rope slacken a fraction.

'Jean-Francois Thiland, bachelor of this parish.' The boy whipped the cap from his head and gave a flourishing bow to his audience.

'It's J-F!' a woman whispered to her neighbour. This obviously meant something to many of them because the name was passed one to the other,

121

accompanied by a smile and a nod.

'Citizens, I appeal to you! What has the girl done but come out a trifle unprepared? My maman does that when she's had too much to drink—would you hang her too? Not very chivalrous, no?'

A few in the crowd laughed.

'Besides, I believe her when she says she's one of us,' the boy continued, strutting like a pigeon on the pavement in front of me.

'How do you know she's one of us?' my judge-cum-executioner asked, glaring at him.

The boy pouted, evidently annoyed to find his word doubted. 'Citizen, what fine lady would know that sign? And I may not have understood her, but I know a girl swearing like a guardsman when I hear it. At home, I hear it night and day—don't you?'

There was some muttering behind me and a titter of laughter. The boy was playing his audience well, transforming murderous anger to good humour. Standing with a noose around my neck, I was heartily thankful, though I could not help but think him foolhardy to risk intervening: he could so easily end up joining us in this little death party. On the other hand, he seemed to wield a strange authority over the crowd; he acted like someone used to performing in front of others. A whiff of the theatre about him perhaps? As they say, it takes one to know one . . .

The boy they called J-F scanned the faces before him, and then judged the moment was right to bring forward his demand. 'Release the English into my hands, citizens, and I promise that I will examine the matter carefully in my court.'

His court? What did that mean?

'If they are guilty, they will not survive until

122

tomorrow; if blameless, then innocent lives will have been spared.' The boy turned to each side of the audience in turn, hands held out in graceful appeal. His eyes then fell on Frank, who was being restrained by a burly porter, his face tinged blue as an arm choked his throat. 'But I wish to let them speak on their behalf and to speak I believe they need air, citizen.' Frank's captor grinned sheepishly and loosened his grip. Frank gasped and staggered. 'Now, if you will oblige me in untying that noose from the girl, I will summon help to escort these foreigners to their appointment with justice. The next session in the Court of the Thieves of the Palais Royal is about to begin.'

With immense relief, I felt the rope being removed from my neck. The boy gave a piercing whistle and six lads wormed their way to the front of the crowd and saluted him like soldiers reporting for duty.

'Take the men, my friends,' he commanded. They surrounded Frank and Joseph and began to hustle them through the crowd before anyone had time to change their mind. A final thought struck my saviour and he turned back to the crowd who were now smiling and laughing, their bloody mood giving way to a carnival atmosphere. The king's flight had turned everything upside down, so why could beggar boys not preside over a court?

'Oh, and if any worthy citizen wishes to view the trial, let him proceed to the Golden Balls.'

With that, he gave another bow and held out his hand to me. I stepped hesitantly forward, wondering what was going to happen next. J-F smiled at my bewilderment, kissed my fingertips, and then led me away from the lamp post that had

123

so very nearly become my scaffold.

'Follow me, firecracker,' he said.

SCENE 4—THE THIEVES' COURT

I looked sideways at my escort. He was only a few inches taller than me. He had an alert face, eyes darting this way and that, sharp like a sparrow on a tray of crumbs. Prominent ears stuck out from matted brown hair like handles on a toby jug. He moved with confidence, swaggering down the street with the bearing of a little prince, tipping his cap to all the ladies.

'Monsieur, thank you for saving us,' I said when we turned into a quieter street of close-pressed houses and rank gutters off the rue Saint Honoré. It reminded me of home.

'My name is J-F, mademoiselle. And I haven't saved you. You have the wrong idea about me if you think that.'

Was he being modest? It didn't seem his style.

'Then why did you step in to stop them lynching us?'

'Why waste three perfectly good suits of clothes—possibly jewels and money too?' He gave me a searching look, eyes flicking up and down as he assessed my finery. 'If I hadn't, someone else would've nabbed them before you were cold. I'm no friend to aristocrats—I just like their stuff.' His face was hard, inscrutable. I didn't think he was joking. 'You look shocked, mademoiselle.'

'Not shocked, disappointed,' I said sourly. I now realized the adventure was far from over as we

124

walked back to this hideout of his. The thought crossed my mind that, for the moment, I only had him to deal with: I should run for it if I knew my own best interests. But what about Frank and Joseph, being marched off to their appointment with the Thieves' Court?

J-F appeared to be following my internal debate from the expressions passing across my face because he tightened his grip on my arm. 'I am sorry to disappoint a lady, mademoiselle. Does it make you feel any better to know that I also wanted to see the firecracker go off again?' He winked and gave me a grin that a gargoyle would've been proud to own.

I didn't smile back. There was something in his expression that told me that he was not to be crossed. He would need careful handling—neither Frank nor Joseph would know how to do this. Resolving not to abandon them, I allowed J-F to lead me into a tavern adorned by three golden balls that hung over its entrance. We walked straight through the empty taproom and out to a yard at the back. It was stacked with barrels and had that distinct odour peculiar to inns: a perfume consisting of beer and wine slops trodden in by muddy boots. Frank and Joseph were already there, surrounded by a group of at least twenty boys, all of whom were pawing at their clothes with greedy fingers. Two girls appeared from a side room and greeted J-F with a kiss on each cheek. He muttered something in their ears and then clapped his hands.

'Search the accused for evidence!' he ordered. 'Marie, Annette—take the little redhead to your room.'

Frank looked alarmed to see me being separated

125

from them. 'I beg you not to harm her!' he shouted after me. Marie and Annette tittered.

'He's so gallant,' Marie, the dark-haired one, whispered to me.

'Frank, don't worry. I'll be perfectly safe. Just behave and it'll be all right,' I assured him in English.

Marie and Annette led me into their lodgings and closed the door. We eyed each other cautiously like dogs trying to work out if the stranger would bite.

'Mademoiselle, if we could trouble you for the dress,' said Annette with mock-politeness. She was a pretty girl with white-blonde hair and blue eyes.

'Of course.' I gave them not even a growl as I slipped out of the gown—I'd hated it from the start. They took one look at my shift and turned up their noses in disappointment. No doubt they had been hoping for something much finer.

'We won't be bothering with that—not a bit of lace on it,' said Marie. 'No jewellery either. But the shoes—we'll have those.'

They turned to each other and began to chatter away, valuing my goods between them. Though they seemed quite content to leave me standing barefoot in my undergarments, I had other ideas.

'You know, I think that dress would look really good on you, mademoiselle,' I said to Annette, the shorter of the two. 'Pink was never my colour but it'd look lovely on a girl with your hair.'

Annette giggled and turned to Marie for permission to do what she longed to do.

'Go on, Annette. I'm sure J-F won't mind,' encouraged her friend.

Annette wriggled out of her patched clothes and

126

donned my dress with a smile of pure delight, unconcerned that it fell well short of her ankles. She fingered the fine material, her eyes shining.

'I was right: it does look better on you,' I told her. 'You don't mind if I make myself presentable?' I picked up her discarded dress with an enquiring look at my two guards.

'Not at all,' Annette replied, preoccupied with tweaking the bows on the bodice.

Her old dress was on the large side, the hem trailing on the ground, but it was plain and serviceable. I was not unhappy with the exchange.

'May I have this?' I asked, pointing to the cockade pinned on the front.

'Go ahead: we've some to spare,' said Marie. She reached into a box at the end of their rickety bed and pulled out another. 'I don't suppose you want to be seen without one again?' She grinned, showing wide gaps between her teeth.

'I'm sorry I don't have anything for you to wear,' I told her.

She shrugged. 'Don't worry, English girl, I'll sell the shoes. They'll fetch a nice price. Come, let's go back to J-F before he sends someone after us.'

We emerged into the courtyard to find the thief lounging on a makeshift throne of barrels, toying with a pink ribbon I had not so long ago had in my hair. I hadn't even noticed him pilfering it: he must be good at his craft. He tied the bow around his own head, making his followers laugh.

Frank and Joseph had not fared as well as me: they were both stripped to the skin with only a rag to keep their modesty covered. Frank looked mortified to appear before company in this fashion; Joseph incensed. As both were bound and gagged, I guessed they had resisted the attempt to part them from their belongings. Well really, what did they expect? When you fall among thieves, it's wit and cunning that'll keep you safe, not moral outrage. As they seemed in no immediate danger, I stood back, arms folded, to watch the little thief order his court. I had admired his pluck in front of the mob at the lamp post; it would be intriguing to see how he held sway here. I also had to think of a way to extricate us from this situation.

J-F sat up on his throne. The laughter died. He waved a hand to one side as if talking to an imaginary person.

'What are the charges?'

Assuming a stern expression, he answered himself: 'The accused are charged with being stuck-up foreign nobility not wearing the cockade.'

His followers cheered, enjoying the performance.

'Defence?'

He now assumed a wheedling, hand-rubbing persona: 'The tall one's a servant, your honour.'

'But he calls the other "Milord",' J-F said, switching to the prosecutor's voice. 'That means the buckskin boy is an aristocrat.'

The crowd booed and jostled Frank.

'And what about her?' the judge voice asked.

J-F stared hard at me, his hazel eyes perplexed. 'Don't know—she remains a mystery,' he concluded in his normal tone. 'Girls, what did you find?'

'Nothing of value, except the dress,' said Marie, coming to sit at his feet. Annette blushed and gave a twirl.

'Very pretty—keep it. I found this on him,' announced J-F, tossing Frank's purse into the air and catching it so that it chinked. 'So, to the verdict.' He looked around the room, gauging the mood of his followers. 'The man's acquitted. The boy's condemned for being a filthy aristocrat.'

Condemned? Frank gave me a desperate look but J-F hadn't finished with us yet. He waved at me.

'Girl—stand forward.'

I stepped into the centre of the court. I wasn't afraid for myself, not like I had been when surrounded by the mob outside the palace, but I was worried for Frank. How far would J-F carry this charade?

J-F twirled the ribbon at me. 'Who are you?'

'I've already said. I'm English. I'm a friend of the revolution—or I was until you all tried to string me up this morning. Since then, my feelings have cooled somewhat.'

Marie laughed. 'Don't blame you, girl,' she called out.

'That's who I am. And I'll tell you who you are for nothing,' I continued.

'Oh yes? And who's that?' asked J-F, sitting forward as if expecting to be handed a treat.

'You're a complete idiot.'

Frank struggled with his bonds, groaning through his gag. He was trying to warn me to show more respect for our captor but I knew exactly what I was doing.

J-F smiled, apparently not disappointed. 'And how did you work that one out, English girl?'

'Since when have all aristocrats been your enemy?'

He tossed the ribbon carelessly into the air. 'All rich people are. It doesn't matter to me who's in power—they all turn out to be the same: protecting their own, stamping on the likes of us.'

'If you really think that, it just proves what a dimwit you are. Frank's been my good friend for two years now—he's helped me out of many fixes.' J-F did not look impressed by this so I took a different tack. 'Tell me, are all thieves in Paris the same?'

J-F smiled slyly. 'Redistributors of wealth, please. And no, we most certainly are not.'

'That's right,' agreed Marie. 'We're much better than that lot from Notre Dame—bunch of nasty cutthroats, they are.'

The crowd cheered themselves.

'Well, then,' I continued, 'why expect all aristocrats to be the same? Surely you know better than that here in the Palais Royal? As the judge in this court of yours, Monsieur J-F, I'd've thought you'd know the importance of not being prejudiced against people without evidence.'

'Perhaps,' the little judge conceded with a bow.

'And where would a good thief be without the rich to steal from? A dairymaid needs a cow to milk; a thief a fat purse. If you do away with them all, you do away with your livelihood.'

'Hear, hear!' muttered a few in the audience.

'So you see, you shouldn't let a pair of fine breeches bother you: you should see the wearer as an opportunity for enrichment.'

'Oh, I'm not bothered by him,' said J-F lazily, nodding at the duke's son. 'It's you I can't work out. State your name before the court.'

'Catherine Royal.'

'Ah, that Royal again. Very suspicious. Father?'

'No idea.'

There was a cheer from behind me.

'That's more like it,' said J-F with a pleased

smile. 'Mother?'

'Not the foggiest.'

Applause greeted this statement.

'So what is a base-born girl like you doing walking round with a noble like him?'

'Well, I'd have told you from the start if you'd given me a chance.' I rolled my eyes with obvious exasperation. 'I was abandoned as a baby on the steps of the Theatre Royal, Drury Lane—'

'A very honourable start to life,' commented J-F to Marie.

'I was raised by the theatre folk and that was where I met Frank. We're friends—just friends,' I added severely as Annette giggled. 'A couple of weeks ago, the theatre closed so I've come to learn to be a ballet dancer with a troupe belonging to a Madame Beaufort.'

'A dancer? The most respected profession,' J-F remarked, rising to pirouette on the spot, ribbon rippling behind him.

'As Frank was coming here to visit his family, we decided to travel together.'

'So who is he, this Frank?' J-F circled my friend, flicking the ribbon at him, a gesture at once playful and menacing. Frank flinched back.

'A theatre-goer.' I kept very quiet about the dukedom.

J-F let the ribbon flutter into Marie's lap, and scratched his head. He seemed on the point of letting us go but something was bothering him. Suddenly, he leapt back to his throne and announced with a sweep of his arm:

'It's no good. Kill them!'

'What!' I'd thought I'd won him over. I had begun to congratulate myself on my cleverness.

131

'I don't like them. Get rid of them!'

'*You* don't like *us*!' I shouted as two boys sprang forward to restrain me from slapping his face. 'Well, at least I'm not a lice-ridden dwarf with an inflated sense of his own importance.' J-F stopped scratching and sat down with a delighted smile, infuriating me even more. My French was not quite up to the task of insulting someone properly, but I was giving it my best shot. 'I can't understand how your mates stand it: you stink like the poisonous gas from a cow's backside. You're nothing more than a grub on a rat's posterior.'

The thieves were now laughing and cheering me on. J-F was gazing at me as if I was the most marvellous thing he'd ever seen. 'Go on, firecracker, keep up the crackling. If you give me just two more up to that standard, I'll let you all go.'

So he'd done this on purpose to make me explode! 'You're a pile of rotting offal from a diseased pig.' His mouth twitched. I was on to his game. I had better make the last one my best. 'You're a lying, thieving . . .'

'Now, now, don't spoil it with compliments,' J-F said modestly.

'. . . low-down steaming pile of dog dirt fired from the behind of a rabid mongrel.'

This got the biggest cheer yet. I heard several 'hear, hears!' from the crowd. Marie was wiping tears of laughter from her eyes.

J-F jumped to his feet, bringing an imaginary gavel down on the barrel beside him. 'Free them. The prisoners are acquitted on the grounds that she is as foul-mouthed as the best of us—and they because . . . well, because they're her friends and, as she had said, I should not be prejudiced.' He

132

skipped over Marie to land beside me, grabbed my shoulders and saluted me on the cheeks three times. 'Welcome to France, sister.'

'A drink for our guests!' announced Marie, following J-F in kissing me.

Annette reappeared with five mugs balanced on a tray. The little thief-king took two, handed me one and clinked his own against it. 'To the nobility of the gutter everywhere!'

I raised my drink in return, noticing as I did that my friends were still bound like chickens ready for the oven. 'Isn't it about time you freed them?' I suggested. 'And . . . er . . . got them some clothes?'

J-F frowned. From the flash of scarlet among the crowd of boys, I guessed that Joseph's livery was now adorning some fortunate favourite. Another was dancing about with the footman's wig askew on his head. 'I understand that you may still require the original garments as . . . um . . . evidence . . .'

'Ah, yes, evidence . . .' echoed J-F archly, his eyes sparkling.

'. . . But, as they've been acquitted, perhaps the court could spare them the indignity of walking the streets of Paris in their birthday suits?'

J-F grinned and clicked his fingers. Four boys descended on Frank and Joseph, whipped off their gags and ropes and produced a motley selection of clothes to cover the bare essentials. Joseph looked outraged, Frank amused, to find themselves trans-formed into working men of France, complete with floppy red caps and cockades. Joseph, being a man of great stature, was now wearing trousers that ended halfway up his legs and appeared none too pleased at the exchange for his smart Avon livery. He shot me an angry look. But what did he imagine

133

I could do about it? He was lucky to be decently clad.

Frank held out his arms and turned round for my benefit. 'What do you think, Cat?' he called over the heads of J-F's boys.

'Very good, citizen. I'm sure it's what every self-respecting monsieur on the left bank is wearing this season.'

J-F did not like us switching into English. 'What did the English boy say?' he asked me, taking my arm possessively. I suppose he was right to be wary: his prolonged existence depended on sharp wits and keeping one step ahead of the law.

'He only asked if I admired his new suit of clothes,' I replied, trying to soothe his ruffled feathers. 'I told him I thought them very chic.'

J-F flung himself back on his throne. 'But what did he call you, this . . . this "Cat"?'

So that was what was bothering him. 'Oh, that: that's my nickname. Cat—that's English for *le chat*. My friends say I have nine lives and I always fall on my feet.'

J-F's grin returned. He turned to Frank who had pushed his way through the crowd to join me. 'And has she?' he asked him.

'Has she what?' asked Frank, taking a gulp from the mug Marie handed him.

'Has she got nine lives?'

'I'd say she's used up two or three of them if you count today.' Frank watched with equanimity as his breeches went by on the legs of a tall black lad with tattoos on his face.

J-F took out Frank's purse, poured the contents into his palm and handed the wallet back. 'You have this. I'll keep the rest as payment for your clothes.'

134

'Of course, that's very reasonable,' said Frank, exchanging a look with me.

'Reasonable, my lord!' spluttered Joseph. He didn't need to understand French to realize that his master was being asked to pay for the privilege of being deprived of his belongings. 'This is daylight robbery!'

'Of course it is,' Frank replied, thrusting a mug in his footman's hand. 'Or we could look on it as the price for saving us from the mob. It's going to happen anyway, so we might as well make the best of it as Cat has.'

'Look and learn, Frank, look and learn,' I replied with relish.

'What did the giant say, milord?' J-F asked Frank.

'He was just expressing his thanks for your hospitality,' said Frank with a bow to his host.

J-F laughed and clapped Frank on the back. 'I like you, *le chat*—Cat—and Milord. You both understand how the world works.'

'Sometimes I do, sometimes I don't,' I admitted. 'I think I got it slightly wrong this morning.'

Frank snorted into his drink. 'Slightly! Not wearing the cockade and almost getting us all killed, she means.'

J-F shrugged. 'Ah well, we all make mistakes and, in fairness to her, it's not every day that the king goes missing.'

My own personal danger having driven the events of the day from my head, I now remembered I was supposed to be finding out for Mr Sheridan what the common people of Paris made of these developments.

'And what do you think about losing your royal

135

family, J-F?'

He gave me a long look before deciding to answer. 'Don't care as long as it doesn't mean too many of the National Guard on the streets. If they are kept busy running about after Piggy Louis and off my back then I'll be happy.'

'So you're not bothered that the king has gone—possibly to return at the head of a foreign army?' asked Frank, intrigued by this casual attitude to whether or not the head of state was on the throne. His upbringing among English nobility had not allowed for the possibility that the common man might not care two hoots for the doings of his sort.

J-F rubbed his nose thoughtfully, pondering all facets of the situation. 'I'm not sure what it'll do for business. A bit of confusion is good, but blood running in the streets—soldiers—panic—no, I don't like the sound of that. If he's gone, I hope he's gone forever. But it might not be a good time to be a foreigner in Paris.' His eyes met mine, his expression serious: was he giving me a warning or merely referring to the events at the lamp post?

Frank put down his drink. 'In that case, I think we had better be going before anything else happens to us. And I still have to call on my parents.'

I rose to take my leave. 'Thank you, J-F. It has been most . . . illuminating meeting you and your people.'

The little king conducted me to the door. 'Come back any time, Cat—Milord. You have my word of honour that you will have safe conduct through my kingdom.'

'For a price, no doubt,' I added.

'For a price,' he agreed, kissing my hand.

Transformed by our experiences among the thieves into the garb of lower class Parisians, we attracted no attention as we made our way back to our lodgings. The pavements were busy; everywhere I looked I saw people gathered in huddles to debate the day's news, but no sign of panic.

'Well, that was a most educational experience. The lengths you go to to get rid of a dress you hate astound me, Cat,' commented Frank as we stood on a street corner to allow a messenger to gallop past. Frank glanced at his map. 'He's heading away from the National Assembly. I wonder who's in charge now?'

Now that the head of the country had chucked in his crown and scarpered, he meant. Would old London be as calm under similar circumstances? I wondered. Mind you, we chopped the head off a king last century—that was before having the cheek to invite his son to come back a decade or so later to pick up where his dad had left off. We seemed to have survived the episode so I supposed that the French would too. Now I came to think about it, as I studied the kingless streets of Paris, what were royalty for really? ~~Perhaps they weren't needed after all?*~~

'Frank, have you ever wondered what purpose a king serves?' I asked, speaking my thoughts aloud as we passed a group of men gathered around a notice pasted up on a brick wall.

My friend eyed me shrewdly. 'What's this? Treason, Cat?'

It felt wonderfully liberating to think the unthinkable—and then to say it out loud with no fear of reprisals. 'Answer the question, Frank. If a king has real power, isn't it stupid to trust to chance that his parents won't produce a dunce?'

Frank shrugged. 'It's tradition. Besides, it's all in the hands of God.'

'And if the king's only a figurehead,' I ploughed on, 'then what's the point of that? Isn't it an expensive luxury—all those princes and princesses, palaces and servants to pay for?'

'I can't believe you just said that, Cat, you sound just like a republican.' Frank shook his head as if diagnosing me with some incurable disease.

'What's wrong with that?'

'Everything. England is not—and never will be—a republic. Oh, it's all right to think like that for new countries with tiny populations like America, but for big countries like ours and France, it would be a disaster.'

'Why? From what I can see around me the world hasn't come to an end for these people. Look, she's still carrying her basket to market and he—well, he's found time to pick his nose.'

'A most uplifting spectacle. I'm sure we'd all just love to be ruled by the likes of him. Without a king to unite the country, this place will fall apart. You need a strong man in charge.'

He sounded very pompous—not like the normal Frank.

'Stop talking to me as if you've got a poker stuck up the proverbial. Strong man, indeed!' I scoffed.

'Well, look what happened when we had a woman in charge of our walking party this morning!' he said wickedly. 'Almost hanged by your oh-so-enlightened masses and then fleeced of all our worldly goods by a dwarfish thief and his bunch

138

of merry men.'

'And what happened when we had a man in charge of map-reading yesterday? Scared a flock of nuns, deafened a beggar and frightened some poor soul out of her wits by leaping out upon her in the dark . . .' I stopped suddenly. 'You don't think . . . No, it can't have . . .'

'What are you rambling on about?'

'That woman—in the alleyway behind the palace last night—remember how well-spoken she was? You don't think that . . . ?'

Frank realized where I was going with my speculation. Our argument forgotten, he said nothing for a few moments. 'Well, if she did have anything to do with the royal family's disappearance then we'd better keep quiet about it. We almost got killed this morning on a whim; we wouldn't want to get tangled up with all this. Who knows what revenge they'll take on anyone connected with the king's flight?'

Argue though we might about kings, I certainly agreed with Frank on this. We would mention what we'd seen to no one and just hope the drunken coachman would do the same.

*　　　*　　　*

We arrived back at Madame Beaufort's lodgings as a nearby clock sounded midday.

'Oh blast! I'm *so* late: she'll kill me!' I exclaimed as it dawned on me that I had missed two hours of ballet while I had been making my acquaintance with death Parisian style.

'Poor Cat,' grimaced Frank. 'I completely forgot you have balletic duties. You'd better go straight

139

up.'

Leaving Frank and Joseph to make themselves decent for a call on the Avons, I ran upstairs, two at a time, and burst into the practice room where all the dancers were gathered. They were standing in a long line, looking at themselves critically in a wall of mirrors, bending and swaying like willow trees in a breeze. In contrast to the hustle of the streets I had just left, the quiet in the room was a shock.

My entrance broke the concentration in the room as surely as a hot pin lancing a boil lets the pent-up unpleasantness spurt out.

'If there is one thing I cannot abide, it is lateness,' rapped Madame Beaufort, bearing down on me like an angry poodle, her mass of hair wobbling in time with the shake of her head.

'I am sorry, madame, but I have a very good excuse. When you hear what happened—'

'I do not want to hear excuses—there is no special treatment for anyone in my ensemble.' Her gaze alighted on my new clothes. 'And what is that you are wearing?'

I opened my mouth to explain.

'Never mind, no time to change now. To the barre and copy Belle.'

'But don't you want to hear about the king . . . ?'

'Quiet! Dance! By Saint Anne, you have more than enough to learn without being the only one to miss our lessons!'

Clearly nothing short of an earthquake would prevent Madame Beaufort from putting her girls through their paces. I took my place at the end of the row of dancers and turned to face the mirror. I looked so out of place, it was laughable. Belle, my neighbour, was tall and graceful, dressed in a loose

140

white practice gown; I was short, angular and decidedly rumpled in my patched striped skirt and apron. As for learning to dance, who did Madame Beaufort think she was fooling? I had no more chance of succeeding than a monkey of writing *Hamlet*.

Swish! The rod tapped my wrist.

'Bend it so, Cat. Imagine your hands are exclamation marks to your movements, not full stops.' Madame Beaufort curled her own palm over the back of my wrist, easing it into the required shape. I was taken aback to hear anything so poetic from her. 'See, you can do it when you try.'

Gazing at myself in the mirror, I understood what she meant. If I thought of myself as awkward, my body behaved accordingly; if I forgot myself and let the music flow through me, I became far more elegant.

Oh no, I'm beginning to think like a ballerina! Help! It must be the after-effect of the events of the morning. I frowned at my reflection. Thank goodness nothing else could possibly happen today.

Just as this comforting thought had floated through my mind, the door banged open and Frank erupted into the room. Seizing me roughly by the arm, he dragged me after him, knocking dancers over like ninepins.

'Apologies, madame, but I have to speak to Cat urgently,' he shouted over his shoulder.

'My lord!' she exclaimed in protest, but he slammed the door behind us.

My heart was in my mouth. Frank looked absolutely terrified. Taking me by the shoulders, he announced:

'They've arrested my family—all of them: Mama,

141

Father and Lizzie—on suspicion of helping the king
to flee.'

Interlude—A Country Dance

Paris, 22nd June 1791

My dear Patron,
I had not expected to have so much to write after being here only a day, but Paris has turned out to be far more interesting than I had imagined and I can wait no longer with my news. The chief point is that the king and his family fled last night, leaving the city in confusion. Fortunately the streets, with a few exceptions, are calm. My impression is that most care little for the king himself but no one wants war. Death and destruction is bad for business, one entrepreneur told me.

This is not my only news. A disaster has struck much closer to home: our friends from Grosvenor Square have been arrested on suspicion of aiding the king's escape. On what grounds I know not, other than the unfortunate fact that they are English. Please do all you can through your channels to secure their release; I'm doing what I can here. I'll be meeting our friend, the Captain, as soon as possible. He may be able to help.

Your Diamond.

P.S. By the by, Frank and I almost got hanged today and were robbed by a charming gang of thieves so there is no need for you to worry that I will feel homesick for old London.

P.P.S. I hope you agree my first letter is not devoid of interest and worth a guinea.

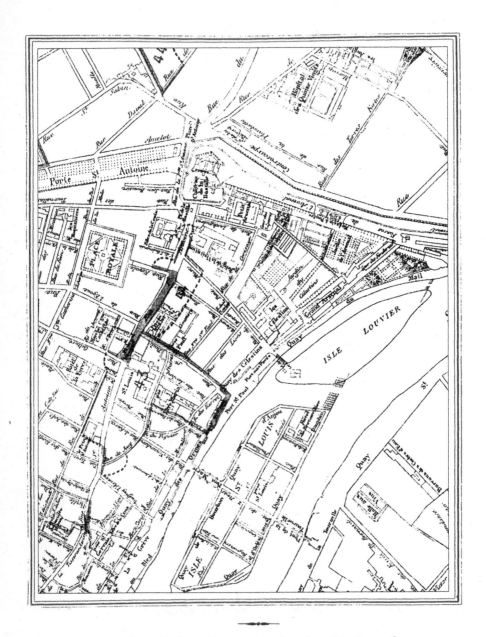

Act III - In which the Bristol Nightingale sings once more . . .

Act III

SCENE 1—CAPTAIN SPARKLER

'The first thing we need to do, Frank,' I told my friend as we huddled together in my little room, 'is we need to disguise you. If they're after the Avon family—and they can't be too particular if they took Lizzie—they might just arrest you to make it a round number.'

Frank nodded, staring blankly at his feet, not yet recovered from the shock of finding his parents had been led off in chains. Joseph stood sentry at the door, on the watch for any snooping ballerinas, but he kept casting anxious looks at his master. Neither of us liked this dejected mood: Frank was normally so full of life you usually wished someone would sit on him to keep him quiet.

'Why the handcuffs?' I asked Joseph when I realized that I was going to get very little from Frank for the moment. 'I thought they'd treat a duke with more respect—he must have *some* sort of standing, even in France.'

'It wasn't for the duke, miss,' said Joseph solemnly. He need say no more: I could see it as if I'd been there. The duchess was not a woman to allow herself to be dragged off without a struggle.

'How many did she injure?'

'The butler said that she felled two guardsmen before they resorted to the irons, miss. The duke also sustained an injury to his nose, possibly broken.'

'What! They didn't dare mistreat him, did they?'

Joseph shook his head. 'Not them. Her grace

accidentally caught him with a punch right in the face when he tried to restrain her.'

'Ah. And Lady Elizabeth?'

'Distressed but otherwise calm.'

Of course. I expected nothing less of my friend.

I got up from the bed and walked to the window to think. We'd already sent a message to Johnny and were expecting an answer at any moment. After that, the next step would be to find out where they were being held and see if they had any immediate wants; I knew from my own brief experience of prison* that it would be short on any comforts. We also needed to inform the British representative in Paris. My letter would take days to reach London and we had to have help much faster than that. Secretly, I was hoping that this would all be over before Mr Sheridan even had time to break the seal on my letter. The Avons were bound to be released before the day was over, weren't they?

I gazed at the sun setting over the rooftops, shafts of light spotlighting the smoke twisting up from the cooking fires. A sparrow hopped on to the ledge beside me, looking hopeful. I had nothing to give him; in fact, I realized I'd eaten nothing since breakfast. My stomach rumbled.

'I'm going down to the kitchen,' I told my companions. 'I'll see if I can arrange a place for you to stay. It's best, I think, that we say nothing to Madame Beaufort about this until we are sure of her—she's been acting strangely since she returned home and I couldn't swear that she won't hand you over to the authorities.'

Frank nodded glumly.

'At least, sir, we have our disguise already provided for us,' said Joseph brightly. 'Courtesy of that extraordinary young gentleman we met this morning.'

'Thanks, Joseph,' I said, patting him on the back as I passed. 'Keep an eye on him for me, will you?'

'Need you ask, miss?'

'No. Of course not.'

*   *   *

The kitchen was quiet. The ballerinas had already dined and gone out with Madame Beaufort to visit the Opera, the place where they were to perform. Only the old concierge was there, stirring the fire with a long black poker.

'There you are, mademoiselle,' he said gruffly. 'Your dinner is still in the pot, if you want it.'

My growling stomach decided rapidly that I might as well have some before sorting out supper and lodgings for my friends.

'Thank you, monsieur.'

I helped myself to the stew and broke off a piece of bread from one of those long sticks the French prefer, a little too dry for my taste but not bad when dipped in the gravy.

'What have you done now, miss?'

'What?' I was surprised to be interrupted by the concierge. 'I mean, pardon, monsieur?'

'Those little madams were talking about you as if you were the worst of the worst. "What, her? That little thing?" I thought to myself. You must have done something very bad to earn their dislike.'

'Oh.' I put my spoon down, my appetite vanishing.

'So what did you do?' The concierge took the poker from the fire and dipped it in a mug of wine

149

at his elbow. The smell of nutmeg and cinnamon wafted into the air as the liquid fizzed. I thought of Caleb Braithwaite, who is partial to warm porter, which he heats in the same manner by his little fire at Drury Lane. Used to heat, I corrected myself. His post by the stage door was probably rubble by now.

'Speak up, mademoiselle. I like a story. I can't believe anything too bad of you. I've a grandson who must be about your age—you remind me of him.'

I sighed. I needed some allies just now and he seemed a pleasant fellow. 'Well, monsieur, I'm not exactly sure what I've done, but I think the root of the problem is that I've been telling too many stories about myself for their liking. They think I think I'm better than them.'

'And do you think that?' He took a mouthful of wine and spluttered. '*Mon dieu*, that's hot!'

I passed him a jug of water from the table.

'Of course I don't. I'm no better than anyone. No parents, no home, no situation in life; I can't even dance like they can—how could I possibly think I am superior to them?'

He smiled, his wrinkles deepening into little valleys.

'That's not what I heard. I was told—by a friend of mine, you understand—that you are one of the royalty.'

'You're joking?'

He shook his head. 'Street royalty. A certain king took a shine to you this morning.'

'That's not all he took.' I smiled ruefully, remembering my dress, Joseph's livery and Frank's money. I shook myself. 'How did you know that?'

He touched his finger to the side of his nose.

150

'What do you think an old thief king does when he gets too old to play the game?'

'He . . .' I looked around me. 'He becomes a concierge?'

The old man nodded. 'Guarding empty buildings is a fine job for a man with, shall we say, interesting connections. The old king recognizes the authority of the new, even if he is the cheeky offspring of his no-good son.'

'You're J-F's grandfather?'

'For my sins. Pleased to meet you, Mademoiselle Firecracker. He's asked me to look after you.'

I was astonished: this seemed a very sentimental gesture for the thief king. 'Why?'

'So no one else robs you blind, of course, my girl. He thinks of you as his property now—you and the young lord: he called you his milk cows.'

'Thank you, monsieur.' At least, I think it called for a 'thank you'—I wasn't too sure. This surely couldn't be a coincidence?

He sipped his drink. 'Call me Renard.'

Meaning fox. Yes, that fitted.

'Thank you, Renard.' I scowled at him. 'You told J-F about us, didn't you?'

He gave a grunt of laughter. 'Not much escapes you, does it? I must admit I thought the young lord's purse needed slimming down. I suppose it is possible that I may have given my grandson a tip that three clients would be out on the streets this morning, heading for the rue de Clichy.'

'So he followed us,' I muttered, more to myself.

'It was your good luck that he did. I had nothing to do with the discussion at the lamp post—you can take all credit for that yourself.'

He stretched his legs out and sat back in his chair.

151

'Now tell me, mademoiselle: what do you want me to do for the boy you've smuggled up to your bedroom now his family has been arrested?'

Nothing gets past a thief king—even a retired one.

*   *   *

'Now, don't fly off the handle, Frank, but I've got a suggestion for you.' I had waited until Frank and Joseph had their hands occupied with their supper before I broached the subject in case either of them wanted to throttle me for what I was about to say.

'Oh yes?' said Frank suspiciously. 'What kind of suggestion?'

'A safe place for you to go to ground while we try and sort this out.'

'That's good, miss,' commented Joseph, far more trustful of me than he should have been.

'I've been having a talk with the concierge and it appears he knows J-F—he's his grandfather, in fact . . .' I wasn't sure I had the courage to continue.

'Really? That's a strange coincidence,' remarked Frank.

I coughed awkwardly, not thinking it an opportune moment to explain how we were set up this morning by our friendly concierge.

'Go on,' prompted Frank.

'He . . . well, no, *I* suggested that the safest place for you at the moment might be at the Golden Balls . . . with J-F.'

'What!'

'He won't let anything happen to you—not if we pay him well,' I added in a lower voice.

'Cat, you can't be serious! That boy is a

152

menace—a charming one, but still a menace. He will sell me out sure as my name's Francis.'

'Well, it's not any longer. You're François.' He seemed about to protest again. 'Look, Frank, do you have a better idea? It's only for a few days.' His objections died before they passed his lips. 'Joseph, you don't have to go with Frank but . . .'

'Of course I have to go with him,' the footman replied indignantly.

'I thought as much. But please don't anger J-F. He's doing us a favour.'

'How much?' asked Frank bitterly.

'What?'

'How much is this costing me?'

I twisted my hands together. 'He understands that you may be low on funds at the moment . . .'

'Yes, since he stole all my money, you mean.'

'So we've put aside the matter of payment until later. He's promised that it won't be more than we can afford.'

Frank gave a snort.

'You could look on it as a chance to broaden your horizons,' I said over-brightly. 'You always loved exploring the streets of London with Pedro; why not Paris?'

'Yes, but Pedro isn't a ruthless thief who'd cut your throat if the fancy took him.'

'You don't know that about J-F.'

'Don't I? I bear the scars from this morning's encounter even if you got off lightly, Cat.'

'Still . . .'

'You're sweet on him, aren't you?'

'That's ridiculous.'

'You are—don't you deny it!'

'What? Sweet on a boy with ears like pitcher

153

handles and hair full of lice? Give me more credit than that, Frank.'

'You can't fool me. You admire him—I can tell.'

'I might admire him—just a little, mind, but that doesn't mean I like him in that way.'

'Rubbish—you do!'

'Don't!

'Do!'

'I don't, you stubborn . . .'

'What? Do my ears deceive me or is that the dulcet tone of my Catkin?'

Frank and I spun round to see a tall, dark-haired man lounging against the doorpost.

'Johnny!' I shrieked and threw myself at him. He hugged me tight, rocking to and fro.

'It's so good to see you, Cat. Has Sheridan been treating you well, eh?'

I shrugged, grinning up at him. He hadn't changed a bit: still the same handsome Lord Jonathan Fitzroy—sorry, plain Johnny now he had emigrated to America and Captain Sparkler to all lovers of radical cartoons.

'And Frank. I'm so sorry to hear about your parents and . . .' he gave a cough to clear the catch in his throat '. . . and Lizzie. I'm sure we can sort it all out.'

Frank got up to shake his hand. 'Thank you, Johnny. I'm glad you're here. Perhaps you can knock some sense into Cat for me.'

Johnny kept his arm around my shoulders and gave me a squeeze. 'I doubt that.'

'She's suggesting I hide among a gang of thieves we met this morning.'

'They saved us from being lynched,' I chipped in.

'Only to rob us,' Frank finished.

154

'Sounds an excellent idea to me,' said Johnny with a chuckle. 'I trust Cat's judgement about people. Don't you?'

Frank opened his mouth to say something then shut it.

'I can't hide you,' Johnny continued. 'The authorities are aware that I know your family—I've hardly thought it necessary to hide the fact until today. If they are looking for you, they may well come knocking on my door. But I would bet my last dollar that they won't look for an English lord among thieves. They'll think you're far too proud to mingle with the poor. You're not, are you?'

Frank put his head in his hands, his shoulders hunched with worry. Then he let them drop, took a deep breath and looked up. 'Sorry, everyone, I'm being a bit of an idiot, aren't I? Of course I'm not too proud. I mingle with Cat, don't I?'

I poked Frank in the ribs, very pleased to find Johnny still placed his confidence in me. 'So, you'll do as I suggest?'

Frank nodded.

'In that case, Marie is waiting in the kitchen with Renard to escort you. You'll need to change back into the clothes you had this morning. Leave the rest here: I'll look after them.'

'What are you going to do?' he asked as he shooed me out into the corridor so he could undress.

I glanced at Johnny. 'I guess we're going prison visiting.'

*   *   *

Johnny hired a carriage to take us over to the

155

Conciergerie Prison on the Ile de la Cité. It was twilight but the streets were still busy with people shopping and chatting. If I had been at home I would have said there was a holiday mood in the air, but perhaps I just didn't understand them yet.

'Corpus Christi tomorrow,' Johnny commented, nodding to a church where some nuns were brushing the steps. 'There'll be a huge procession through the streets. I just hope there's no trouble. I'm amazed it's been this quiet so far.'

'I wouldn't call it quiet,' I muttered, rubbing the rope burn on my neck. I proceeded to tell him what had happened that day, sparing no details.

'Poor Catkin,' said Johnny, pulling me to him. 'You really do need looking after, don't you?'

'I thought I did quite well extricating us from J-F's court with a full suit of clothes each.'

He laughed and tapped the end of my nose. 'You know what I mean. You shouldn't have been there in the first place. I'll have words with Sheridan for sending you off to this den of thieves.'

I snuggled against him. Once I thought I loved Johnny like an older brother. Seeing him today, I realized I had developed a hopeless devotion to him—so hopeless that it hardly hurt to know that his feelings were all for Lizzie. When I was with him, I need not look over my shoulder wondering if I was safe and accepted—I just knew I was.

'Mr Sheridan did me a favour giving me this job,' I confided. 'I made a terrible mess of looking after myself when the theatre closed.'

'Do you want to tell me about it?'

I nodded. Then it all came tumbling out: sleeping rough, Mr Tweadle, my stories, even the stupid bargain with Billy Shepherd. Johnny was silent for a

156

long time. I listened to the hooves clattering on the cobbles and the squeak of the carriage. Did he think badly of me for letting everyone down?

'When this is all over, you could come back to America with me, you know,' he said at last. 'I'm not concerned about that Tweadle fellow—Sheridan will sort him out for you, I have no doubt—but Shepherd worries me.'

'He's always worried everyone. I expect even the midwife had second thoughts and wanted to put him back the moment he was born.'

'I'm being serious, Cat. He won't rest until he's got you under his thumb.'

'I rather thought he'd end up killing me,' I said with a shrug.

Johnny sat up and took me by the shoulders. 'Why are you treating this like a joke? Don't you realize what you're up against?'

Of course I knew: I'd watched him beat Johnny to a pulp and had felt his razor at my throat.

'I'm not joking, Johnny,' I said seriously. 'I know he's dangerous—I know what he wants and he's not getting it.' Johnny shook his head. I could tell he thought I was naïve. 'Look, he could've got rid of me any day over the last year but he hasn't. I refuse to live in fear of a wart like him.'

'Come to America, Cat. You'd like it there,' urged Johnny.

I paused. Could I really go? I'd said it a few times but could I bear to watch him and Lizzie starting their married life together? I loved them both: wouldn't it sour all that if I tagged along, an unwanted third in their nest?

'Well?'

'If I go to America, it'll be because I want to, not

because Billy Shepherd has driven me away.' The words surprised me but as I said them I knew I meant it. 'I'll get the better of him, just you wait and see.'

Johnny refrained from commenting. We had more immediate problems to worry about than Shepherd but we would return to the subject later, I had no doubt.

The coach clattered to a halt. Johnny poked his head out of the window.

'Here we are. Now let's see if I can talk our way in. I suggest you remain silent.' He'd clearly forgotten what I was like if he thought I was going to leave so important a matter to him. 'I'll tell them you're my sister if anyone asks.'

I looked up at the building looming in front of us. It was nothing like I expected: this wasn't a prison, it was a palace—many storeys high with a steeply pitched roof outlined against the night sky and two towers facing the river. Faint lights glimmered in the windows. Only the heavily armed guards and frequent patrols across the forecourt signalled the building's more sinister use.

'Do you think you can get us in?' I asked. The Conciergerie gave me the creeps—all that fine stonework used to imprison people. I preferred my gaols to declare their purpose straight out, show themselves to be brutal and ugly, like Newgate.

Johnny scratched his chin thoughtfully. If he had been a cracksman, I'd swear he was looking for a way to break into the place. 'Well, I have a vague diplomatic status as I'm attached to the American delegation. They might let us in on the strength of that.'

I'd forgotten how innocent he was to the ways of

158

the world.

'Don't be daft, Johnny. Haven't you learnt anything yet? Papers will help to get you in the front door, but you'll have to bribe them.'

He patted his pocket. 'I've come prepared.'

'But it seems to me that we also need a good story.' I thought for a moment. 'Look, why don't you tell them that I'm a friend of Lizzie—that I've been badgering you witless all day to bring me here so I can see for myself that she is all right.' I tapped the basket of food we had brought with us. 'I insisted on bringing her something to eat as she's only just recovered from . . . from the flu. Tell them she's delicate—they don't want their star prisoners to fall ill on them, do they?'

Johnny nodded to show he'd got all that and offered me his arm.

'I'll play it young and innocent,' I whispered, continuing with my stage directions. 'Don't forget, we must look as if we think we have every right to be here—don't let them see our doubt.'

We approached the sentry on duty.

'Yes, monsieur?' the guard said coldly.

'We would like to see the prison governor, if it is not too much trouble,' said Johnny politely.

The man frowned. 'He's busy.'

I trod on Johnny's toe. 'Demand,' I hissed.

Johnny cleared his throat. 'Not too busy to see me, I'm sure. I demand to see him.' He thrust his papers at the guard—a good move for I doubted the man could read.

The guard's expression changed as he saw the official seals at the bottom. 'Follow me,' he grunted.

We crossed the courtyard and were shown into a dimly lit office. A corpulent man was sitting at the desk with his feet up, chin on his chest as he snoozed. Busy indeed!

'Monsieur le Concierge!' barked the guard in a voice designed to carry across a parade ground.

The governor sat up with a jerk, dislodging a stack of papers so that they crashed to the floor.

'Monsieur,' said Johnny, bowing.

'*Sacŕe bleu?*,' asked the governor, his chubby face flushed. He stood up and straightened his rumpled uniform.

'I apologize for disturbing you. I will not keep you long. I'm with the American delegation to Paris.' Johnny presented his papers with a flourish.

'I don't care if you're with the Archbishop of Paris. What are you doing here?'

The governor's eyes slid to me. I curtseyed and then smiled what I hope was my most charming smile, hiding behind Johnny as if shy. I tugged his jacket, like a child trying to get her parent's attention. My friend leant over and I whispered in his ear. Johnny stood up straight.

'Sorry about that, monsieur. My sister here was just asking me if you were a general. She said she'd never seen so impressive a man before.'

The governor smiled despite himself.

'No, no, I'm not a general, mademoiselle. Just a humble steward—the Concierge of the Conciergerie.' He came round the table and handed me into a chair. 'Now, what was I asking? Oh yes, would you please state your business?'

'It concerns a prisoner who was brought here today,' said Johnny.

The governor stiffened.

'Are you a family man, sir?' Johnny asked quickly. 'Maybe you have daughters? If you do, you'll know what loyal friends little girls are to each other. My sister here is a close companion of the English girl who was brought here this morning. She gave me no rest until we came here to see that Lady Elizabeth was well looked after.'

'But meeting you, sir, I'm sure she must be,' I lisped, looking up at the man with wide, trusting eyes.

'According to my sister, her friend has been ill and Catherine fears she'll have a relapse without proper food and warm clothes. We took the liberty of packing a basket and wondered if we could be granted a few moments to take it to her.'

I presented the basket with another curtsey (thank goodness for my ballet lessons—at least now I could pretend to be elegant), lifting the cloth to show its contents.

'Catherine's really devoted to Lady Elizabeth. It would mean everything to her if you'd let her see her friend.'

'Well.' The governor scratched his chin, looking down at me. Poking a finger in my eye, I raised a tear-filled gaze to him and let one droplet escape— I hadn't lived all those years among actresses without learning a trick or two. 'I'm ordered to keep the prisoners isolated until they've been questioned, but I suppose I could make an exception. It's not as if the little girl is an English spy or anything!' he joked.

'Then we can see her?' asked Johnny eagerly.

'Not you, monsieur—I cannot bend the rules that far. No, just the little one. I'll send for a guard to take her up.'

Johnny hid his disappointment. 'Thank you, monsieur. You are very kind.'

161

My escort took me into the prison by a side entrance. We emerged into a huge vaulted chamber with four fireplaces, one on each wall. I did not need a history lesson to know that this room must date from many centuries before our modern age. Whatever noble use it had once, however, had been superseded by present requirements. The stone floor was muddied by the continual passage of boots; the sconces hosted cheap tallow candles, staining the ceiling with smudgy soot marks.

The guard led me from this vast chamber into the maze of passages where the prisoners lived. The lower floors were occupied by the poor who slept on straw like beasts, three or more to a cell. One man gazed at me hopefully through the bars on the door, hand outstretched as I passed.

'Mademoiselle, for the love of Saint Geneviève, have pity!'

I looked down at my feet, embarrassed that I could offer no relief. The guard batted the man's arms away with his rifle butt. We mounted a stone staircase. The upper floors had been given over to those who could afford to pay for the privilege of a private room, bed and furniture. Though it was night, it was still stuffy and airless up there; it must have felt like an oven during the summer day. You could not ignore the smell of too many bodies cramped together with no other sanitary arrangements than a bucket. Lizzie wasn't built to withstand these conditions. We had to get her out quickly.

'Voilà, mademoiselle,' said the guard, pausing

outside a door on his left. A sheet had been tacked to it, listing the occupants—the duke, duchess and Lizzie. 'Monsieur the Concierge said to give you fifteen minutes. I will wait outside.' He passed me a lantern.

'Merci.' I bobbed him a curtsey and waited for him to unlock and let me in. The door shut smartly behind me and the key turned.

'Who is it? What do you want?' demanded the duke. It was very dark in the cell and the light I was carrying must have blinded them for an instant.

'Your grace, it's only me—Catherine Royal.'

'Cat!' Lizzie leapt from her bed and threw herself on me. 'What are you doing here? I didn't know you were even in Paris.'

'My dear!' The duchess enfolded me in a hug. 'Don't say they've locked you up too?'

'No, no. It's not my turn this time,' I said, shaking my head. 'No, Johnny brought me.'

'He's here?' Lizzie looked over my shoulder, expecting to see him at the door.

'Yes, but he wasn't allowed to see you. I'm not supposed to be here either but I convinced the governor I wouldn't sleep without visiting you. He seems to think I'm about five, the way he's treating me.'

Lizzie took the lantern and placed it on a table. 'I don't suppose you had anything to do with that, did you?'

'Oh no,' I said, eyes round and innocent.

The duke stepped forward, took my hand and said in a whisper, 'We are very glad to see you, Miss Royal, but you should know that it is dangerous for you. If they arrested us, they must think any foreigner is under suspicion. You're not safe.'

'I'll be fine, your grace. Don't worry about me. Is there anything you need? I've got a basket here with some basic supplies.'

'Thank you. That is very thoughtful.' The duke sighed and moved back to the tiny window that let in only a faint breath of air. 'I can hardly believe this has happened to us. I thought my rank . . . well, it seems not. I assume that your friend downstairs has alerted the English representative?'

'Yes, sir—and I wrote to Mr Sheridan. I'm sure you won't be kept here long. They'll find out that it was all a mistake.'

'Hmm.' The duke sounded sceptical.

'What's wrong?'

Lizzie led me to a seat beside her on the bed. 'We only wish we knew what our cousin, the Comte de Plessis, has been up to the last few days. He did take delivery of a large carriage the day before yesterday in our name—he said it was for touring, but it appears this was not the case.'

'Ah.'

'And he is a close friend of Count Fersen.'

Fersen? The name was familiar. Where had I heard it before?

'From what we can gather, Count Fersen is a particular friend of the queen and was involved in arranging their departure. The carriage was used by the royal family in their escape.'

'I see.' This didn't look good for anyone who'd been within a mile of that coach. 'It sounds as if you need a lawyer.'

'Correct, Miss Royal,' interjected the duke. 'Would you ask Lord Jonathan to arrange one?'

'You should call him just Mr Fitzroy, your grace. It's better if the people here think he's American.

164

I'll ask him right away.'

There was a lull in the conversation and I had a chance to observe my friends more closely. Lizzie was pale, but otherwise calm. The duke's nose was swollen and there was blood on his shirt front. The duchess had a distinctly rumpled look, with bruises on her wrists. It looked as if she had not adapted well to the indignity of imprisonment. Perhaps a few words of advice might not come amiss? After all, I'd been in their shoes once.

'Have you thought, your grace,' I began tentatively to the duchess, 'that they may treat you better if they understood that you are not really a—forgive the term—a stuck-up aristocrat?'

The duchess turned her imperious eyes to me. 'I have laboured for years to be treated with respect. I thought you of all people would understand that.'

'I do understand, but this isn't England. As I learnt today, they look on rank very differently here.'

'What do you expect me to do? Renounce the title I assumed on marriage?' She was bristling with indignation.

'Of course not. I just thought that maybe you . . . you could sing for them, you know.'

The duchess had met her husband some twenty years ago when she was plain Maria Rivers, an ordinary girl whose talent earned her the title 'The Bristol Nightingale' and made her a star of the London stage.

'Sing?' said the duchess coldly. If looks could kill, I would be in my coffin.

'It's just a suggestion, but I think they'd feel more favourable towards you all if they knew that your husband had the good judgement to marry a

165

commoner. At the moment, they're just convinced you're like all the other blood-sucking aristocrats— saving your grace's presence,' I added quickly, casting an apologetic look at the duke.

'Well! Of all the—' muttered the duchess.

'Listen to Cat, Mama,' Lizzie interrupted. 'I think she's right. Since you hit those two guards this morning they've given us the worst possible food and denied us even a candle. It can't do any harm, can it, if you were to try to charm them?'

The duke went to his wife and kissed her hand. 'You certainly charmed me, my dove, when I first heard you.'

The duchess touched his cheek gently, biting her lip as she saw his battered nose. 'Perhaps you would have been better off with a true lady, Sam— someone who wouldn't have done that to you.'

'Rubbish, my darling. I chose you and have never known a moment's regret. All I ask is that you listen to Miss Royal and Lizzie.'

I could hear shuffling outside the door—my time was almost up. 'Sing now. They're bound to ask me where you learned to do that and I can tell them.'

The duchess smiled sadly. 'My first concert in twenty years—a prison in Paris.' She stood up and composed herself. 'Well, I think a lullaby would be appropriate for our little visitor here.'

Taking a deep breath, she began. I had never heard her sing and, even though it had been my suggestion, I was taken aback by the richness of her voice—it poured from her, banishing the dingy cell. At that moment, we could have been anywhere. The key turned in the lock and the guard stood transfixed on the threshold. He had been expecting the virago who had assaulted his colleagues earlier.

Now he found an angel.

When the duchess finished, we were all silent.

'Thank you, my dear,' said the duke hoarsely. 'It is too long since I last heard you sing—I had almost forgotten.' His eyes were shining—I could see that he was falling in love with his wife all over again.

Lizzie gave her mother a hug.

'That was beautiful, your grace,' I said, an eye on the guard. 'Thank you. I'll sleep better tonight for hearing you sing.'

The guard gave me a nod. As I rose to go, I remembered I had forgotten to give them a vital piece of news, but I could not risk my escort understanding English. 'Oh, the chimney sweep from Syd's gang is here too,' I said airily, kissing Lizzie on the cheek. She gave a gasp. 'He's staying with new friends. Big Jo's looking after him. Goodbye.'

And leaving Lizzie to explain my cryptic remarks, I followed the guard out of the cell.

SCENE 2—PALAIS ROYAL

Johnny dropped me back at my lodgings with a promise to call for me the next day. I crept in, anxious not to disturb any of the dancers as I had no desire to answer questions as to where I had been all evening. I have to admit, Reader, that I was shaken. To see one of the highest noblemen in England locked up, with so little ceremony, challenged the world I knew. France had turned everything on its head—peers in prison, kings in flight and the common people left to sort things out

167

as best they could. I had thought the revolution a tame beast as the old regime rolled over to do the bidding of the masses, but now it seemed the creature had teeth and would savage anyone who stood in its way. I had not forgotten that I had almost been hanged from a lamp post today over a bit of ribbon; I hoped Lizzie and her family would not meet with so rough a judge as I.

'Psst! Mademoiselle Firecracker!' Renard put his head round the kitchen door. 'You have some visitors.'

Who could they be at this hour? I wondered. Messengers from Frank perhaps?

'Thank you, monsieur. Where are they?'

He jerked his head inside the kitchen. I followed him and found an ill-matched gathering. On one side of the table, looking very much at his ease with his legs crossed and a slice of bacon in his hand, was J-F. Perched on a stool opposite him was a smartly dressed figure, violin case clutched on his knees.

So Pedro had already worked out that these two rogues would steal anything they could lay their hands on.

I rushed to Pedro and gave him a hug. 'It's so good to see you! When did you arrive?'

'Only today. We stopped in Chartres to give some concerts. Signor Angelini has taken lodgings not far from here. I saw Madame Beaufort at the Opera this evening—she told me where you were.'

J-F gave an annoyed cough at being ignored and excluded from a conversation carried out in a foreign language. Remembering how much we were relying on his goodwill, I bobbed a curtsey.

'Monsieur le Roi, may I present my good friend, Pedro Amakye?'

If Pedro was surprised to find I was acquainted with the little thief he did not show it. He stood and bowed.

'He is a friend of yours?' J-F asked suspiciously.

'Indeed, monsieur.'

'To whom does he belong?'

'I don't belong to anyone,' Pedro declared proudly. His French was rudimentary, but he understood the gist of what we were saying.

'Freeman or a runaway?' asked Renard shrewdly. I could see him swiftly calculating the bounty for returning Pedro to his master.

'Both,' said Pedro with a smile at me.

'It's a long story,' I explained hurriedly. 'But he really is free.'

Used to taking life's disappointments in his stride, Renard gave a shrug and, instead of bundling Pedro off to a bounty hunter, offered us a glass of tea.

'So what brings you here?' I asked, making sure I was paying J-F my full attention, as he expected.

'I came to say milord is safe and well,' said J-F, still glaring at Pedro.

'I am very grateful.'

'And what of Milord François' family? Grandfather said you'd gone to visit them in the Conciergerie.'

Pedro's eyebrows shot up. 'What's going on, Cat?' he asked in English.

I quickly explained the events of the last two days.

'But Johnny's on the case,' I concluded. 'With his help, I'm sure the Avons will soon be released.'

'I'd like to see Johnny again,' said Pedro.

'You will. He'll be here tomorrow.'

'No more English,' said J-F petulantly, flicking crumbs off his lap in the direction of Pedro. 'I do not like to be in the dark as to what you are saying. For all I know you could be plotting to call in the law officers.'

'You know I wouldn't do that,' I answered indignantly, annoyed by the little king's treatment of us. He could not bear to be sidelined for a moment.

'No? I know no such thing!' he exclaimed, waving his hands in the air. 'They could be outside now, clubs in hand, waiting to haul me off to the executioner.'

'Don't be such a muttonhead.'

'Don't you call me names!'

'I'll call you names when you deserve them.'

Pedro looked taken aback to find me going hammer and tongs with a complete stranger. Renard chuckled. J-F rounded on his grandfather.

'Shut up, old man! She's a little vixen. I should've let them string her up today and good riddance! We can't trust her—one moment she's defenceless, about to meet her maker, the next she's riding in carriages with American gentlemen and hugging strange African boys!'

So that was it: he was jealous of my friends.

'You really are the most ridiculous boy I've ever met,' I snapped. 'I thought you had to be sharp-witted to be king of thieves, but it seems not.'

J-F sulked over his glass of tea, pretending not to listen.

'You think I'd call in the law officers? Why, for heaven's sake? You're protecting one of my best friends from them.'

He frowned and took a sip.

'The American gentleman is an old friend. We saved his life last year: he owes us one.'

J-F nodded. Debts he could understand.

'As for Pedro here—he's not a stranger. He's like a . . . like a brother to me.'

Pedro looked up and smiled, having understood the description. He felt under the table and gave my hand a squeeze.

'In fact,' I continued, holding on to his hand, 'we're the only family each has so of course I'm going to hug him when I see him. Nothing you say can change that.'

'Don't like him, don't trust him,' J-F grumbled.

His attitude called for desperate measures. We could not afford to make him Pedro's enemy. Time to call on our weapon of last resort.

'Pedro, play for them.'

My friend opened his violin case and took out his bow.

'What's he doing?' J-F asked.

'What do you think? Stirring the stewpot?'

Renard guffawed and settled down to listen.

J-F stuck his fingers in his ears. 'Hate music.'

'Suit yourself.' I put my feet up on the fender and prepared to be entertained.

Pedro cast an appraising look at Renard and began to play a French folk tune he must have recently added to his repertoire. After only a few bars, Renard began to hum and mumble the words under his breath, foot tapping in time. I relaxed: we'd gained one supporter at least.

'What do you think, monsieur?' I asked Renard, giving J-F the cold shoulder.

'Me? I think that—we need to do the dance!' The old man leapt to his feet and pulled me up. 'Here,

171

Mademoiselle Firecracker, this is how we do it in Paris!' He seized my hand and began to show me the steps of a lively jig involving much clapping and jumping. Pedro picked up the beat in honour of the dance. Renard shouted with laughter as I clapped on a jump and jumped on a clap. Even J-F's face cracked into a reluctant smile.

'Get it right, mademoiselle, get it right!' Renard urged, 'or they'll never let you on stage at the Opera.'

I laughed with him. 'Slow down, slow down: you're doing it too fast!'

It was no good: he was remorseless. His feet shuffled and stamped as if he were twenty, not sixty.

'Allow me, mademoiselle.' J-F appeared at my side and took my hand. Pedro glanced at us and slowed to match the little king's pace. 'It goes like this.' He took me through the steps, twisting and turning me skilfully. 'Got it now?'

I nodded. Pedro began to pick up the tempo again. The music filled the kitchen. I was tired after a long day, but the tune seemed to carry me along with it, providing me with the strength to match my tutor. J-F was a very good dancer. Deprived of his partner, Renard picked up the mop and began to twirl it around. I only hoped I was a little more elegant than it was.

Pedro concluded the dance with a flourish and I curtseyed to J-F's bow. The mop inclined its head as Renard blew it a kiss.

'*Eh bien*, what is this?' asked a man's voice in the doorway. 'A party?' Our noise had disguised the fact that we had an audience. Madame Beaufort was standing with a handsome gentleman dressed in white breeches and a dark coat.

'Le Vestris!' muttered J-F in excitement, bowing low to the visitor. Renard dropped the mop with a clatter.

'No, no, monsieur, you must not treat your partner like that!' The man moved lightly across the floor and swept the mop-dancer up in his arms. 'Mademoiselle, you were enchanting.' He twirled the mop and placed it reverently back in the corner. 'Until I next have the pleasure. Gentlemen, ladies.' He bowed to the company and left, a bemused Madame Beaufort trailing after him.

'Who was that?' I asked.

'That? That was only Maria-Auguste Vestris, the principal dancer at the Opera,' said J-F, his eyes shining with admiration. 'He is the master— admired throughout Paris and beyond. There are few who wield more influence over the people than Le Vestris: when he dances, he is our heart and soul. We would all do anything for him. Surely you've heard of him?'

I was amused by J-F's unexpected admiration for a ballet dancer—but then perhaps the arts were more valued in Paris than in London.

'I think I have. I think he came to Drury Lane when I was little.'

'Littler than you are already?' queried Renard, giving the fire a poke. I could tell he was delighted to have entertained a celebrity in his kitchen so I did not begrudge J-F and Pedro the laugh at my expense. At least the ice between them had broken.

'Thank you for my lesson.' I suppressed a yawn. 'I'd better get to bed before madame tells me off for consorting with strange mops in the kitchen.'

J-F stood up. 'I'll escort your friend home, Mademoiselle Cat.' Pedro looked doubtful but J-F

173

slapped him on the arm. 'Remember, Monsieur Pedro, a friend of the Firecracker is a friend of mine.'

So now he remembered!

*   *   *

The news that the famous Monsieur Vestris had discovered me dancing in the kitchen with a young stranger had filtered through to the ballerinas. At practice the next morning, I could not ignore the whispers as I tried to concentrate on the exercises. Madame Beaufort was kinder than I anticipated: apparently we had impressed her guest with our show of 'animal spirits', as he had put it to her, so she did not reprove me. That left Mimi, Belle and Colette to make up for it.

'I suppose the little moll is going to put it all in her next story—how she cavorted with a guttersnipe before the great Vestris himself,' whispered Mimi loud enough for me to hear.

'Going down in the world, isn't she?' answered Colette. 'I thought she had her cap set at that lord— now it seems she'll pick anyone off the street.'

'What do you expect? It's where she came from. Like is attracted to like, they say.'

I tried to imagine their gossip as nothing more than the clatter of knives in a cutlery drawer, but some of their words cut me. I wasn't used to being the object of envy. The girls wanted to think the worst of me and there seemed very little I could do to mend their opinion.

It was a relief to reach the end of lessons. Rather than dine with the dancers, I took a bowl of stew and sat on the front step with Renard. He pointed out the people on their way to take part in the Corpus Christi celebrations.

'The processions are going ahead even with the king's flight?' I asked, watching a red-faced priest hurrying towards the centre of town, a rosary swaying at his side.

'But of course. When we lose one certainty, we must cling to another.' He crossed himself automatically.

I'd never been in a Catholic country before but had heard much of the extravagance of their festivals, and so was eager to see for myself. I could now hear the tantalizing strains of music in the distance.

'What's that?'

'The choirs. The churches all parade their statues in the streets, seeing who can sing the loudest—it's a fine show. Lots of pockets for the picking,' he reminisced fondly.

'So J-F will be busy?'

'Yes, indeed.'

'There's one pocket I hope he has not picked.' I spotted Johnny approaching on foot.

'Off to see the show with him?'

'Sadly not, monsieur. I've arranged to meet Frank to see how he is surviving in his new life.'

Renard chuckled. 'Milord will certainly remember his time in Paris. No feather beds, no silks and satins where he's staying.'

Johnny drew level with us and tipped his hat to my companion. He looked as if he'd passed a sleepless night—doubtless fretting about Lizzie. He still managed a smile for me. 'Ready, Cat?'

'Of course.'

'So where are we going?'

'The Palais Royal—it was J-F's suggestion,' I added to Renard.

Johnny presented me with his arm. 'Why there?'

'It's the only place the police aren't allowed to go, thanks to the king's brother who owns it—royal privilege,' explained Renard.

'Ah, of course, murmured Johnny. 'Philippe fancies himself as the opposition to his older brother so it's the favourite place of all rogues and rebels.'

'That'll suit us then,' I said.

We made our way south towards the river, heading for the rue St Honoré.

'Did you make any progress today?' I asked Johnny as we shouldered a passage through the crowd waiting on Place Louis le Grand. Johnny clapped his hand to his coat pocket automatically as a skinny girl darted between us. The girl turned round.

'Don't worry, monsieur: you're safe while you're with her!' she called over her shoulder.

Johnny looked down at me. 'What's that?'

'My friend, the king of thieves of the Palais Royal—he's given me special privileges.'

'So it would seem.'

'As I was saying, any news?'

'No,' he sighed. 'I'm trying to track down this Fersen character who had the coach taken round to the rue de Clichy but he's disappeared—fled, they say. My next step is to confront the coach builder and see what he knows.'

'My guess is he'll know nothing for his own good.'

'I'm afraid you're right.'

We rounded the corner into the rue St Honoré. Outside the convent of the Jacobins a man in a powdered white wig worn in two side rolls stepped out of the crowd to shake Johnny's hand. They exchanged a few brief words while I stood back.

'Who was that?' I asked Johnny when we set off again.

'Only a lawyer I know by name of Robespierre. Very committed to helping the poor. Bit of a cold fish but useful.'

'Can he help with the Avons?'

'I doubt it. He's in parliament but doesn't really have the ear of the men that count.'

'Who does?'

Johnny thought for a moment. 'Hard to say with the king gone but I suppose Lafayette—he's a soldier, head of the National Guard—and Mayor Bailly. I've been trying to get to speak to them, so far to no avail. They're both too busy dealing with the crisis to talk to an unimportant foreigner like me. But I won't give up.'

We arrived outside the colonnade leading into the Palais Royal.

Johnny patted my hand. 'Ready? Take a deep breath.'

We launched ourselves into the crowd pouring into the pleasure palace beyond. To a Londoner like me, it looked like Vauxhall Gardens and Piccadilly combined: two covered promenades full of clubs, cafés and shops, reverberating with noise and laughter, stretched on either side of the park. In the centre of the open space created by the galleries, tree-lined avenues were crowded with people coming to see and be seen. Here there was a mixture of high and low life such as I was used to at Drury Lane: guardsmen, gamblers, hawkers, students, women of good repute and of no repute

177

at all.

'Like it, Cat?' asked Johnny with an affectionate smile at my expression.

'Like it? I love it!'

He could barely pull me past the window of the little waxwork exhibition as I admired the bust of the pope and the king. I noticed that someone had knocked the latter's crown askew. I was next absorbed by the poster for the Palais theatre that occupied a large part of the wall next door:

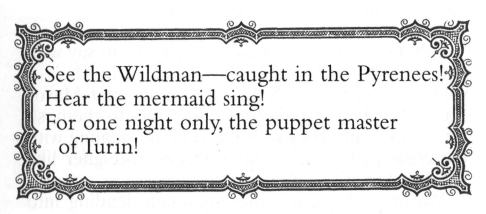

See the Wildman—caught in the Pyrenees!
Hear the mermaid sing!
For one night only, the puppet master
  of Turin!

Johnny wrinkled his nose. 'Come on, Cat, I thought you had better taste than a freak show. I thought you were all for Shakespeare and Dryden.'

'But a real mermaid, Johnny! I've never seen one of them.'

'And you won't here, believe me. It's just some poor scantily clad woman squeezed into a costume.'

I let him pull me away but I couldn't help wondering. This was France, after all, not London. Maybe they had mermaids here?

Johnny led me to a seat at the Corazza café and ordered some refreshment. Watching me, he began to laugh.

'Stop it, Cat! Your eyes are out on stalks!'

I had been staring at a very fat man wobbling along like old gooseberry, accompanied by a tall, thin lady with a deep voice.

'There's something not right about that lady,' I said, puzzled.

'That's because his name is Louvet—he's in parliament. He likes to dress as a woman.' Johnny snapped open a newspaper that was lying on the table as if it were perfectly normal to see members of the legislature walking round in evening gowns.

I felt a tap on my shoulder.

'How are you, chérie?' It was Annette, still wearing my old dress. With her was Marie and a rather sombre looking Frank. Joseph was standing aloof, keeping watch.

Marie shrugged at the footman as she took a seat. 'I told Jo there was no need, but he doesn't trust us.'

'Oh, why would that be do you think?' I asked innocently. 'Was it because you stripped him of all his worldly goods and left him standing naked yesterday?'

'Perhaps,' she conceded.

I introduced Johnny to the girls. They gave him their most charming smiles and began to flirt with him—a game I discovered Johnny was skilled at playing. Their attention diverted, I had a chance to talk to Frank.

'So, Frank, how are they treating you?'

'Fine, Cat, fine.' Frank seemed distracted.

'What's up?'

Suddenly, it all burst from him. 'Do you know how these girls live? Imagine it: they don't even have a bed to sleep in! Marie here—her father's

179

blind, lost his sight in the army, and has to beg for a living. Annette—she had to run away because her uncle used to beat her. Can you believe it?'

Of course I believed it, but it seemed Frank had only just discovered how the majority live. He had only been playing in London when he'd run with Syd's gang, going home at night to his ducal residence; he'd obviously not stopped to think what the rest of us were going home to.

'They don't know where their next meal is coming from, they have no money unless they steal, they get treated like dirt on the streets. I've never known anything like it! No one I know lives like that.'

'That's not true, Frank,' I said quietly, thinking back to my days sleeping rough.

'Who do we know in London who has to put up with that?'

Poor, dear, innocent Frank. I felt both angry and sorry for him for being so blind. 'Me for one. Most of Syd's gang for two.'

Frank opened his mouth to protest, looked at me and closed it.

'You've never noticed, have you? Never noticed that I survive on charity?'

'You—charity? No, you always lived in Drury Lane Theatre. I can't think of a better place.'

'But did you ever look behind the gilt and velvet, Frank, and ask how we theatre folk got by? Where was my bed? Where did my meals come from?'

'Well, erm . . .'

'Exactly. You're only seeing it now because you're having to live it. Most people of your class never do that so they don't see it either.'

Frank tugged at the ragged neckerchief he had

knotted round his throat.

'I suppose I am guilty of an acute lack of imagination, Cat. I'm sorry, I never thought to ask.'

'None of us wanted you to. We have our pride.'

At that moment, a man ran into the café where we were sitting, waving a piece of paper over his head.

'The king has been found! The royal family were overtaken at Varennes!' he shouted, leaping over a table in his passage through.

An excited babble broke out and several political gentlemen of Johnny's acquaintance jumped to their feet and ran off. Johnny poured himself a fresh glass of wine and raised it to us.

'Let's pray this means peace. No foreign invasion. No war. And freedom for your family, Frank.'

'Do you think so?' asked Frank hopefully.

Marie plumped herself down on his knee and ruffled his hair. '*Pauvre François*, I'm afraid not. We Parisians will not want the conspirators free to plot another escape.'

'But they're not conspirators!' Frank protested, blushing deeply as she caressed him.

Marie shrugged. 'Then they have nothing to fear.'

Annoyed seeing her take such liberties with my friend, I said rather more waspishly than I intended, 'For someone who spends most of her time avoiding arrest, you seem to have strange faith in your law officers.'

Marie cast me a knowing look and cuddled up closer to Frank. 'But I would be guilty, *n'est-ce pas*? François says his family is innocent. I believe him.' She kissed him on the cheek.

I turned my eyes away only to see Johnny looking amused by Frank's discomfort. I glared at him, trying by the force of my gaze to remind him that it was Lizzie's little brother that he was laughing at. Johnny winked at me.

'Enough, mademoiselle,' Johnny said, patting his knee. Annette was already leaning against him on the other side. 'You have tested that young man's modesty enough for one evening. Come sit here and behave yourself. We have work to do.'

From my point of view, the exchange did not improve matters. I now had the distraction of watching the two girls hovering round Johnny like bees to a honey pot. Cudgelling my brains into order, I tried to concentrate on our predicament. Lizzie would not thank me for wasting time fuming over a couple of flirtatious girls. Instead, I told Frank about Pedro's arrival.

'That's good,' said Frank. 'I've been wondering how we can get to see my family again. They'll obviously not let either of you in—I daren't show my face—but I had thought that maybe Pedro could take a message for us. No one would suspect him. But how to get him into their cell—that's the real challenge.'

The suggestion prompted me to an inspired thought. 'Your mother.'

'Pardon?'

'Your mother. She's rediscovering the power of her voice. I bet they wouldn't be able to resist the offer of a free concert—her and Pedro: an unbeatable bill. It's almost worth being arrested to hear it.'

'That's not bad, Catkin,' commented Johnny, brushing a strand of Marie's hair off his face. I bit

182

my tongue. I only wished he had his hands more worthily employed.

Now there's an idea.

'If Marie's right about the Parisian people wanting to keep the conspirators locked up,' I said, 'we've got to do something to make the public feel differently about the Avons.'

'I know, Cat. It'll be too easy for the authorities to blame it all on foreigners,' agreed Johnny.

'Well then, what do you think about Captain Sparkler coming out of retirement and beginning a new campaign on behalf of the Duke of Avon: the English peer who had the good taste to marry one of the people; the innocent swept up in the scandal around the king's flight?'

Johnny leaned forward quickly, dislodging Marie from his knee. He apologized and helped her on to the seat next to him. I hid a smile.

'You know, that's a brilliant idea!' he said eagerly. He turned to his admirers. 'Mesdemoiselles, do you know a good printer of political cartoons in Paris?'

Annette giggled. 'Of course, Monsieur Johnny.'

'Where?'

'Here. You're surrounded by them. They're at liberty to print whatever they like in the Palais Royal.'

Johnny kissed her hand. 'Thank you, mademoiselle. I am indebted to you.'

What about me? It was my idea, I thought grumpily.

Johnny got to his feet. 'Let's go, Cat. No time like the present. I'll escort you home and get drawing.'

Giving me only time for the briefest of farewells to Frank, Johnny dragged me off in the direction of the Opera quarter.

'You can't wait to sharpen your pencils, can you?' I asked.

'Indeed I can't. It's been too long since I picked up my drawing things for a cause I believe in.'

I could see he was already planning the cartoon in his head. In this mood I was forgotten, so I had plenty of time to contemplate my foolish jealousy as I trotted to keep up. Marie and Annette were harmless—I knew that—so why did I feel so envious seeing them treating my friends in their free, affectionate manner? I knew my feelings for Johnny coloured my reaction to anything that concerned him, but Frank? What was that about?

Then the truth hit me, bringing me to a standstill as I saw myself for what I really was. The last few weeks seemed to have stripped me down to my essentials, revealing some unpleasant truths. I was afraid, mortally afraid, of being usurped. If other girls became special to Johnny and Frank, where did that leave me? Without my friends, as I had discovered since losing Drury Lane, I really had not a thing in my life that meant anything: no family, no home, no roots.

Johnny noticed I was no longer following and came back to fetch me. 'Are you all right, Cat?' he asked.

'Of course.' I gave him a false smile.

Johnny wasn't fooled. 'No, you're not. Something's up. You're jealous, aren't you?'

I coloured. What I felt was nothing as simple as jealousy. He wouldn't understand how vulnerable I was feeling just at the moment.

'Don't be silly; I'm not jealous.'

'Of course you are. I saw your face when Marie

flirted with Frank. It's nothing to be ashamed of—I can think of many worse people for you to be sweet on.'

He thought I was in love with Frank! This was getting too much.

'You've got it all wrong . . .'

'Aha!' Johnny tapped the side of his nose. 'You want to keep it a secret—I understand. But I think I should warn you that even with the Avons being so progressive, I imagine they'll think twice about letting the next duke marry a . . . a . . .'

'A what?' I was feeling angry with him—both for his stupid guesses and for his inference that I was not good enough for Frank even if I'd wanted him. 'A beggar? A base-born street child with no family? Don't you think I know I'm rubbish without you telling me?'

I pulled away from him and started to run up the street. I didn't want to talk to him—or anyone else who had a peerage and a fortune as a cushion to protect them from the life I knew. To hell with the lot of them—dukes, kings, rich men all!

I heard pounding footsteps and my arm was caught from behind. Johnny swung me round to look at him. He was furious.

'Don't you ever call yourself rubbish in my hearing, Cat Royal! I will not put up with you spitting on your own reputation like that!'

'So I should just let others do it for me, should I?'

'Don't be silly, no one's called you that!'

'No? What about Mr Tweadle, the ballerinas, half of London—and you—you were about to say it in so many words—admit it!'

'I was not.'

We were beginning to attract a crowd with our

185

raised voices but I didn't care. Johnny pulled me down a side alley and out of sight.

'So, tell me, what were you going to say then?' I challenged him.

'I was just going to say that they wouldn't want him to marry a commoner.'

'That's it exactly. Common as muck, bred in the gutter—I've heard it all before, Johnny. I know what you mean—it's all right, you don't need to explain. It's fine for aristocrats like Frank to play at being poor, even all right for you to pretend to be a man of the people with your simple Mr Johnny Fitzroy routine, but when it comes to someone like me rising above her station, then alarm bells begin to ring.'

Johnny was lost for words. He didn't know he'd just walked in on a very private battle I was having with myself as to my own worth. As ever though, my mouth continued to run on long after it should have shut up.

'You aristocratic revolutionaries can only bear so much change, can't you? It's just skin deep—literally! If it's an African or Indian—or, heaven forbid, a woman who wants her equality, then you start to panic.'

'That's not true, Cat.' He had gone pale; I had struck a nerve.

'Isn't it?'

'Not with me.' He seemed confused that I had leapt from my opinion of myself to politics. 'What's all this about, Cat?'

'It's about you telling me I'm worth something when I know that you and everyone else don't really think so. I count for nothing—I have no property, no vote, no blue blood. I have nothing because what little I once had has been stolen and twisted to benefit someone else's pocket. So don't you go telling me I'm not rubbish! If I say I am, then I am.'

I had argued myself into the absurd position of defending my right to put myself down. I can't blame Johnny for being confused.

'Stop it, Cat, stop it!' he said, running his hands through his hair in exasperation. 'Why are you saying all these terrible things about yourself?'

'Because they're true! If you hear it enough about yourself from everyone, then you start to believe them.'

'But you mustn't.' Johnny grasped my shoulders, then gathered me into his arms and gave me a hug. 'You've certainly had your confidence knocked out of you by that Tweadle fellow, haven't you, Catkin?'

I clung to him, like a castaway holding on to the last bit of flotsam that stood between me and drowning.

'You mustn't let rogues like that tell you what you're worth. In fact, you shouldn't even listen to me or your other friends.'

'Who should I listen to then?' I felt so lonely—I knew that at any moment he would let me go. I wished I could continue standing in his arms forever.

'In the end, Cat, all of us have to listen to our inner self. The voice that tells you you're worthless isn't the real you—it's from outside. Think—what does Cat really think of herself?'

'I don't think you'll be pleased.'

'No? Try me.'

'I think that I can't be worth much because my parents abandoned me.'

'Ah.'

'I'm nine parts stupidity to one part wit.'

'That's not bad—most of the population cannot claim even that much.'

'And I suppose I'm loyal, a good friend and have my moments of bravery,' I conceded.

'Hear, hear.'

I pushed him gently away, thinking it better that I broke willingly from his hug while I still could. 'Sorry, Johnny.'

'Sorry for what?'

'For shouting at you. It's just that when I think about the future, I keep panicking. It's like falling from the top of the stairs in the dark, not knowing where I'll end up.'

He put his arm around my shoulders. 'I understand. Life is precarious for most of us, but more so for you. What you forget is what most of your friends see in you.'

'What's that?'

'The ability to beat the odds . . .'

'And fall on my feet?'

He nodded.

'I just hope that lasts.'

'It will, Catkin, it will. It wouldn't dare fail you.'

*   *   *

But for all Johnny's optimism, my luck had just run out. We arrived at Madame Beaufort's to find two members of the National Guard at the door. It was too late to make a run for it even if we had known which of us they were after. They leapt to their feet.

'Mademoiselle Royal?'

'*Oui*, monsieur?' Johnny's grip tightened on my arm.

'Will you come with us, please. The mayor would

188

like to ask you a few questions.'

'What about?' I asked, my heart thumping.

The guard shrugged. 'No idea, mademoiselle. I am merely doing my job.'

I looked up at Johnny, my expression asking, what should I do?

'Don't worry, Cat,' he said in a low voice. 'This isn't an arrest—it's just to help with their enquiry. They're bound to release you after the interrogation.'

'What do you think they want with me?'

'I guess it's about our friends. Be discreet and you've nothing to fear.' He turned to the guard. 'Monsieur, my companion is only young. May I come with her?'

The guard raised his eyebrows. 'And who are you, monsieur?'

'Jonathan Fitzroy—an American citizen.'

'So you are no relation?'

'No, monsieur. A friend.'

'Then I'm afraid not. We will take good care of her. If she is released, you can come and fetch her from the Town Hall later.'

If!

'Come along, mademoiselle. Quickly now: we mustn't keep the mayor waiting.'

For all his encouraging words, Johnny looked alarmed to see me frogmarched off by two tall members of the guard.

'I'll be fine!' I called to him, knowing he had enough on his hands worrying about Lizzie. 'Just tell the concierge where I am.' And there was no harm letting the king of thieves know I had been taken. Who knew what connections he would have that might prove useful?

SCENE 3—THE BISHOP OF THE NOTRE DAME THIEVES

It was a long walk from the Opera quarter to the Town Hall—a humiliation I had to go through before the eyes of all the people on the streets celebrating Corpus Christi. My escort said nothing to me, leaving me free to hear the suspicious whispers that followed our passage through the crowds. I was relieved when we arrived at our destination: a palatial building level with Notre Dame on the right bank of the Seine.

'Voilà, mademoiselle,' said my guard. 'We are here.'

'A moment please.' I sat down on a stone bench outside and took off my shoe, ostensibly to remove a pebble, but really to see if anyone was watching. I would've been surprised if the thieves had not taken action by now. Sure enough, a familiar sharp face was watching us from a doorway across the square. J-F nodded when he saw that I had spotted him. Restoring my shoe after much shaking, I thanked the guard for waiting and let them lead me inside.

It was reassuring that they had taken me into the public area of the building, an ornate space of polished floors and grand staircases. If I had been in worse trouble, surely I would have been put in a cell? I had enough experience of falling foul of the law to know that they didn't waste carpet on suspects.

I followed the guards upstairs, having to run to keep up with their strides. The place was buzzing with activity and few spared us a glance as they went about their business keeping the City of Paris ticking over during the crisis.

My guard opened the door to an antechamber furnished with white and gilt chairs that stood against the walls like ladies in a ballroom waiting to be asked to dance.

'Remain in here. The mayor will be with you as soon as possible.'

This was to be expected. Questioning one English girl was doubtless at the bottom of the mayor's 'To Do' list. I remembered Johnny had told me he hadn't even been able to get an interview with Mayor Bailly. Perhaps I should look on this unwelcome interruption as an opportunity to learn more? The questions he asked me were bound to give a clue as to what connections the authorities thought the Avons had with the whole business of the king's flight.

Time passed. It was getting dark outside now and a servant came in to light the candles, giving me a friendly nod as he left. I kicked my heels and hummed the tune we had danced in the kitchen the night before. Still no one came. I took off my shoes and rubbed my tired toes. Perhaps they had forgotten me? Getting bored of sitting on the same chair, I stood up in my stockinged feet and began to go through the steps I had learned, turning and hopping as J-F had taught me.

A door banged open just as I finished a pirouette. I sprang to attention to find myself under the gaze of five gentlemen. Thinking I might as well make the best of it, I swept them a low curtsey as instructed by Madame Beaufort—hand curved elegantly to my breast.

'Who's this?' barked a harassed-looking man

191

standing at the front.

'The English girl. The ballerina, Monsieur le Maire,' said a young man clutching a sheaf of papers.

Mayor Bailly directed a thin smile at his companions. 'I can see the latter part for myself, Donville. Remind me why she's here.'

'The Duke of Avon, monsieur.'

Mayor Bailly clicked his fingers. 'But of course. It's been a long day. Follow us, mademoiselle.' He began striding down the corridor.

Hopping into my shoes, I cursed all men who forgot that short girls do not possess the same long legs as them.

Bailly marched into his office and threw himself into a chair behind a desk piled high with papers. I took my first good look at the man in charge of Paris, wondering what he would do with me. Johnny had said that Bailly was a distinguished astronomer before the revolution swept him to his current position and I thought that he still had the earnest look of a scholar: high cheekbones, a strong, slightly hooked nose and heavy lidded eyes that had probably spent far more time than was healthy staring through a telescope. Indeed, his gaze did seem as though his thoughts were fixed on something beyond the room rather than on those present. Was he merely thinking of the king coming back under escort from Varennes or the craters on the moon that he had been the first to spot?

'Well, mademoiselle, what can you tell us about the whereabouts of the Duke of Avon's son?' he asked, his eyes losing their dreamy look and focusing on me as he dragged himself back to business.

'Me, monsieur?' I said with wide eyes, wondering how far injured innocence would take me.

'Perhaps it would save us all a lot of time if I told you that we know that you arrived in Paris in the company of this young gentleman on the very night that the king and queen made their escape. A coincidence, perhaps, but I for one do not like coincidences.'

So he knew rather too much for comfort. I would have to think up a plausible story—and quickly.

'We went our separate ways shortly after arriving, monsieur. I believe the gentleman in question was intending to travel for his education, taking a year away from studies before he went to university. I think he may be heading for Italy.'

'Really?' I could tell Bailly did not believe me. 'We have no record of a young Englishman leaving by any of the city gates. My impression is that he is still in Paris—gone to ground because he knows we have his parents and sister in custody. What I want to know is where is he and what did he have to do with the king's flight?'

'Nothing, I'm sure, monsieur,' I said answering the second part of his question.

Bailly's eyes narrowed. 'How can you be so certain?'

'We got lost on arrival and spent most of that night trying to find my lodgings.'

'So what was your coach doing by the palace? You were seen by General Lafayette's attendants when they were doing their inspection. We've questioned the driver and he has only a suspiciously hazy recollection of events, but he told us enough to know that you were nowhere near the Opera quarter.'

'Precisely, monsieur.' My hands were fluttering so I clasped them behind my back. 'We were lost.' My most vacuous smile wreathed my lips.

'Hmm.' The mayor tapped a pen on a piece of parchment thoughtfully as he looked at me. I could tell he was trying to work me out.

Please think I'm just an empty-headed ballerina, I urged him silently.

'I have here a warrant for the young man's arrest.' The mayor dipped his quill in the inkpot and signed it. 'I am giving you the benefit of the doubt, mademoiselle. Whatever your companion was up to that night, I judge that you were ignorant of it.' He handed the paper to his secretary. 'However, you should think of yourself as under suspicion. Your behaviour must be exemplary or you will be expelled from France. And if I find you have been hiding anything from me—protecting the young lord for whatever reason—you will be prosecuted. Do you understand?'

'*Oui*, monsieur.'

'That's all. You may go.'

I turned, half expecting to be escorted off the premises, but not one of them bothered to follow me. Thinking this odd, I made my own way downstairs. I paused in the foyer, hoping my friends had come to fetch me, but there was no one there. I wasn't sure what to do; it was foolhardy to walk the streets of a city at night, especially a foreign one. Before I had made up my mind, someone collided with me from behind, making me stumble.

'I'm very sorry, mademoiselle.' It was Pedro, acting as if he didn't know me. 'Are you hurt?'

'No harm done, sir,' I said stiffly, trying for disdainful but not sure I carried it off.

'I believe you dropped this.' He handed me a piece of folded paper, bowed and walked on out of the building.

Taking a seat in a secluded corner to give the impression I was waiting for someone, I carefully opened the note.

Catkin,

Your remarkable friend J-F says there is a reward out for Frank. He thinks that they called you in with the hope that you'll lead them to him as you rush to alert him to the danger. It is therefore highly likely that you will be followed—as will anyone you are seen with. We decided it was best that my connection with you was not too publicly demonstrated so I'm sorry that I have not come to fetch you as I said I would. J-F will see you home safely—but from afar, as he says he has a natural antipathy for officialdom and does not want to be brought to their notice. Leave the building and look for him. Keep your distance and he'll make sure that anyone on your tail soon loses you.

Send me a note with Pedro to say you have got home safely. He'll wait with Renard for your return.

Johnny.

I folded the note again and tucked it into my bodice. So that was why no one had escorted me to the door: they had wanted me to believe I was free to go and of no further interest. Well, if they wished to follow me that was their look-out. They didn't stand a chance. J-F and I were about to lead them on a merry dance.

Giving a histrionic sigh, as if giving up waiting on my friends, I walked to the door. Once back on the square, I looked about me, not finding it difficult to play the confused tourist seeking her bearings. My survey revealed J-F waiting in the same doorway. As soon as he saw me, he set off, heading north. Hesitating slightly, trying to seem as if I was having difficulty deciding my route, I followed him. If my pursuers had any decency they would prevent a lone stranger heading off in completely the wrong direction, but it seemed that decency was in short supply in Paris at the moment. And if I was being tailed, I could not tell it. They were good at their job, whoever they were.

J-F turned left, then right, leading us into a warren of alleyways. They stank of the familiar scents of piss and dung, intermixed with the acrid odour of rotting fish and garlic—something the streets of London lacked and, in my opinion, it did nothing to improve the bouquet. Thinking it would look suspicious if I seemed too obvious in my attempt to lose my pursuers, I stood at the corner of the street indecisively, trying to make out the sign. A gaggle of rouged women pushed past me, giving me a dirty look. This was clearly their spot and they thought I was invading. I quickly started walking again but, in that short interval, I had lost sight of J-F. It was no laughing matter to lose one's guide in such a neighbourhood. I stopped again, this time because I really was undecided as to where to go next. An arm reached out from a doorway and yanked me inside, smothering my cry.

'Quiet,' whispered J-F. 'You have two trackers. Let's give them a little time to realize they've lost you.'

Taking my hand, he led me under the wooden stairwell and out of sight. We crouched together in the dark, saying nothing as we listened to the sounds outside. I heard feet running past and then back again. Shouts. Curses. I was shivering but J-F was unconcerned. He played with my old pink ribbon, knotting, unknotting, and reknotting it into increasingly complicated patterns.

'What's going on?' I whispered. 'What if they start searching the buildings?'

'They won't. Just about now, Annette should be appearing at the end of the street dressed in a cloak like yours. She's going to lead them into the Marais and then turn back so they can see they've been chasing the wrong goose.' He flicked the ribbon into the air, letting it fall back into his lap. 'You were in there for hours. Did they give you a hard time?'

I shook my head. 'No, it was just very boring. They kept me waiting.'

J-F frowned. 'See, I told you: rich men, rulers—they're all the same. They all keep the common folk waiting.' He ducked his head around the staircase. The sounds had died down. 'Come on, Cat, time to go. I don't like hanging around here longer than is strictly necessary.'

'Why not?' I asked, following him out into the passageway. Suddenly J-F stiffened.

'Because, mademoiselle,' said a man's voice, 'this is not his patch and he knows it. Our rules say that he should ask permission from our bishop before setting a foot here.' The speaker stepped into sight, blocking the route to the courtyard. He was a young man of about twenty, the length of his face marked by a scar that pulled one eyelid down. Quick as an eel, J-F spun round to bolt for the door but three men dropped lightly over the banisters from above, sealing off that exit. J-F grabbed my arm.

197

'We have a slight complication, Cat,' he whispered.

Complication! I knew an ambush when I saw one.

'Keep quiet. This is not about you—it's about me,' J-F warned.

'Who's the bishop?' I asked.

'The bishop, Mademoiselle Anglaise,' declared the scarred man, 'is the leader of the Worshipful Company of the Notre Dame Thieves.' He pulled me away from J-F. 'Your friend here is the King of the Vagabonds of the Tuileries and Palais Royal.' He gave a nod to his men and they pinned J-F's arms to his side, slipping a hood over his head. 'And right now, the bishop wants to have a few spiritual words with the king.'

'You're not going to harm him, are you?' I asked anxiously as they dragged J-F into the street.

Scarface gave me a bitter smile. 'No, mademoiselle, we have you for that.'

'What!'

He produced a second hood and whipped it over my head before I could cry out. Next he threw me over his shoulder and jogged off after his mates, taking so little care that I was thrown against the doorpost with a stunning blow. Dazed and half suffocated, I bumped up and down on his shoulder. Only now did I regret that I had been so eager to throw off my government followers: surely even they would have intervened to stop this? Scarface had indicated that I was there only as leverage on J-F and I did not relish a role that pitted the amount of pain the little thief king could bear to see me suffer against whatever business it was they wanted to conduct.

After what seemed like hours of this treatment,

198

though it was probably only minutes, I was bounced down a flight of stairs and thrown to the floor. Bruised and humiliated, I reached to pull off my hood.

'Don't touch it!' said Scarface brutally. 'No one sees the bishop face to face unless he says so!'

I wasn't going to stand for this—I was going to breathe at least. I freed my nose and mouth. 'Why? What's wrong with him? Has he got a particularly ugly face? Warts? Snout like a pig?' Scarface aimed a kick at me but I heard it coming and flinched out of the way. 'You should tell him that good cosmetics can do a lot for even the most hopeless cases.' I scrambled to take cover behind something. 'Then the rest of us might be able to breathe in his oh-so-holy presence.'

'Firecracker, this is not a good time to go off!' hissed J-F somewhere on my right.

Someone came to stand before me, two brown boots in line with my knees. A hand reached down and took off my hood. I blinked in the light.

'You'd like to give me beauty tips, would you, little redhead?' said a man's voice. The accent wasn't Parisian—it reminded me of an Egyptian snake charmer who'd once performed at Drury Lane.

Still on my knees, I looked up at six foot of brightly coloured person towering over me. A coat hung with ribbons and silk handkerchiefs like some kind of robe draped from his shoulders to the floor. A mane of shaggy black hair hung down his back. I stood up, straightening my skirts, gaining little advantage as I still did not rise above his chest. A pair of shrewd dark eyes in an olive-skinned face inspected me. He had the cruel beauty of a bird of prey. I had no doubt he had killed before and would again.

'Well, Monsieur Bishop, with a face like yours, you really don't need any advice from me,' I said, seeing what flattery would do for me, 'but neither do I understand why you would want to deprive anyone of the pleasure of looking at you.' I glanced to my right and saw that J-F was strapped to a post. We were in some kind of underground cellar with a vaulted ceiling, surrounded by barrels of wine. J-F looked worried. Not a promising sign.

'You are too kind, mademoiselle,' the bishop replied, taking my arm and leading me to sit on the step up to his chair. He moved with powerful grace like a lion pacing his domain. 'But if you live like us, you will understand that the fewer who can identify you, the safer you are. I don't like having too many people running around Paris knowing what I look like.'

I gulped, working out that I had now joined that endangered group. 'I suppose it's not too late to put the hood back on?' I asked. 'I have a terrible memory for faces.'

'Unfortunately, mademoiselle, you strike me as just the kind of person to have an acute memory and besides, we all want to see you—J-F, I have no doubt, wants to have a clear view of you as we conduct . . . our business. It will help concentrate his mind.'

If concentrating his mind involved putting me in distress I wasn't planning to stay any longer than I must. I knew I was in the presence of a very formidable person and his intentions towards me did not appear benign. Escape seemed the best option. Continuing to listen hard, I looked for some way out. The cellar was crowded with at least eight of the bishop's men, three of the burliest standing by the door. No escape through them. I'd have to do this by my wits and not by hoping to make a lucky dash for it.

'Well, *Petit Roi*, I am delighted you could make time to come to confession,' said the bishop glibly, settling down on his chair.

'I'm pleased you are pleased,' said J-F with an attempt at his old bravado.

'So, tell me, why were you in my territory?'

'I was showing my friend here the sights of Paris.'

'Indeed. And giving Bailly's bulldogs the slip into the bargain.'

J-F smiled nervously. 'That too, your eminence.'

'You know I have the right to slit your throat for being out of bounds,' said the bishop in a friendly tone, putting his feet up—on my shoulder. 'But I like you and don't want to do away with such an adversary for so slight a thing.'

'Adversary?' queried J-F quickly. 'I always looked on us as business associates occasionally in competition with each other.'

'In that case I have a business proposition for you. I understand that a foreign traitor has gone to ground in your patch—possibly with your connivance, but I can't believe that of you, good citizen that you are.' J-F bowed. 'I am minded to pick up the reward for him to help tide me over some temporary monetary difficulties I'm experiencing. Send him along to me and we'll forget about today's little incursion.'

'You are most kind. But what makes you think that once out of here I will hand anyone over to you?' J-F's eyes glinted with a hardness to match the bishop.

The bishop smiled. 'I thought we would get to that—and I think you know the answer.'

J-F glanced at me.

'That's right. Your little friend will pay the penalty you should've paid for your trespass.'

J-F shrugged. 'So be it. She's nothing to me.'

I wasn't sure if he was lying. It's always best to deny the value of a thing if someone else has it. On the other hand, perhaps I really was of no matter to the mercurial J-F—a sigh of regret, a frown and then he'd forget me.

'In that case, you can collect her body from the Seine when we've finished with her. You have until midnight tomorrow to decide just how much she's worth to you.'

This wasn't good—not good at all. My life for Frank? Or would J-F just abandon me, hand Frank over to the authorities himself and pocket the money? I mean, what did I really know about the king of thieves except that he was good at stealing?

'Cut him loose and boot him out the back door,' said the bishop.

Scarface seized J-F by the scruff of the neck, but he twisted free and scrambled to stand in the space before the Bishop.

'Ibrahim, think!' J-F said breathlessly, sweeping a hand at me. 'Where's your gallantry to a female? She's nothing to do with us. It's not fair to use her like this.'

He must be on very shaky ground if he was appealing to a rival's better nature. My heart sank a fraction deeper.

'First names, J-F? We must be desperate,' chuckled the bishop, stretching lazily in his chair, dislodging me from my step with his boot. 'And I'm sure she's everything to do with the business or why was Bailly having her followed? I was intending to have a little discussion with her about this while we were waiting for you to decide what to do. Hurry along now.'

J-F cast me one last anxious look before he was unceremoniously bundled back up the stairs. His expression was too close to an apology for my liking. It seemed I was on my own.

Silence fell in the room as the bishop and I listened to the sounds of J-F being escorted from the premises.

'So, mademoiselle,' said the bishop at length, 'how are you enjoying Paris?' He stroked the bridge of his nose thoughtfully. It looked as though it had been broken several times.

I took off my shoe to rub my blistered feet. 'Oh, it's just delightful. Every crowd I meet tries to hang me and every villain to rob me. And as for the night life, I've never been so entertained with threats to my own person since . . . well, I can't remember when.'

The bishop laughed. 'You have spirit, mademoiselle. What is your name?'

There seemed little point in hiding it from him. 'Cat Royal.'

'Well, Mademoiselle Cat, it is late and I've some work to do. If you would do me the honour of breaking your fast with me, we can postpone our little discussion until then.'

I shrugged. 'As you wish. I hardly have any say in the matter.'

He stood up, taking off his ridiculous cloak and folding it. 'Come, come, we must keep up appearances. You are my guest. I invite you to eat with me—I do not command.'

'And where am I to wait for this much-to-be-anticipated tête-à-tête?' I wondered if I was managing to convey sarcasm speaking in a foreign language. It was the only power left to me.

'Here, of course, mademoiselle. I will have my men bring you some blankets. Is there anything else I can get you?'

'Apart from the key out of here?'

His smile was thin—I was sailing dangerously close to annoying him. I buttoned up my tongue.

'Thank you, monsieur. I would appreciate pen and paper. If tomorrow's to be my last, I've letters I'd like to write.'

'Of course, mademoiselle. And I'll promise to deliver them whatever happens to their fair writer.'

'You are too kind.'

'You see, gallantry is not dead, even if you will be.'

Interlude—Set to solemn music by Handel

Paris, 23rd June 1791

My dear Patron,
    I am writing what might turn out to be my last letter to you. I thought it best to complete it to earn another guinea as it might at least help pay my funeral expenses. That was meant to be a joke but unfortunately it is too close to the truth to seem funny even to me.

    Here are the facts as I understand them: our friends from Grosvenor Square are still enjoying French hospitality; one sprig of the tree is at large but under threat; a bunch of cutthroats are holding me to ransom in the hopes of claiming the reward for turning him in.

    That's all the news from the family. As for the rest, you probably do not need to be told that the king is returning to Paris. The city remains quiet. My gut feeling is that people are beginning to realize that the sky did not fall on their heads when the Bourbons left town—this does not bode well for Louis. He, like me, might learn soon what it means to be expendable.

    I have never forgotten your many years of kindness towards me. I send my love and best wishes for the future,

Your Diamond.

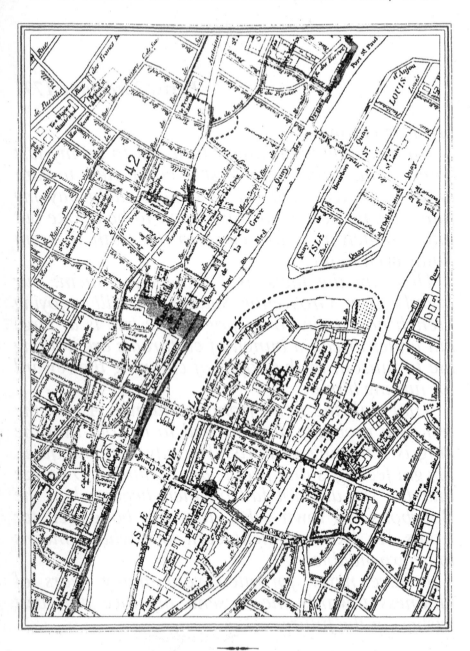

*Act IV - In which Cat surprises
even herself . . .*

Act IV

SCENE 1—ENGLISH SPY

Woken by the sound of a door closing, I wriggled out of my cocoon of blankets and found myself alone. A fresh candle, two cups, a coffee pot and a basket of bread stood on a barrel. I guessed that meant it was morning. Rubbing the sleep from my eyes, my recollections of the previous night returned and with them my fear. It was hard to know exactly what to think or feel. This wasn't about me, as J-F had told me, but still I was the victim. I was a foot soldier caught up in the battle between two empires—forces beyond my control were in charge of my destiny. I didn't like it one little bit.

Pacing the cellar, I tried to imagine what my friends were feeling—that's if J-F had chosen to enlighten them to my plight, and I wouldn't put it past him to remain silent if it suited him. Frank would demand to be exchanged for me—and he would be right as his fate was only prison with a good chance he might be freed when the truth about the king's flight came out. But the reward skewed everything.

Relying on thieves for your safety was not a good idea, I decided. If I got a second chance, I wouldn't do so again.

'Bonjour, mademoiselle. I trust you slept well?'

The bishop was back for his breakfast. He was standing at the top of the steps looking down on me. I hadn't heard him come in. He was carrying a sack

207

over one shoulder.

I gave a contemptuous shrug.

He jumped down the steps, the bag clanking on every bound.

'I presume you've brought the church plate with you?' I asked, nodding at the sack.

'Indeed so. I relieved some affluent citizens of their surplus as a donation to the poor. After all, it is harder for a rich man to enter heaven than for a camel to pass through an eye of a needle.' He gave me a wicked grin. Charming he might be but I knew that those shining eyes of his were like wrecker's lanterns: the sort to lure you off course on to the rocks of your destruction.

'That was very charitable of you.'

He chucked the sack into a corner and turned to the breakfast tray. Lacing his fingers together, he bent them back, cracking his knuckles in preparation for the meal.

'Has anyone ever told you that that is a very unattractive habit?'

'Oh yes,' he said with a wolfish grin, 'two people. So I put them out of their distress.'

I decided to laugh at this, though for all I knew he really did kill people on such flimsy pretexts.

'How thoughtful of you.' I poured myself a cup of coffee from the pot on the tray, adding a couple of spoonfuls of sugar to mask the bitterness.

'Now you understand me, Mademoiselle Cat.'

'I don't pretend to do that. I don't have a clue, for example, what's going on between you and J-F.'

He devoured a piece of bread, folding it to fit inside his mouth in one huge bite.

'You should understand, mademoiselle, that Paris is a divided city. Each faubourg or district has its own identity—even its own government. Likewise, we gentlemen of the night have our own way of distributing the territory between us.'

It sounded like home. I was beginning to get an inkling of what was happening.

'But J-F seems very young to be running a kingdom,' I ventured. 'Why hasn't someone taken it over?' In London, I couldn't imagine quick wits and an entertaining manner keeping anyone in charge of a gang of thieves.

The bishop scratched his chin thoughtfully. 'Now there's an idea.'

'No, don't get me wrong!' I said hurriedly, not wanting to be blamed for starting a gang war in Paris. 'I wasn't suggesting anything.'

Monsieur Ibrahim showed a fine set of white teeth as he threw back his head and roared. 'Don't worry, mademoiselle, I'll do no such thing without provocation. It's tradition that the thief king of the Palais Royal is a merry fellow like our J-F—he rules by consent. The bishop of Notre Dame,' he tapped his own chest, 'rules by decree. Each to his own.'

Paris struck me as a very mixed up-place with all these contending underworld rulers. In my city, the person with the biggest fists commanded the most respect. We liked to keep it simple.

'But you shouldn't underestimate J-F,' continued M. Ibrahim as if he could read my thoughts. 'He has people loyal to him. It would be more difficult than you might imagine to walk in and declare that you've taken over his kingdom.'

'I see.' I remembered the hulking lads who had walked off with Joseph's livery—yes, J-F did have his troops even if he preferred to live by his wits rather than fists.

'But this will not do, mademoiselle,' declared M. Ibrahim, pouring me a second cup of coffee. 'I was supposed to be asking you the questions, not the other way round.'

'Of course, your eminence. I am at your service.'

He grinned and stroked the lip of his cup. 'You're an interesting creature, Mademoiselle Cat. Who are you really? I don't buy this story that you're a dancer.'

'Me? I'm no one—just an orphan brought up among theatre people, now having to find my own way.'

'Really?' His tone was sceptical.

'Yes, really.'

'You see, mademoiselle, our beloved authorities are convinced that there is an English agent at large in Paris.'

I choked on my coffee. 'Oh yes? How do you know this?'

'Naturally, I've a source in the City Hall.'

'I see.'

'Certain incriminating correspondence has been intercepted mentioning the king's flight and the imprisonment of those English aristocrats. Mayor Bailly is under the impression that the most likely source for these reports is someone close to the Avon boy, perhaps a servant or the boy himself. It's one of the reasons they are so eager to lay their hands on him. What do you make of that?'

'That's very . . . interesting.'

'Isn't it? I don't suppose you'd care to show me what you were writing last night?'

I put down my cup and discreetly checked that the letter was still in my apron pocket.

'Actually, your eminence, I'd prefer to keep my

letters private.'

He leaned forward. 'That is a shame, mademoiselle, because I have a theory that if I handed the authorities the English agent, they would still give me the reward.'

'What's that to do with me?'

'Think about it, mademoiselle. J-F won't part with the boy without profit for himself so I have scant hope of receiving anything that way tonight. This means you will die unless you can persuade me that it's worth my while to let you live.'

'And I thought we were getting on so well.'

'Oh, but we are. I think we understand each other completely.' He rose and yawned. 'I'm going to sleep now. Think over what I've said. I'll be back to hear what you have to say this evening.'

The first thing I did when he left the room was burn the letter I'd written to Mr Sheridan. The bishop doubtless knew that I'd destroy any evidence I had on me but he was confident I'd prefer confession of my guilt to death. Curse Mr Sheridan for saying there was only slight danger involved in setting up a confidential correspondent in Paris!

Mind you, I reflected as the paper curled into ashes, he'd said that was before the king took it into his head to flee, leaving an anxious and suspicious government behind. I should've taken this into account before I started firing off my missives. Why did it not occur to me that in these dangerous times any letter to a well-known English politician such as Mr Sheridan would be opened as a matter of course? I should be cursing myself—so I did just that as I sat curled up in a ball on the bishop's chair. I'd got myself into this mess, so I had to think of a way out of it. As far as I could see, there were two possibilities: J-F would surprise me with his loyalty and think of some way of rescuing me or I would do it myself. Of the two, the latter was the most likely.

I explored the cellar again: there was only one way in and out: up the stairs. The top of the steps was secured by a heavy wooden door that would've withstood a pounding from Syd, let alone yours truly. The best I could think of was to lie in wait and try to slip past the next person to come in. To this end, I made a Cat-shaped mound out of my blankets and returned to the top step.

I hate waiting. I am the least patient person in the world. Add to that my fear at what I was about to do and I hope you can understand, Reader, what an uncomfortable day I passed. I knew my plan was a shaky one: I didn't even know what was on the other side of the door—more barricades for all I knew. But I had to try something.

After many hours, I heard footsteps in the corridor outside. I flattened myself in the space that would be behind the door once it was opened. It's fortunate that there's not much of me—few would manage this without being squashed flat. A key turned in the lock and the door swung open. Someone entered carrying a tray—that suited me as it meant they did not have a hand free to shut the door behind them.

'Mademoiselle, your dinner is served,' called Scarface to the mound of blankets.

I crept out from behind the door and into the corridor. I was in a passageway. Left or right? I ran to the right as a shout echoed behind me. My trick had been discovered. Turning a corner I mounted a second flight of stairs. I could hear Scarface cursing. A door at the top—I pushed it open and emerged

212

into a twilit cloister. In the centre of the quadrangle was a lawn and sundial. I dashed down the avenue of pillars heading towards the grand door at the end. Overhead, the bells of Notre Dame in her twin towers began to chime for the evening service—I must be very near the cathedral. Where there were people, there was hope. I grabbed the door handle and pulled. It did not move. I could hear Scarface running towards me. I had only seconds left.

'Come on, damn you,' I cursed. 'Shift!'

'Tut, tut, mademoiselle. From the few words of English I know, I do believe you were swearing.' The bishop sauntered into view from the aisle to my left, picking his nails clean with a knife. He didn't seem surprised to see me there.

Scarface reached me and slammed my shoulder into the door as he grabbed my arms.

'Sorry, your eminence,' he said breathlessly. 'She tricked me.'

'I expected no less of her. Though why she thought I'd put only one lock between her and freedom, I cannot guess.'

'Didn't your mother teach you that it's rude to pick your nails?' I spat at him.

'And didn't yours tell you it's rude to leave your host without even saying goodbye?' He tickled my cheek with the point of the knife.

'I just wanted a breath of fresh air.' Scarface had my face pressed against the wooden planks of the door. I could hear voices, echoing footfalls, tantalizingly close.

'Really? Because I could've sworn you were trying to escape. No matter. Something has come up, mademoiselle, that requires your presence here in any case. Luc, stop squeezing our guest to death.'

The pressure on my back was instantly removed. I rubbed my bruised arms. 'Perhaps you would care to accompany me?'

Ibrahim held out an arm. I hesitated—until Scarface Luc prodded me in the back.

'Where are you taking me?'

Ibrahim produced a key from his pocket and opened the door that foiled my bid for freedom.

'There are summons that even a bishop cannot ignore,' he said, pushing me through.

The door took us on to the square in front of Notre Dame. I had scant time to admire the pale stone of the carved arches and statues and the two soaring towers as Ibrahim marched me into the cathedral itself. In contrast to the twilight, it was dark inside. Light seeped through the stained glass, glowing with jewel-bright colours; candles flickered beneath icons. The sounds of the street outside were swallowed up. Like Jonah in the mouth of the whale, we had entered another world cut off from all else, swept along on a tide of darkness to plunge into the very belly of the beast.

Monsieur Ibrahim led me to the chapel behind the main altar. By the rail knelt a man I recognized: it was none other than Maria-Auguste Vestris, principal dancer at the Opera, last seen bowing to a mop in Renard's kitchen. The ballet master looked up on our approach and rose fluidly to his feet. He seemed unabashed to meet so threatening a person as the bishop, and advanced confidently towards us. I had a second chance to study one of Paris's most famous sons. I was impressed by the intense expression of his eyes and a sense of hidden vigour—he was like a bow bent, ready to fire. And he was here to meet us of all people. What did this mean?

'Ah, here is my missing dancer.' Le Vestris smiled enquiringly at me.

Ibrahim bowed respectfully before the great man and pushed me towards him. I curtseyed, hovering in the no-man's-land between them. 'Monsieur, I am sorry if I have inconvenienced you by keeping her as my guest,' said the bishop sourly. He was clearly doing this with some reluctance.

'Not at all, not at all.' Le Vestris turned to me. 'And how are you, *ma chérie*? Still able to perform the country dance I saw you doing the other night?'

'D-dance?' I stammered.

'I certainly hope so, as I think it will be a most charming addition to *La Fille Mal Gardée*—two miniature dancers to complement the adult soloists. It's going to be a real *coup de théâtre*! I understand your host here had some difficulty believing you were a ballerina so I've invited him to see the evidence with his own eyes on Saturday night.'

My brain was slowly catching up with what was happening here. The personal appeal of so celebrated a man had secured my freedom—but the price was a performance at the Opera.

Ibrahim seized my hand and raised it to his lips. 'Forgive me if I have mistaken you, mademoiselle.' His lips brushed my fingers. 'I've agreed to sacrifice the pleasure of your company temporarily to allow you a chance to prove your innocence. I have promised Le Vestris to drop all claim to you if you impress me on Saturday.'

'And if I fail?'

'You will not fail, mademoiselle,' said Le Vestris, taking me by the elbow and shepherding me away from the bishop. 'No one taught by Le Vestris ever

215

fails.'

But Ibrahim's sardonic smile told another story. He clearly suspected some trick of J-F's lay behind this rescue. If I failed, he would have further evidence to denounce me to the authorities as a play-acting spy—which was exactly what I was, of course.

'Until Saturday, Mademoiselle Cat!' called the bishop, signing a blessing in the air as I left.

Le Vestris showed me into his carriage and within seconds we were rattling out of the bishop's diocese. I sank back against the cushions, still reeling from the abrupt changes in my fortune. It was as if I was on a merry-go-round, faces spinning before me as my dizziness increased with every turn of fate. Feeling giddy, I closed my eyes for a moment. When I opened them again, I saw my rescuer watching me with fatherly concern from the seat opposite.

'Did they mistreat you, mademoiselle?'

I shrugged. 'No more than I'm used to.'

'So I remember—you were never a cosseted child.'

'Pardon, monsieur? I don't understand . . .'

'Little J-F reminded me today of my time at Drury Lane. I think we have met before, Mademoiselle Cat.'

I felt an ache for my home as he spoke—a glimpse of a paradise from which I was now shut out. 'We did?'

'Perhaps you do not recall my season in London? I was guest dancer at the ballet in your Theatre Royal; I believe I met with some acclaim,' he added modestly. 'But you were an infant then—how could you remember? Still, I recollect you very well: Sheridan's little ginger stray, they called you. You

216

were always in sight, either curled up at his feet or tucked away somewhere backstage—three or four years old, I guess. You were not a favourite with everyone though—I seem to remember seeing you chased off from time to time, scurrying up the ladders out of reach of a sharp tongue or the back of someone's hand.'

I grimaced. 'That's true enough.' I had to admit it was by no means always a paradise for me.

'And perhaps that little girl would not have stuck in my memory if it hadn't been for your remarkable curls: they were what bobbed to the surface when J-F told me all about you. Now, it seems our future lies together for a short while and if so, then we will have to hide those for the performance.' Le Vestris pointed to the bruises blooming on my arms from where Scarface had squashed me against the door. 'Fortunately I have prepared a character costume for you.'

I could hardly believe what I was hearing. The principal dancer of the Opera de Paris was serious! This wasn't a ruse dreamt up by J-F. I knew from my time among the ballerinas at Drury Lane that a character costume was an adaptation of a peasant dress—bodice with mid-calf full skirt. At least it was a relief not to be making a fool of myself in the filmy robe of the danseuse or sheath-like dress of the demi-caractère. There were strict rules of dress for ballerinas reflecting their role in the production—presumably my role was to expose how accomplished everyone else was.

'Are you sure this is a good idea, monsieur?' I asked.

Le Vestris smiled. He had an expressive face, well used to projecting emotion to the back rows of the

Opera. Even off-stage every gesture he made was exaggerated and graceful. 'You have done me a favour, mademoiselle. I have had my eye on that little rogue J-F for months—he's a natural dancer, as you saw the other evening. Before he rose to his current eminence, he used to dance at the Palais Royal theatre. So, when he asked me to act as go-between, I knew at once what my price would be.'

'J-F sent you?' That was unexpected. My faith in humanity was partially restored after the serious battering of the last few weeks.

'Of course. He believed I was the only one who could persuade that young Arab to surrender you in one piece. It seems he was right. It is rather flattering, I must admit, to find my reputation has earned me so much respect in the more . . . er . . . interesting classes in our city.'

I looked out of the carriage window. It was true. Those that recognized the dancer's carriage stood to attention and removed their caps as he passed. They were in awe of their favourite celebrity. Le Vestris waved a cheerful acknowledgement.

'If you do not mind, mademoiselle, we will proceed directly to the Opera. You have much to learn if you are to make a creditable debut on Saturday.'

He could say that again.

SCENE 2—CONCIERGERIE PRISON

Fortunately, all I was expected to do that night was watch the show. Le Vestris led the way backstage and sat me in the wings next to the man in charge of the curtains. From this side view of the stage, I could see a segment of the boxes filled with chattering Parisians, the cello players tuning their instruments, a piper warming his fingers by playing flourishes like outbursts of bird-song. A large chandelier lit the stage, light spilling out into the auditorium, picking out the gilt and glitter of the decorations edging the boxes, flashing off jewels and opera glasses. Swags of red, white and blue looped the walls, declaring the Opera's allegiance to the revolution. Behind me, the ballerinas were limbering up, touching their toes and stretching their arms above their heads. I felt at home: the stage was on a larger scale than Drury Lane, but the smells and the sounds—all these were essentially the same. My heart beat with sympathetic excitement as the moment of performance approached.

'So, the little stray has returned.' Mimi was at my back, looking none too pleased to see me, behind her Colette and Belle. They were dressed in peasant costume with their long hair wound into plaits over their ears like badly made croissants.

'Why, were you missing me?' I asked, tired of their banter.

'How they let you get away with it is beyond me,' tutted Colette. 'Marched off to the city hall, out all night with a band of vagabonds—I can't imagine Madame Beaufort allowing us to do that.'

'Mesdemoiselles, positions please!' Mimi's words were cut short by the stage manager. The ballerinas scurried off in a patter of cork-soled shoes. I was pleased to see the back of them: their constant sniping at me was beginning to depress my spirits. It seemed they were never going to accept me.

The conductor entered to the applause of the house. As he took his place, I noticed a small black violinist sitting near the podium. So Pedro had landed himself a new job.

A hand landed on my shoulder as I craned forward to catch a better view of my friend. I jumped.

'Careful, Catkin: the stage manager won't be pleased if your head is spotted by the audience.'

'Johnny!'

He pulled me back with him into the shadows of the wings as the strains of the overture began. Taking my shoulders, he turned me round and inspected me.

'Those thieves didn't hurt you?'

'Not much. But I've got so much to tell you.' I quickly informed him of the suspicions running rife that there was an English spy in the Avon circle. 'It seems I only made it worse writing that letter to Sheridan to ask for his help. The bishop suspects me—but I think Mayor Bailly has his eye on Frank or Joseph. The mayor seemed to think I was too empty-headed to be a threat—he let me go with nothing more than a telling-off.'

Johnny frowned. 'And this bishop: what is he like?'

'He's a street Arab—as sharp as they come. Ruthless and charming.'

'Well, at least we know where we stand with him.

We know we can't trust him, whereas I must say your little friend J-F has kept me guessing all day. I wasn't sure I could believe him when he said he knew how to rescue you. You've given us a terrible time since last night—we've all been worried.' Johnny bit his lip. He looked tired out with fretting about me and Lizzie.

'You weren't the only one, Johnny. I wasn't sure my luck was going to hold. But how's Lizzie? Did Pedro get in to see the Avons with a bribe of a free concert?'

Johnny nodded. 'Though I doubt he should go again—we don't want them suspecting him of spying after what you've told me. He didn't mention your predicament to the Avons—we didn't want to alarm them, thinking they had enough to worry about.'

'And how are they?'

'In some ways, much better. The duchess has charmed the governor with the recital she and Pedro gave him and his lady wife, and as a result their conditions have improved. They now have access to a courtyard; the food's edible and they've been given candles. The English representative visited today and is pounding his fist on the desks of the bureaucrats to get the Avons released. Things might also move faster when we get this printed.' He pulled out a scroll of paper from his jacket pocket: it was a rough of his cartoon of the Avons, the duke portrayed as a loyal friend of the revolution trapped with his songbird (the duchess) in a cage. 'Marie is seeing it through the press for me.'

'Excellent! I can't wait to see it in print. And Lizzie?'

He frowned. 'As well as can be expected. A little pale, according to Pedro, and she has a bad cough, but she's not complaining.'

'Oh, Johnny.' I squeezed his hand. Lizzie was the last person who should be locked up in a pestilential prison.

'So we'd better hurry up and get them out, Catkin,' he said with a brave smile, returning the pressure on my fingers. 'I'll see you at the end of the performance and walk you home.'

I watched the ballet from the wings with growing despair. Not only did the prospect of participating in it in a few days fill me with dread, but I couldn't stop thinking about Lizzie. Sitting so close, I could hear every thump and squeak of the boards as the dancers leapt and twirled. They flitted by, masking the effort they were making with bland smiles; they were like my friend—putting on a false air to deceive the onlooker as to their true feelings. Lizzie was doubtless trying to hide her illness in order not to alarm her parents. What if she became dangerously sick? I couldn't bear it if we lost her, especially when she was so close to realizing her hopes of happiness with Johnny.

A light touch like a spider tickled my neck. I shivered.

'Mademoiselle Cat.' J-F bowed and grinned at me. 'I freed you from the clutches of the church, no?'

I curtseyed, returning his smile. 'Indeed, monsieur, I am in your debt.'

He linked arms with mine, bobbing on the balls of his feet in time to the music. 'Unfortunately, the bishop still claims you as his parishioner. Why would that be, do you think? He knows I'll never

222

give up milord for so little profit to myself.'

The unspoken confession that J-F would betray Frank if enough were offered gave me a sudden alarm.

'J-F, what have you done with Frank?'

'Don't worry,' he patted my arm. 'He's safe. But you haven't answered my question.'

'Which one?' I knew full well what he meant but I did not want to mention the bishop's suspicions about me. Who knew what opportunities for himself J-F would see in this little bit of information?

'About the bishop.' J-F was looking shrewdly at me but I kept my eyes on the dusty toes of my shoes.

'Perhaps he just wants to see what a terrible dancer I am.'

'But you won't be terrible!' J-F put his hand around my waist and began to dance me around the wings in time to the music. 'We are both born to do this. Your mother must have been a dancer like mine—or your father perhaps?' He wove around Mimi and Belle, giving them a wink as they made an elaborate fuss about him brushing against their skirts. 'Maybe Terpsichore herself gave birth to you.'

I had to smile. 'I doubt it—most people think my mother was a beggar or worse.' We spun into the corridor leading to the stage door.

'Down with most people, Cat!' J-F stopped dancing and gave me a stern look. 'If you have no origins, you are free to invent something that has poetry—indeed, it is your duty. I, King of the Thieves, command it!'

I then realized that, for all the dancing around each other the last few days in our strange game of trust and mistrust, I was looking into the face of a kindred spirit. How often had I made up parents for myself, believing that such dreams did no harm and much good, a defence against the unpleasant truth that I had been abandoned? J-F was the first to have ever encouraged me to do this. He understood.

'I will, your majesty.'

He took my hand. 'You might not know it, Cat, but you are luckier than some. I have to invent my stories to do away with a parent I wish I didn't know. At least you have a blank canvas to work on.'

I shook my head, puzzled. 'I don't understand.'

He mimicked ducking a blow. 'My father used to beat my mother and me—how else do you think I learnt to dance out of the way so quickly? It was a relief when he left and Grandfather took us in. Now, if he came back, I'd be ready for him.' He gave me a confident smile. 'But he won't come calling, not now I'm the king. He knows what that means for him.'

'And your mother?'

'Oh, I've made sure she's free of him too. Earns her keep as a mermaid at the Palais Royal. See, peddling dreams is in the family.' And with that, he winked and disappeared into the shadows outside.

*   *   *

I spent most of the next few days in the practice rooms at the Opera. Le Vestris's idea was that J-F and I should lead the dancing in the village festival scene. Our dance was to be copied by the lovers, played by Le Vestris and the prima ballerina, concluding in a high spirited competition of agility

224

between the two pairs.

'You see, mademoiselle,' Le Vestris declared, waving his silver-topped cane in the air, 'this ballet is about us—the common people. I want to show the audience that, from our cradle, we can all belong to the aristocracy of talent. Even our children can dance like the greatest among us.' He gave a modest bow, hand to his chest.

'He thinks you and I can rival him and Mademoiselle Angeline?' I muttered to J-F. 'Is everyone mad in Paris?'

'At the moment,' said J-F sagely, 'I'd say we're all a little out of our minds: daring to think the unthinkable, to do the impossible.'

'Well, this certainly counts as impossible.' I lost my concentration and stepped on J-F's toes. 'Sorry.'

'Mademoiselle Cat, what was that supposed to be?' Le Vestris descended on me and prodded my errant leg with the cane. 'You have ability, but you lack discipline. If you believe you will fail, you will fail. I cannot allow that. You must believe that you will succeed.'

'Fat chance,' I said under my breath. It was hard to concentrate on thoughts of success when my mind was so full of anxiety. News from the prison was worse: Lizzie was now ill enough for her gaolers to agree that she required the attendance of a doctor. Johnny's pleas for her to be released had fallen on deaf ears. The mayor's men were still searching for Frank and I had a bishop to please to avoid denunciation as a spy.

I stumbled again.

J-F gripped my hand. His expression was almost tender. 'What would it take, Cat, to clear your mind for the dance?'

225

I gave him a rueful smile. 'I suppose I'd be a lot happier if only I knew my friends were out of danger.'

'If I promise to have them released by Saturday, will you promise to concentrate for the rest of the practice?' He stroked my cheek, seeming quite confident he could keep his word. It was strange being so close to a boy in the sanctioned intimacy of a dance—I wasn't sure how to behave.

'You can do that?'

He nodded. 'Being the king of thieves does have some advantages. You must put your trust in my influence.'

'But if you can do this, why haven't you done it before now?'

'You didn't ask—and besides, your Monsieur Johnny had to prepare the ground for me.'

'So how are you going to do it? The officials aren't listening to the British representative or anyone else. What hope do you have?'

'Ah,' J-F gave me a mysterious smile, 'they will listen to me. Paris is now governed by its people— not by official representatives.'

'Cat, Jean-François, pay attention!' Le Vestris clapped his hands together. The pianist had been tinkling away on the practice pianoforte for some time now while we'd been conducting our negotiation.

'I am sorry, monsieur.' J-F bowed to the master. 'But I feel sure that now I've put her mind at rest, Cat will dance flawlessly for us.'

'Indeed, monsieur, I promise to try my best,' adding under my breath to J-F, 'though I'm not sure about the flawless bit.'

And we swept off into the dance one more time.

226

At breakfast on Saturday, Renard sidled up to me on the pretext of filling my cup.

'Mademoiselle, I think you should ask to be excused from practice this morning. Tell Madame Beaufort you are resting before the dress rehearsal this afternoon.'

I swallowed my mouthful of milk too quickly. 'Why? What's going on?'

'Just let us say that my grandson keeps his promises. You will be going on a little walk with us, that's all.'

I wanted to ask how a stroll with the two thieves would secure the release of the Avons, but the ballerinas were watching me. They had stopped mocking me since Le Vestris had taken an interest in my dancing and they now regarded me warily. I think they were worried I was overtaking them, being exalted into the realms of the stars while they still plodded away in the chorus line. If only they knew how limited my abilities were, they wouldn't lose any sleep on that count.

Having secured Madame Beaufort's blessing for my excursion, I accompanied Renard to the local market.

'Why are we here?' I asked as Renard sniffed a melon with professional interest.

'Well, little one, there's still the matter of your tail. As you are not a real cat, you do not need the mayor's men dangling behind you.'

'They're still following me? Why didn't you say?' I glanced over my shoulder and caught sight of a dark-jacketed man pretending to read a playbill.

227

'Yes, that's one of them,' Renard said with a chuckle. 'We didn't feel we needed to mention it, believing it was better they were waiting around the Opera than causing problems for milord searching for him near the Palais Royal.'

I grinned. 'True.'

'But now it would be better if they lost sight of you for a few hours, and the market is the best place to do this.'

With that, he ducked between two vegetable stalls as a flock of housewives passed, baskets in hand. I followed and found that he had led me into a narrow alley. At a smart pace, we made our way out the other end, leaving the noise of the market behind us. Renard handed me into a doorway and stood watching the alley for a moment. No one appeared at the far end.

'Good, they are still scratching their heads then, wondering if you've been turned into a pumpkin. Let us hurry.'

We proceeded at a trot towards the Palais Royal.

'Will you tell me what's going on now?' I panted beside him.

Renard patted my arm which was linked through his. 'Nothing for you to worry about, mademoiselle. My grandson is rabble-rousing.'

'He's what?' I'd experienced the French mob once already; I wasn't certain I wanted a repeat performance.

'He's calling the people of Paris to demand justice.'

'How's that going to help?'

'It's the people who rule now, mademoiselle. We ruled when we knocked down the Bastille; we did it again when we dragged the king from his hiding

228

place in Versailles. It'll surely be but the work of a morning to raise enough people to free a few foreigners, particularly with the promise of a free show.'

As we turned into the courtyard of the Palais Royal, we were greeted by the sight of J-F standing on a barrel outside a café, addressing a crowd of onlookers. Annette and Marie were passing through the people handing out copies of Captain Sparkler's latest cartoon.

'Citizens,' cried J-F, 'we must not let this happen. One of us—a woman of the people—has been locked up with her husband and daughter at the whim of the bureaucrats. These English visitors came to pay their respects to our revolution and have been thanked with a prison cell. I thought we had kissed goodbye to such abuses when we broke down the walls of the Bastille, but already our new rulers resort to the same methods.'

The crowd shouted their encouragement to the little orator. There was a holiday mood in the air.

'What's J-F up to?' I heard a woman ask her neighbour.

'I don't know. Something about an opera singer. He's said she'll sing for us if we get her out.'

I could tell that few cared about the cause, or really understood it; they were just enthusiastic to exercise their political muscle again, to prove they were still a force to be reckoned with.

'Will you come with me,' J-F called, 'come with me to demand the release of the songbird? Such talents should not be caged but let loose for all of us to hear.' He jumped down from his barrel, holding aloft a stick with a familiar pink ribbon on one end. The crowd gave a huzzah and turned to follow him.

For the second time since coming to Paris, I found myself swept along with a mob, this time bound for the Conciergerie.

'What if the national guard take it into their heads to send us packing?' I asked Renard nervously.

'Don't worry, mademoiselle. That's why I'm here.'

'Oh?'

'Yes, J-F said to keep you safe.'

'That's kind of him.'

'He doesn't want to lose his dancing partner, does he, so close to the big night?'

'Oh.'

As we crossed the Seine, my arm was seized on the other side.

'Frank!'

'How are you, Cat? I hear you're to dance for us tonight. See, I told you you could do it.'

'You haven't seen me dance yet. But should you be here? Isn't it dangerous for you?'

'You think they'll spot me as an English lord in this crowd? If they do, they deserve to catch me.'

It was true. Almost a week of living with the thieves had roughened Frank's polished edges. He looked dirty, a little hungry, he even walked with a slouch—in fact, he now resembled the rest of us.

'I suppose not. Do you think this'll work?'

'It's got to.' His expression was grim. I had the impression that Frank had grown up a lot over the past few days.

We arrived outside the gates of the Conciergerie. Our number had swelled in our passage through town as people flocked to find out what the fuss was all about. J-F hoisted himself on to the shoulders of an all too recognizable footman and shouted to the guard inside, 'Release the English woman and her family! You've got the king back—let these people go!'

The guard tried to ignore him.

'Listen to your brothers and sisters, citizen!' cried J-F. 'The people want no friends of the revolution behind bars!'

No one replied; a guard even turned his back—a very bad move for it was this contempt for the people that infuriated the crowd. The masses started to beat on the gates, whistling and booing.

'We'll make them listen,' shouted a black-bearded man. 'Oi, citizen, if you don't bring them out here now, we're coming in to get them.'

'Remember what happened to the gaoler in the Bastille!' shrieked a woman.

'Bastille! Bastille! Bastille!' chanted the crowd.

This had the desired effect: the guardsman darted inside to fetch the governor. The concierge himself appeared on the steps and held up his hands, appealing for calm.

'Citizens, what can I do for you?' he said with an entirely false smile. He was shaking with nerves—as well he might as his predecessor at the Bastille had ended up with his head on a pike.

'Let the innocent go!' called J-F.

'Innocent? That is not yet decided.'

'Where's your proof they were involved? You have none. But we have proof that they are friends to our cause. Bring them out—let them pledge their support before us, the people, and let them go.'

At this point, the crowd helpfully surged against the gates, which groaned on their hinges.

The concierge wiped his brow. 'I want no trouble

today, my friends. The king is returning—the streets must be quiet to show him that we can govern ourselves in his absence.'

'Then do as we say and we'll return peacefully to our homes, and this will be remembered as a mere discussion between friends,' J-F replied shrewdly. 'You can take the credit for righting an injustice.'

The concierge was clearly weighing up the options: risk a battle on his patch or release a few prisoners who were at the most only marginally involved in the king's flight.

'All right, my friends, I will bring them to you. But how shall they make their pledge?'

J-F was ready with his answer. 'Let the British songbird sing the *Ça ira*, the people's anthem. That will be proof enough.'

The crowd cheered this suggestion. The concierge nodded to his guard who disappeared inside.

Frank squeezed my hand. 'I can't believe it. It's working.'

'It's not over yet,' I warned. 'Do you think she'll do it—sing the song, I mean?'

'She must, or she'll be lynched,' said Renard cheerfully, chewing on a handful of sunflower seeds an enterprising salesman had just sold him.

A few minutes later, the Duke of Avon appeared, supporting Lizzie on his arm. His wife followed, listening to the explanations of the guard. She was frowning and shaking her head.

'I'm not sure she knows it,' said Frank.

'Quick, Renard, tell me how it goes,' I begged. 'Whistle the tune.'

'Oh, it is easy to learn.' The Frenchman began to trill the notes. The melody bounced along,

232

proclaiming that the people would come out on top of aristocrats, priests, and all who stood in their way. I only hoped that would prove the case today.

'Get everyone to sing it,' I urged.

'What?'

'She's not heard it before. Sing it—please! The duchess is trained for the opera: she'll pick it up if she hears it even once.'

Catching on, Renard took a deep breath and began to boom out the words. His neighbours joined in with gusto, rollicking through the tune like a victorious army returning home. The song echoed off the walls of the prison—a magnificent, impromptu concert hall. Up on the steps, the duchess was concentrating hard, her hand pressed to her brow. Then, as we returned to the chorus again, she dropped her arm and clasped her hands loosely before her. A sublime voice joined us, rising over the song of the crowd like a seabird gliding over a rough sea. Our voices fell away to listen.

'Ah, ça ira, ça ira, ça ira!'

When the duchess finished, the crowd cheered and stamped. Even the concierge applauded. The duke and Lizzie were both smiling.

'Encore! Another!' chanted the crowd.

The duchess bowed and, moving to safer ground from a song about hanging aristocrats from lamp posts, sang an aria from Handel's *Messiah*. Chairs were produced for Lizzie and the duke. A tumbler of water was handed to the duchess. It seemed that the Conciergerie guard had as much appetite for a free concert as the crowd. The duchess sang to us for a full half hour, before finally bowing a last time and looking across at the concierge. He leapt up, took her hand and kissed it.

233

'You are free to go, madame. All doors will spring open before such a voice.'

'God bless you, monsieur,' she said.

The duke offered her his arm, and the Avons walked out of the Conciergerie, freed by the power of song.

SCENE 3—LA FILLE MAL GARDÉE

By popular demand, the Avons were to be given a box on the side of the stage at the Opera that night. I was the only person in Paris not to be cheered by this prospect: if I was going to make a fool of myself, I'd prefer to do it in front of strangers.

'I'm sorry not to see you dance,' said Lizzie, wrapped up in shawls as she sat up in her bed in the rue de Clichy, 'but Dr Montard thinks I should rest until I'm fit to travel.' She succumbed to a fit of coughing which she covered with a lace-edged handkerchief. She looked so fragile sitting there, her pale skin almost translucent. I was seized with the fear that my friend might fall into a consumption and never live to see happiness with Johnny. It looked as if the merest puff of wind would blow her away.

'Dr Montard is a clever fellow then,' I said brightly, hiding my thoughts. 'Don't worry—you won't be missing much, except perhaps my utter humiliation. But when will you be fit, did he say?'

Lizzie shook her head and lay back on the pillows. 'Mama and Papa think we should leave Paris as soon as possible. With Mayor Bailly returning to town with the king's family this

234

afternoon, they are worried that he might reverse the will of the people and lock us up again. Your little friend doesn't think that likely, but I don't know—things seem to change on a whim here. After all, our cousin is still in detention. Her fate rests on that of her husband, which in turn depends on what the king has to say for himself on his return.'

I nodded. 'I think we could all do with putting some miles between us and Paris, if the truth be known. You've heard about the spy, of course?'

She smiled. 'Of course. How absurd to suspect Joseph and you!'

I fiddled with her silver-backed hairbrush. 'Not so silly as you might think,' I mumbled.

'Oh, Cat . . .'

'Why else do you think Mr Sheridan paid for me to come here? It was just supposed to be a little bit of discreet sniffing around for him, but I turned up in the middle of a political crisis and stupidly added more fuel to the flames with my letter.'

'You weren't to know . . .'

'Oh yes, I was. I should've at least sent it under a cover to Mr Kemble or Syd's parents. I deserve everything I get for scrawling "Sheridan" on the envelope. I can't seem to get anything right at the moment.'

Lizzie reached out and took my hand. 'What will you do when you return to London?'

I shrugged. It was too difficult a question to answer.

'There'll be a spare bedroom—that is, one more than normal—in our house. I'm sure Mama and Papa would like you to stay. It'll help them get used to it.'

'You don't mean . . . ?'

'Yes, I do. I'm not coming back to England. Johnny and I are to marry as soon as I'm well enough, then we'll take a ship to America. We'd like you to be there at the ceremony too, if you can. I'd like you as my bridesmaid.'

'Thank you, Lizzie, I'd be honoured—if I can be there, that is.' My voice was strangely hoarse. 'I always thought that a duke's daughter should have peeresses falling over themselves to hold her posy.'

'Who wants peeresses when they can have you, Cat?'

There was a soft tap on the door and Frank put his head round. He had bathed and was now dressed in neat but unremarkable civilian clothes, perfect for blending in on the Parisian streets. We didn't know if anyone would try and execute the warrant on him now the Avons were free, but it was clearly sensible to assume that they might so we were keeping his presence in the house a secret.

'Are you coming, Cat? There's just time to see the procession pass before we head for the Opera.'

'But we've got to hurry!' called Pedro from the corridor.

'Off you go, Cat,' said Lizzie, releasing my hand. 'Good luck for tonight.'

*　　*　　*

Pedro, Frank and I emerged on to the rue de Clichy by the back door and headed towards the Tuileries Palace once again.

'Like old times, hey?' said Pedro cheerfully, linking arms with me. 'Remember when we went to the boxing that first time?'

236

'How could I forget?' I asked, tweaking my cockade displayed for all to see on my bodice. I was taking no chances this time.

Frank took my arm on the other side. 'Did Lizzie ask you then?'

'About being her bridesmaid? Yes, I'm really touched to have been chosen.'

'It's no more than you deserve.'

'Thanks, Frank, but unfortunately, I have my doubts I'll be able to be there. I haven't told you yet, but the bishop suspects me of being the spy—not a bad guess on his part—and he's itching to denounce me to the mayor. It looks as though I should leave Paris as soon as possible.'

Frank frowned and glanced over his shoulder. 'What's stopping him then?'

'Le Vestris stepped in and half-convinced him I really was a dancer. I have to prove it to him tonight.'

Pedro whistled. 'We'd better organize an escape for you then.'

'Nice to see you're so confident I'll succeed, Pedro.'

'Well, Cat, I've been at the rehearsals.'

We arrived at the main road. The crowd lined the pavements, chatting in subdued voices. This was no celebration—it was more like an audience in a courtroom: we all wanted to see for ourselves that the king was well and truly back.

Frank patted me on the shoulder. 'I think Pedro's right. We need to prepare ourselves for the worst. Even if—I mean, when—you triumph tonight, it doesn't mean that Bailly might not be persuaded that you are as talented a spy as you are a dancer. I can imagine that the concierge's decision to let my parents go will not have pleased the mayor: he'll still be looking for someone to prosecute.'

I groaned. 'I wish I'd never come to Paris.'

'No you don't,' said Frank firmly. 'You wouldn't've had half so much fun staying behind in London. And, besides, who would've got my parents out of gaol? If it hadn't been for your quick thinking today, it all could've ended very differently.'

The jingling of harness and clip-clopping of hooves could now be heard approaching. The buzz of talk died away. A large coach, much stained by travel, appeared at the end of the street, surrounded by national guardsmen. Frank reached up to remove his hat, but I nudged him in time. Not a single man in that crowd showed the respect due to a monarch by doffing his cap. Standing sullen with their heads stubbornly covered, the people of Paris demonstrated to the king exactly what they thought of his treachery. As the coach passed, I caught a glimpse of Mayor Bailly, sitting with his knees almost touching the monarch's. The woman I had talked to briefly in that dark alley on Monday night sat beside King Louis, her face stern but resigned. The king himself looked confused. He glanced out of the window, seemingly unable to understand why no one was cheering him.

'I suppose,' I said as the procession clattered out of sight, 'it was better than rioting and insults.'

'Do you think?' remarked Frank. 'If I was him, I'd want at least some sign from my loyal subjects that I was welcome back.'

'But they're no longer subjects,' said Pedro as the crowd filed away. 'They're citizens.'

'And they won't be loyal to him if he's proved to

have betrayed them,' I added.

'But that's terrible!' Frank, heir to a dukedom, shook his head.

Pedro and I exchanged glances. 'Perhaps. I think it's just very sad,' I said. 'If they treat him like that then France no longer has a king. Come on, let's go.'

*   *   *

The curtain was due to rise in fifteen minutes and I was busy feeling sick in the dressing room. When I raised my eyes to the mirror, my face was horribly blotched. I caught sight of Mimi watching me from the other side of the room. I couldn't bear it if she had a go at me now so I closed my eyes and sat with my head in my hands.

Who did I think I was fooling? No way should I be allowed out there tonight. I'd be a laughing stock.

'Here!' It was Mimi's voice. I felt something drop on the table beside me. I looked up: it was a bunch of mint. 'Chew some. It helps.'

'Thank you.' I was so amazed I didn't move.

'Go on. I'm not trying to trick you.'

'I didn't think you were.' I took a leaf and crushed it so that the sweet smell of mint wafted in the air. She was right: it did quell the nausea. 'But why are you helping me?'

Mimi shrugged and rejoined Colette and Belle tying on their ballet shoes. 'I've been talking to Marie, J-F's girl. She told me what's been going on.'

'We all know why you've got to dance tonight, Cat,' said Belle, stretching her arms above her head. 'She said it was J-F's fault for getting you tangled up

239

with his rival.'

'So we thought you needed all the help you could get,' added Colette, bending to touch her toes.

I smiled weakly. 'I'm afraid that's all too true.'

'And, besides, you're part of the company now, aren't you? If you mess up, we all mess up,' concluded Mimi.

On that thought, the threesome looked at each other. 'Come on, we'd better get her ready,' said Colette.

Before I knew it, they had swooped upon me and taken charge of my appearance. Face powder hid my reddened face. Competent hands fastened my hair back. My slippers were expertly tied.

'There, now warm up. You can't go on stage cold—you'll never get past the first few steps,' ordered Belle.

Obediently, I followed their routine. The worst of the nerves had passed. I no longer had a choice. It was too late to run for it as I had contemplated doing that afternoon. Only my promise to J-F to try my hardest had stopped me fleeing.

'Why be nice to me now?' I asked as we bent to loosen our calf muscles.

'We thought you were here because Madame Beaufort had taken pity on you,' explained Colette. 'Thought you'd jumped the queue to join the troupe just because you're Mr Sheridan's favourite. You must admit you showed no promise as a dancer in London.'

'But seeing you dance with J-F made us realize you're not too bad after all. She was right to give you a trial,' continued Belle.

They talked almost as if they were one person. Clearly the trio had discussed my case and decided on a joint approach.

'Thank you.' My insides as well as my muscles now felt a flush of warmth. Their praise had never been more welcome.

'So you go out there and try to enjoy yourself. What have you to lose?' said Mimi.

What indeed?

Standing in the wings with J-F, I watched the scene before ours unfold. Everyone danced so beautifully. They could do things with their arms and legs that I'd never even dreamt of. It was hard to believe that they were plain old Mimi, Belle and Colette in the dressing room: on stage, they seemed like goddesses.

'Ready, Cat?' grinned J-F.

Too anxious to speak, I just nodded. The strains of our entry tune were beginning. I could see Pedro bowing away next to the first violin, eyes fixed on the conductor. At least, thanks to the demands of the music, there was one friend who wouldn't see the hash I was about to make of my debut. Frank, I knew, was somewhere in the galleries with Marie and Annette, keeping his distance from his parents who were sitting in ducal splendour in the box right opposite me.

'I kept my promise, now you keep yours,' whispered J-F.

'I'll try.'

'Remember,' he muttered as he seized my hand for us to run on, 'for all you know, your mother was Terpsichore, your father principal dancer in the English ballet. This is our moment.'

With that, we were on. Hand in hand, we ran through the crowd of peasant dancers gathered for the festival scene and leapt centre stage.

241

Immediately, the orchestra struck up the popular tune Renard had taught us. It was clearly a favourite with the audience for I heard a mutter of approval from all sides and a smattering of applause. On that signal—and I'm still not sure how it happened, Reader—something lit up inside me. I felt as if I had come home. Drury Lane might have been reduced to rubble, but its spirit lived on wherever there was an audience and performers. I realized that I loved this tune too. I wanted this dance because to me it meant friends in unexpected places, mops twirling in kitchens, freedom, the rush of the crowd through the streets demanding that justice be done. It meant *Ça Ira*—we, the people, will win. It meant Revolution. Le Vestris must have known this too and that was why he had chosen this ballet of the common people to play tonight of all nights: the night when the king returned to Paris with his tail between his legs. I didn't care if I made a fool of myself, I just wanted to dance because I, Cat Royal, was one of the people too. I was going to prove that Drury Lane lived on in me.

J-F must have sensed a change in me for his face blazed with joy. For the first time, I was truly his match in the dance.

'Terpsichore indeed!' he breathed in my ear as I pirouetted into his arms.

'No, just a daughter of the people,' I grinned, catching my breath as Le Vestris moved forward with his partner.

Now we repeated the dance in unison. I didn't even need to watch Mademoiselle Angeline: I just knew I was in step with her. The music was running through us like an electric current through a chain, binding all together. There was something special in the air tonight. I could feel it surrounding me: it was coming from the audience, from Mimi, Belle, Colette, from Madame Beaufort and Le Vestris, even from the Duke and Duchess of Avon as they urged me on to success from their box. But most of all it came from the touch of J-F's hand on mine. Looking back now, I can tell you what it was, Reader: it was liberty, equality and fraternity—the essential ingredients of the spell cast by the stage in all ages. The only difference here was that in Paris this heady potion had spilled over on to the streets and people were trying to rule their lives by it.

The dance ended and the crowd erupted. Cries of 'Encore!' rang out. We had to obey our public. I looked across at Le Vestris and saw him smiling at me. To my astonishment, he handed his partner to J-F and took my fingers.

'Again?' he asked.

I nodded. What else could I do? I was now dancing with the master. When he spun me round, I flew; when he lifted me, I soared. The feeling was so exquisite, it was almost painful. I couldn't bear it when the dance finished. If I could have lived forever in that moment, I would've done. My one perfect moment.

But such stage magic cannot last. J-F and I took our bow and exited with the applause ringing in our ears. Once in the wings, I found I was trembling again—no longer from nerves but from a quiver of excitement.

'Wasn't that fun?' said J-F, rubbing his hands together.

'It was more than fun. It was a revelation. I now understand why they do it.'

'Do what?' He pulled me with him past the

243

scenery waiting for the next scene change.

'Dance. It's always escaped me. To be honest, I always thought the ballet a distraction from the real drama at Drury Lane. How wrong I was.'

'So you are converted?' He paused in front of a flat painted like a gloomy forest. 'Thinking of quitting the life of a spy and making your career as a ballerina?'

His comment was like a slap in the face, waking me from my dream.

'What did you say?'

J-F took my hand again—roughly this time—and led me to the dressing rooms. 'I think you heard well enough.'

My exhilaration was draining rapidly away, to be replaced by dread. My heart was pounding. 'You've known all along?'

'At least give me the credit for not being a complete fool. You, so inquisitive, involving yourself in everything you shouldn't—as soon as the mayor put out the call for a spy, I knew who they really wanted. In here!'

J-F pushed me into his dressing room. It was empty as the other performers were still on stage. I backed up warily against the mirror. J-F's tone was light but that only made me more worried. We both knew that this was no joke for either of us.

'What are you going to do with me?'

J-F began to wipe off his make-up. 'From our first meeting, I was watching you, trying to make you out—and at every turn you've surprised me. I was going to hand you over—that would've been the most sensible thing from a business point of view, naturally—but then . . . then something stopped me. And now? I still haven't decided. Tell me first who

244

you were spying for.'

'It wasn't so much spying. I was just supposed to let my old patron, Mr Sheridan, know how things stood in Paris.' He continued to remove his costume without looking at me. 'I wasn't trying to interfere with what's going on here. I meant no harm by it—neither did he.' His silence was worrying me. 'Please believe me, J-F.'

He opened his mouth to speak but we were interrupted by a knock on the door.

Enter the Bishop of the Notre Dame Thieves, splendid in a purple jacket and candy-striped breeches.

'Oh dear,' I groaned. My wonderful evening was fast turning into a nightmare.

Ibrahim bowed to me. 'Enchanting, mademoiselle, enchanting! You are truly a great dancer.'

'Thank you, your eminence.' I curtseyed. I looked from one thief lord to the other, wondering how this would unfold.

J-F threw his face cloth into the wash basket and perched on the edge of the dressing table, his mouth twisted into a mischievous smile. 'Well, Ibrahim, I do believe you are on my territory now.'

The bishop's eyes glinted. He straightened his cravat. 'By invitation.'

'Of course. But I prefer to negotiate with you here rather than at your palace over the water. We have one English spy to dispose of. I think it will be to our mutual advantage to do it together.'

Dispose of? This sounded grim.

'Please, J-F, I didn't mean any harm,' I pleaded. 'Far from it: coming here has made me realize what the common people can do—I've learnt so much.'

'So it *is* you, mademoiselle,' interrupted the

bishop with a satisfied smile. 'I had almost begun to think I had got it wrong and had cause to regret informing the mayor that you were the one he should be seeking. That's good, as I don't want his men to be disappointed when they arrest you. If I'd been wrong, I would not have received my reward.'

'They're waiting to arrest me?'

'Indeed.'

J-F frowned. 'I cannot allow that. You have no right to take her in my kingdom without my agreement—no right to keep the reward to yourself.'

'Then you hand over the English boy—he'll fetch something, I've no doubt.' The Bishop moved towards me.

J-F leapt from his seat and stood between us. 'He's worthless now his parents are free.'

'Shame, but you have only yourself to blame for dallying with the girl, missing your chance while you had it. It seems you will be the loser tonight.'

J-F looked from Ibrahim to me, his eyes calculating. 'There's another consideration,' he said, not giving way.

'Oh yes, and what's that?'

'That we might think that Mademoiselle Cat has earned her freedom. She proved herself a dancer as you asked, you said it yourself when you came in. I believe her when she says she was doing nothing to harm France. She deserves our trust.'

'Trust? Since when have we thieves done business on the basis of trust?' mocked Ibrahim.

'Since the people of Paris began to think the unthinkable, and do the impossible,' I said softly, remembering J-F's words to me a few days before.

'What?' snapped the bishop.

'That's what I've learnt: you people are rewriting

246

the rules here. Why not risk trusting me?'

'You ask why? Because there's no profit in trust!'

J-F shook his head. 'You're wrong. Her friends will match the reward you would've received for her—perhaps even double it if we're lucky, so we can both emerge richer men.'

'Yes, yes, I'm sure they will. Just ask Frank,' I said eagerly, clutching at this straw.

Ibrahim stroked his chin thoughtfully. 'You know, J-F, I was beginning to fear that you were losing your touch. That's not bad reasoning for a vagabond.'

J-F bowed, his old playfulness returning. He waved his hand as if embarrassed. 'Compliments, compliments, Ibrahim: you'll turn my pretty little head if you go on in this manner. Time is short. Cat must write a note to her friends, pledging their support on her behalf, and we must do our part and get her away. But how to do this? I suppose the mayor's men are waiting outside?'

The bishop nodded. 'I regret to say that they are.'

'Hmm, tricky, very tricky.'

Realizing that J-F was throwing me a lifeline with this deal, my thoughts were employed on thinking of a way out of this dressing room without being seen.

'Should I distract them perhaps?' suggested the bishop, approaching the door to listen to what was going on outside.

'The Merry Wives of Windsor,' I said.

They both looked at me. 'What?'

'Shakespeare, Falstaff—surely you know it?' J-F shrugged; the bishop looked blank. Clearly French education was deficient. 'Falstaff escapes from the house in a buck basket—a wash basket.' I opened

247

the lid and emptied out the contents. 'Put me in here—cover me with something. Ibrahim distracts the guard while J-F and Renard carry me out.'

'Excellent,' chuckled J-F. 'I'll fetch Grandfather.'

'And I'll make sure she writes that letter. She's not going without giving her word of honour that we'll see a reward for this,' said Ibrahim.

'We'd better hurry—the performance will be over soon. We want to get her clear of here before everyone comes backstage.' J-F thrust a bill for tonight's performance in my hand. 'Here—use this. I've no ink so use the charcoal in the make-up case. Washing basket, indeed!' he laughed. 'I could make her my queen for that.'

Ibrahim propelled me to a seat at the dressing table and put the eyebrow pencil into my hand.

'Mademoiselle, it looks as if you will be *la fille mal gardée**** tonight, if this works,' quipped the bishop.

Interlude – A Ballet Pastoral

L'Opéra de Paris
*Donnera aujourd'hui samedi
25 juin 1791
La première Représentation de
La Fille Mal Gardée
Avec un ballet-pastoral*

Dear Frank

Forgive my scrawl – I write this in haste. It appears I have to make a rapid exit from Paris thanks to a bishop and a king. I have promised them that you will advance the expenses incurred in my removal – a sum which I will repay as soon as I can. I hope your parents will pardon my presumption but I have little choice.

Tell Johnny and Lizzie that I regret missing their wedding. I send them both my love.

Your friend,
Cat.

P.S. Bid Pedro farewell for me and say that I'll see him back in London.

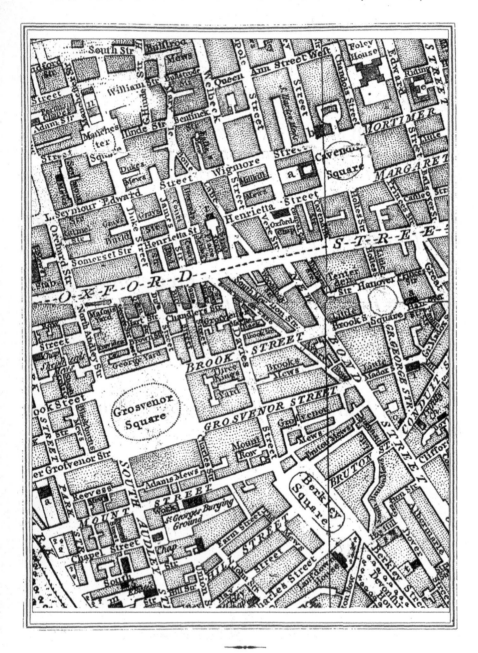

*Act V - In which an old debt is
settled . . .*

Act V

SCENE 1—SLOW BOAT

It was not perhaps the glorious departure from the Opera that I had imagined after my performance, but it was certainly better than the reception that otherwise would have greeted me outside. As I was carried aloft in my wash basket, I could hear the bishop chatting to the guardsmen, telling jokes as he bought them a round.

'To France!' The bishop gave the toast, which was followed by some satisfied glugging.

'Don't worry, monsieur, we'll soon have that little English spy where she can do no more sneaking,' chuckled one man. 'Mayor Bailly is determined to get a result.'

'Can't have any more foreigners sticking their noses into our business,' said the other. 'Here, citizen, where are you going with that?'

'To Le Vestris's personal washerwoman,' said Renard in a wheezing tone, completing his performance with a hacking cough.

'The master's things, eh? Better not get in the way then.' The guard waved us through and turned back to his companions. 'Clever, though, to use a girl. None of us suspected her until you alerted us to her double life.'

Thanks, Ibrahim, I thought sourly as I was jolted past.

'Yes, she certainly is full of surprises,' agreed the bishop.

Once out of sight, I was released from my wicker

prison.

'Where to now?' I asked J-F. It struck me that I hadn't given any thought past escaping the mayor's men, and now I was standing in Paris dressed in a ballerina's peasant costume with no money and no idea how to get home. 'Do we have time to fetch my things?'

J-F shook his head. 'Not unless you want them to catch you. Here!' He threw his cloak round my shoulders. 'Now let's get you your ride.'

'This is where I leave you, mademoiselle,' said Renard. 'I must return to check our friend from Notre Dame does not double-cross us.' He kissed me on the cheeks. 'Farewell, little dancer. I'm sure we'll meet again one day.' He walked swiftly towards the Opera, waving away my thanks.

J-F started off in the opposite direction. 'We'd better hurry. It won't take them long to work out they've missed you.'

We threaded our way through the quiet backstreets to the river.

'I think it best that we take passage on a barge,' J-F explained as he jumped down the steps to the riverside. 'It's slow but all roads are bound to be watched and it's far less likely we'll run into trouble this way.'

'We?' What did this mean?

J-F smiled at my surprise and linked my arm in his. 'I was thinking it was time I took my summer holiday. It's terribly unfashionable to stay in town out of season,' he said, aping the languid tones of the aristocracy. Then he added, in his usual practical manner: 'Besides, though I trust you, I don't trust you to be able to talk your way out of trouble. Your accent's pretty good, but no one

252

would mistake you for a native. No, from now on, you are my silent sister, travelling with her brother to see a sick grandmother in Rouen.'

'J-F, I don't know how to thank you . . .'

'Don't thank me. Milord told me that you have a rare talent for telling tales of your life in London. I'm expecting to be well entertained for my trouble.'

We arrived down on the quayside. I waited in the shadows while J-F ambled on to join some bargemen sitting on barrels, smoking long-stemmed pipes. He was soon chatting familiarly with them. I shivered, glancing nervously behind me: for all J-F's ease, I still feared to hear the sound of pursuit. The discussion ended with him shaking hands with one of the men and handing over some coins. He looked towards me and gave a whistle.

'Oi, sister! Hurry. We've got our ride!'

'A whistle?' I asked in a low voice as we followed the bargeman on to his vessel. 'Since when did you summon me with a whistle?'

'No need to explain to the bargeman who you are now, is there?' J-F was acting very pleased with himself, relishing the adventure and his own cleverness. This struck me as both infuriating and endearing at the same time.

'I suppose not,' I acknowledged. 'So am I allowed to whistle to get your attention?'

'You could try—but I won't answer.' The king of thieves of the Palais Royal had obviously not forgotten the respect due to him, even if we were about to leave his territory.

The bargeman led us to a long shallow-draughted boat moored opposite the Conciergerie prison. The roofs that had so recently housed the Avons were outlined against the dark sky like dunce's caps—a

253

fitting reminder if I needed it of the mess I had made of my errand for Mr Sheridan. It was I that should be wearing the fool's hat, not the building. If ever my patron took the risk of employing me again on a similar journey (which I very much doubted he would), I hoped to act with more discretion. But then, Reader, I know myself well enough to realize that I'll always be a jump-in-without-first-looking girl, so I expect I'll continue to blunder from mistake to mistake. Let us hope I continue to live to regret it afterwards. It had been rather too close for comfort this time and I was still not safe.

It seemed apt that my stay in Paris should have come full circle: I was close to the place where Frank and I had first spotted the towers of Notre Dame but this time I was fleeing the great city. I spared the cathedral a respectful nod as we climbed on board. Directed to a snug cabin in the stern, we prepared to settle down for what we hoped would be an uneventful night.

'I've persuaded our captain to set sail immediately. You sleep—I'll keep watch,' yawned J-F, ever the gallant gentleman.

I was too tired to argue the point. Not used to the frantic activity of the last few days, I felt I could sleep for a week. J-F had not failed me yet: I had learned the hard way that I could put my trust in him. He really was an extraordinary person. But I wasn't so sure that his motive for accompanying me was merely to have a holiday. Somehow, some-where along the journey we had travelled together the past few days, we had become part of each other's lives. Brother and sister, he had said. Perhaps. But why then did my eyes always turn to him when he was in a room, only to find he was

254

already watching me? There was something between us that we hadn't yet had a chance to put a name to; maybe the time on the barge would give me the answer.

'You've surprised me, J-F,' I admitted.

'How so?'

'You seem not to mind that you've spent the last few days getting me out of trouble.'

'But you forget that I'm being well paid by milord—and besides, who said a thief can't have a friend?'

'I won't forget it.'

The last thing I remember before I closed my eyes was J-F sitting by the stairs to the deck, softly humming the tune to which we had danced.

*   *   *

Life slowed to walking pace from the hectic career of that week in June. We saw out the month and the early days of the next making our way slowly downstream on the barge. J-F procured me some shoes and clothes at the first riverside market we came to and now we could stroll arm in arm along the bank among the meadows thigh-high in grass and summer flowers, keeping pace with the horses pulling our vessel along the sluggish waters of the Seine. Two town mice, we learned on that journey to take life more gently, to sit still and watch the water roll by, to cook over open fires under the stars. Every mile separating us from Paris made me feel safer. I was able to relax for the first time since coming to France and enjoy the companionship of my new friend. It was a magical interlude.

Our captain was a taciturn man but he evidently

liked having young people about. His own son had gone into the navy and he spent too many hours alone with no one but his dog for company. At first he divided tasks as he thought best, me to do the cooking and J-F to help about the boat, but when he found I was more skilled at managing the tow ropes than the kitchen, there was a rearrangement of roles to everyone's mutual benefit. J-F cooked some wonderful stews, rich with herbs and garlic, which with the accompaniment of some fresh bread made a feast truly fit for kings.

But as the days passed a question still hung unresolved between J-F and me: what exactly was going on between us? Was the pleasure we took in each other's company just the result of a holiday— a bubble of emotion that would burst at the first prick of reality? I was amazed at how fickle I was! First confused by Syd's kiss, then languishing hopelessly for Johnny, now wondering about the feelings of a funny-looking French boy with a personality so intriguing that it became harder and harder to think I'd have to leave him so soon.

It wasn't as if the prospect of returning to London was so very alluring: all my friends away and only my enemies waiting for me.

'How will I get back to England?' I asked J-F one evening as the bargeman snored gently in his hammock. We were nearing the Channel port of Le Havre and I needed to make plans for the next stage of my journey.

'Are you sure you want to go back, Cat?' he asked, blowing a plume of smoke into the air from his pipe. He swore the fumes kept the mosquitoes at bay but I suspected he was merely trying to impress me.

'Where else can I go? It's my home.'

'You could stay in France—with me.' He glanced at my face to see how I took the casual invitation. I didn't know if he could tell, but my heart was thumping: was this the declaration I had been expecting? I was suddenly no longer sure I wanted to hear it. 'Every court needs a queen,' he concluded.

'You have plenty of candidates,' I said, trying to turn the remark light-heartedly. 'Annette, Marie— either of them would make a worthy companion. If I were you I'd choose Marie—she's a natural leader.'

'True.' He sucked on his pipe stem.

'And I'd be a burden: you'd have to get me out of difficulties all the time.'

'Yes, you would be trouble: I'm sure of that. Perhaps that's why I'm asking you to stay.'

This seemed less than wholehearted. I needed more.

'I don't know, J-F. I'm hardly welcome in Paris at the moment—I can't really stay, can I?'

J-F paused. 'I suppose not.'

Having wanted him to agree and endorse my decision to go, I now felt annoyed that he had. Did he not care enough to make more fuss about my imminent departure? Or did he just feel too much and not want to risk revealing it: a display of weakness was fatal to someone in his position. He'd probably forgotten how to show anyone he needed them.

My confusion made my next words too brisk. 'Well, in that case, I'd better get myself back home where I'll be no trouble.'

J-F shook his head. 'I can't believe that.'

'Can't believe what?'

'You—no trouble. It follows you like a tail does a cat.'

I had to laugh: he was right, of course. I wasn't leaving trouble behind but heading right into a new storm involving Billy Shepherd, some stolen stories and a playhouse reduced to rubble. I didn't relish the thought of facing *that* alone.

'Why don't you come with me, J-F? Come and see London for yourself.'

He sat down beside me and put his arm around my shoulders. 'I can't. I'd be a fish out of water. You wouldn't like me any more if you saw me like that.'

'Who says I like you now?' I prodded him in the ribs. 'You told the bishop I meant nothing to you: you see, I haven't forgotten.'

'I wish you would.'

Silence fell between us: it was a moment that could have gone in any direction—to a kiss, to a joke, to an argument even. It was J-F who broke the spell, turning to practical matters.

'There's no need to worry, Cat: I promise I'll get you home even if I do have to pass up the chance to see your city. I have a useful contact who should be able to get you into England—and he'll do so without alerting our authorities to your regrettable desire to quit these shores.'

Once again, I felt disappointed that J-F hadn't tried harder to persuade me to stay—but part of me was also relieved. I attempted to match his practical turn of mind. 'Oh yes? What kind of contact?'

'A privateer. I help him—how shall we say?— distribute his wares.'

'A smuggler!'

'Why so shocked? I'm hardly likely to know the

town priest, am I?'

'No, I suppose not. But is he to be trusted?'

'If you were on your own, not a bit—you'd end up in the white slave trade in the Levant—but with me of course!'

'And where do we meet this charming individual?'

'I've sent a message ahead. If he's in port, he'll wait for us at a certain house we both know.'

'You're sure about this plan, are you?'

'Sure? On my mother's honour.'

Not having met his mother, I wasn't sure if this was a reassuring pledge. How virtuous were mermaids? In any case, I was sorry to bid farewell to my quiet berth on the barge which had given us the chance to linger in this period of indecision. Now I was to commit myself to depart, swapping the gentle waters of the Seine for an uncertain welcome on board a smuggler's vessel.

*   *   *

'I should warn you,' I muttered to J-F as we made our way through the grimy backstreets of Le Havre, 'I'm a truly terrible sailor.'

'At least your misery will be brief. The *Medici* is the fastest little vessel in the business,' he said with a complete lack of sympathy.

J-F pushed open the door of a low looking tavern. The air was full of smoke. Guttural voices argued in the fog. Dice rattled on the table as coins changed hands. Undeterred, J-F made his way to the bar. Heads turned. I felt all eyes examine us, doubtless gauging the depth of our purse and the depravity of our characters. Rather unflatteringly,

259

we passed the inspection and no one tried to interfere with us.

J-F rapped on the bar with a coin.

'Yes, sweetheart?' asked the barmaid, her false curls jiggling with a life of their own as she swung round to greet us.

'Mademoiselle, is Monsieur Bonaventure within?' He left the coin on the counter.

The barmaid's eyes flicked down to it and it disappeared into her pocket with admirable swiftness. 'Your luck's in, darling. He's through there.' She jerked her head to the back room. 'Says he's waiting for a big man from Paris but you might be able to catch a few minutes with him.'

J-F smiled to himself as we headed through the door.

'Big man? Have you and he ever actually met?' I whispered, feeling slightly panicky.

J-F shook his head. 'Not until today.'

I followed him anxiously into the dark inner chamber. A man sat in the corner by the fire, feet up on a stool, hat pulled over his eyes. A pipe glowed in his fingers.

'We meet at last,' said J-F, knocking the hat off the man's head familiarly. 'How's business?'

The man jumped to his feet, fists clenched, glaring at us in fury. He had a shock of white-blonde hair tied back in a scarlet ribbon and a dark blue silk jacket. Dressed like this, I guessed business wasn't treating him so bad.

'Who the hell are you?' he growled.

J-F bowed. 'Jean-François Thiland, king of the thieves of the Palais Royal, at your service.'

The man rubbed his eyes. 'Is this a joke?'

J-F looked offended. 'What proof do you require,

260

monsieur? You and I have dealt through intermediaries on numerous occasions. Do I need to remind you of that cargo of porcelain that I helped you shift last month? Or the Spanish wine that mysteriously fell in your path only twelve days ago?'

Our sea captain shook his head, half in disbelief. 'It is you, you devil! Pleased to meet you. I'd heard you were young but . . . well, enough said.' He seized J-F's hand and pumped it up and down. 'Take a seat—have some refreshment! Madeleine! Madeleine! Bring my guests some supper!' Monsieur Bonaventure now turned to me. 'And who is this young lady?'

J-F took a seat on the stool. 'The package I mentioned in my message. She needs to return to her native land without the involvement of our beloved authorities.'

'Mademoiselle, I am honoured to be of service.' Bonaventure motioned me to a chair.

'Thank you, monsieur.'

I watched from the shadows as J-F and Bonaventure discussed their mutual business interests over a bowl of soup, washed down with harsh red wine. The privateer drank deeply; J-F barely touched the stuff. I was glad, because I had rapidly decided that Bonaventure was totally unreliable. I noticed that his eyes slid to me from time to time as he tried to work out who I was and why J-F was going to the considerable bother of helping me escape France.

'Mademoiselle, you are very quiet,' Bonaventure said after a lull in the conversation.

'I have nothing to say, monsieur.'

'What?' he chuckled. 'I can't believe that! You

261

look a lively one—those green eyes of yours don't miss a trick, I'll wager. Don't think I haven't noticed you watching me all evening. I imagine there's all sorts of thoughts swirling around in that pretty head of yours—few of them flattering to me.'

'You may be right, monsieur.'

'I know damn well I'm right.' He leant closer to J-F. 'She's trouble this one, isn't she? Too sharp for her own good. If you want to get rid of her, I know someone who'll take her off your hands.'

J-F smiled enigmatically. 'That won't be necessary.'

'No?' He drained his wine. 'So what's to stop me handing her over and getting the reward myself?' His tone was light, but it carried an edge of a threat.

'Just the little matter of the information about your activities that I've left with a reliable contact in Paris,' said J-F with matching levity. 'If I don't send word that all's well, this person is instructed to cast unwelcome light on your—how can I put it?—less than legitimate business dealings.'

Bonaventure gave a false laugh. 'That's good. Just testing, just testing. Right then, now we understand each other, let's get under way.'

J-F and Bonaventure drained their tankards and we set off for the port. The *Medici* was moored at the furthest point from the custom house, looking as inconspicuous as possible behind a smart sloop. In contrast to her neighbour, the ship was in a sorry state, paint peeling and the figurehead worn to an anonymous blank—nothing to catch the eye or make her stand out as worthy of closer inspection, just as Bonaventure wanted, no doubt.

The crew of the *Medici* lived up to my expectations. It looked as though Bonaventure had trawled the taverns in the most disreputable ports of the

262

world and netted a crew of all nations. A one-eyed Chinaman showed me to my cabin, taking me past a silent African manning the wheel with surly ill-humour. Only J-F's confidence persuaded me to place our fate in the hands of this captain.

'How far are you coming with me?' I asked J-F as the vessel slipped its moorings.

'Until I see you safely home. Captain Bonaventure is a man of many talents but honesty is not one of them.'

I tried to ignore the feeling of nausea that gripped me as soon as we left the protection of the harbour.

'I won't forget what you've done for me, J-F.'

'And nor shall I. Some day, you might be able to return me the favour. Now tell me more about this Billy Shepherd you mentioned: he sounds like someone I might be able to do business with.'

* * *

Our crossing was mercifully smooth. We headed west to confuse any pursuit before turning for England. Unlike the interminable first passage, it seemed no time at all before we saw the white cliffs of Dover glimmering rosy-white in the light of the rising sun. J-F stood beside me as we watched them grow closer.

'Our captain wishes to put you ashore by rowing boat to avoid the . . . er . . . formalities of docking in the harbour. He says he knows a quiet cove not far from Dover.'

'I bet he does.'

'This is also as far as I go. I have a kingdom to rule and I know all too well the dangers of leaving it

263

for too long—after all, that's how *I* took over from the last king. Grandfather will be keeping an eye but still, there's always someone wanting to fill my shoes.'

I knew I had a last chance to change my mind, to risk a new life in France, but my instinct was telling me that this was the parting of the ways—for now, at least.

'Thanks, J-F, for everything.' I kissed him French-style on the cheeks in farewell.

He bowed over my hand, English-style. 'So you really are going back?' He sounded genuinely regretful.

I nodded.

'In that case, mademoiselle, it has been a pleasure.' He paused, then, making up his mind, pulled something from his pocket. 'Here: I have a little souvenir for you. From what you tell me of your predicament, you may find it useful. I got it thanks to you, so it's yours really.'

He put in my hand a hard object wrapped in a silk handkerchief.

'What is it?'

'Open it and see, you silly goose.'

I took off the cloth and saw a diamond-encrusted letter opener, engraved with the crest of the French royal family.

'I liberated it from the king's bedroom the day I was following you. I thought, as a letter writer, you might appreciate it.'

I was almost speechless. 'J-F, you know what you've given me, don't you?'

He nodded. 'Yes, the key to your ball and chain. I hope you enjoy the moment of your freedom, Cat. I'm just sorry I won't be there to see it.'

SCENE 2—A PROMISE KEPT

Frank returned with his parents to London some days after my own arrival home. He reported that Johnny and Lizzie had been married at the beginning of August, while J-F and I were sailing down the Seine, and then had been safely escorted on board a vessel bound for America. I was sad to have missed the wedding; it had been a quiet affair as they wished, performed by the English chaplain to the Embassy. I could imagine some of it: Johnny immensely proud, Lizzie still pale from her illness but steady-voiced as she said her vows. There had been no bridesmaids—Lizzie had said she wanted no one else but me and, as I was not available, she was not going to settle for second best.

'Did she really say that?' I asked Frank again as we sat in his carriage rattling through London one morning in early September.

'Yes she did, Cat.' Frank smiled at my desire to hear his sister's words again. 'No one else would do.'

'She needn't have done that.'

'No, she need not, but that was what she really felt. Johnny backed her to the hilt despite Papa's attempts to persuade her otherwise.'

I gave a smile of satisfaction which only faded as we approached our destination.

'Are you sure you don't want me to come in with you?' Frank asked anxiously as the carriage drew up outside a familiar black and white doorway.

I drew on my silk gloves—a present from the duchess, as was my gown. 'No thanks, Frank. You'd better not get involved. It's best that it's just him and me.'

Frank grimaced. 'Shame. I'd like to be there.'

'I promise a full report when I emerge.' Joseph opened the door to hand me out. 'If I don't return in half an hour, send in the heavies.' Frank had thoughtfully brought along all the footmen from my temporary home in Grosvenor Square to act as insurance.

Feeling apprehensive but also slightly reckless, I knocked on the front door of Billy Shepherd's house.

'Yes?' enquired the butler.

'Is your master within?'

'Who shall I say is calling?'

'Catherine Royal.'

The butler bowed me into the hallway. Standing on the chequered tiles as my arrival was reported, I turned J-F's knife over and over in my hand, looking forward to the moment when I could put it to its intended purpose.

'Mr Shepherd awaits you above,' said the butler, showing me upstairs. I slipped the letter knife into my pocket as he ushered me into the white room I remembered from my most recent encounter with my least favourite gang leader.

'Ah, Cat! Returned from your travels, 'ave you?' Billy strode towards me, his arms open almost as if he was intending to embrace me. I stepped to one side, placing one of his fancy tables between us. He turned the gesture into a flourish of his hands, prelude to a mocking bow. 'I've missed you, but I'm glad you've not forgotten our little agreement.'

'How could I?' I noticed that the room had gathered more objets d'art in my absence, including

266

a marble statue of a goddess in the Greek style. 'I see you couldn't afford the arms then?'

He smiled. 'Yeah, I was robbed, amount I paid for that hussy and she comes short of a thing or too. But not you.' He looked at me admiringly. 'See you've fallen on your feet again, coming to me all wrapped up in silk and satin. Just the present I most wanted. So, what's it to be? I've got lots of room for a girl like you in my operations.' He flicked open a pocket notebook, checking on the state of his empire. ' 'Ow about taking over the girls in St Giles? They need a lot of watchin' to check they don't 'old back their earnings.'

'That's not for me, Billy,' I smiled sweetly.

'Now, now, Cat,' he said, wagging his finger at me. 'I can't 'ave you lazin' about the place all day. Everyone earns their keep.'

'I'm not going to do anything for you at all.'

His face clouded. 'That's not wot we agreed. And besides, it ain't 'andsome of you, seein' as 'ow I've not forgotten you while you've been away. I did over that Tweadle fellow's pad while you were out of town—put 'im out of business once and for all, I did.'

This confession momentarily diverted me from my purpose. I sat down heavily in a chair.

'You did what?'

Billy cheered up again. 'I knew you'd be grateful. Can't 'ave 'im takin' the profit from my girl, can I? 'Is shop mysteriously burnt down two weeks back. Strange 'ow fate works, eh?'

'Is he all right?' I asked weakly.

'As if you care!' snorted Billy.

'Well, I can't say I care that much, but still, I don't want no one harmed for my sake.'

'Aw, ain't you sweet.' Billy chucked me under the chin. I batted his hand away. 'Nah, 'e got out with only 'is nightgown—a bit singed but 'e'll live.' Billy's eyes sparkled at the memory. 'Ain't you even a bit grateful?'

I didn't know what to say. I wouldn't shed tears for the end of Tweadle's book emporium, but I didn't like Billy's assumption that he was master of my affairs. I now noticed that there was a pile of familiar cheap pamphlets on the window seat—Billy had made sure he got the complete set before Tweadle's went up in smoke. He saw where my eyes were directed.

'It seems there's money in your stuff. I's thinkin' that we could put together a proper book of 'em. All you need do is rewrite a few things 'ere and there. I'd pay for it to be done all fancy, gold tooled, the works, if you like.'

'Oh yes?' I was now amused. 'What exactly do you want me to rewrite?'

He took a chair opposite me. 'Well, I 'ave me public to consider. You've not always been kind in your descriptions of our past dealings.'

'You mean, like when you tried to cut my throat and when you kept Pedro locked up?'

'That's the ones. Ah, 'appy days!'

I'd had enough. 'Look, Billy, I didn't come here to bargain with you, nor to rewrite history.'

He smiled fondly at me. 'Nah, I don't s'pose you did. You've come to be asked to be let off our little arrangement, ain't you?'

'No, I have not.'

He raised an eyebrow.

'I've come to tell you I've fulfilled it to the letter. Here's a piece of the Crown jewels as asked, direct from the king's own dressing table.'

I pulled the letter opener from my pocket and threw it contemptuously on the table between us. Billy reached out and picked it up, puzzled.

'Wot's this?' He prodded the crest. 'The diamonds look real, I grant you, but I don't want any old bit of glitter: I want the genuine article. Royal or nothing.'

'And it is.' It was my turn to feel smug. 'You didn't specify which royal family you meant when you set me the task, so I picked this up in King Louis's palace a few weeks back. That's his crest. So there you have it: a piece of the *French* Crown jewels for your collection. I've kept my promise. Your hold over me ends now.' I stood up. 'Goodbye, Billy. I hope we never meet again.'

Billy's expression turned thunderous as his brain caught up with what I was telling him. His knuckles whitened as they clutched the handle of the knife. Time to make a quick exit.

'Nah, you don't, Cat.' Billy leapt to the door and held it closed. The knife wavered between us—perhaps it had not been the best choice of gift. 'You can't walk out of 'ere like this!'

'Why not?' Anger flared up inside me. Though afraid, I knew I was in the right. I'd kept my word; by the code of the street he'd have to admit it.

'Because . . . because I want you 'ere with me.' He had a strange look in his eyes, half-desperate, half-threatening.

'Sorry. I'd rather shovel horse dung for a living than stay under this roof with you. You can't keep me here against my will.'

'Oh, can't I? Who says?'

'Eleven footmen from Grosvenor Square, the

Butcher's Boys if necessary, even my old friends, the Bow Street runners, if it comes to that. Look out the window: they're all waiting for me.'

Billy ran his fingers through his hair, eyes darting to the casement.

'It's come to this, 'as it?' he said, feeling the edge of the letter opener.

I began to fear I had misjudged the situation. Was it possible he would be foolish enough to do so desperate a deed?

'Come to what, Billy?' I asked, not proud that my voice quavered.

'I always said I'd 'ave to kill you. Nasty way to go, though: so blunt.'

I took a step back. 'That's not fair.'

'You've called me many things, Cat, but I don't remember "fair" being one of them.'

'No, please!' I made a dart for the window to signal that now would be the perfect moment for the footmen to earn their livery but Billy grabbed my arm. He pulled me to him, his other hand bearing the king's knife at my throat.

I gave a sick laugh. 'I think we've been here before, haven't we?' I could feel that he, like me, was shaking. But I wasn't going to die begging for mercy—not from a lowlife like him. He was breaking every rule of our street code taking his revenge now, and he knew it. 'Go on then. Don't keep a lady waiting.' I lifted my chin and closed my eyes.

The moment of decision seemed to stretch endlessly. Then I felt nothing but heard a clatter as a knife dropped to the floor. Billy's pressure on my arm lessened as his head sank on my shoulder.

'Nah, I can't do it. You . . . you should go.' He

released his hold and I staggered away from him.

He couldn't bring himself to kill me. That shocked me more than his threats. I didn't know what to say to him.

'Billy, I—'

'Shut it, Cat. Just go.'

Not needing to be told a third time, I ran from the room, slamming the door behind me. Close to collapse, I could go no further for the moment. I grabbed on to the leering satyr for support, struggling with the gulping sobs that racked me. A minute later, I heard sounds at the door—and I was off like lightning. As I clattered down the stairs, Billy came out on to the landing.

'I'm not finished with you yet, Cat Royal!' he shouted after me.

'But I've finished with you,' I replied, standing by the street door. 'Get a life, Billy, and leave mine alone.'

EPILOGUE
PHOENIX

Grosvenor Square, London
30 September, 1791

Mon cher ami, J-F,

Today I stood in the ruins of Drury Lane and thought of you. I wish you had had a chance to see my home before the demolition men got to work. I would have liked to show you the place where Mr Garrick once held London spellbound, Mrs Siddons scared us stiff, and Mr Kemble thrilled us with his eloquence. All that is gone—what remains is just rubble and swirling dust. If the theatre is to be reborn like the Phoenix, I'd say it is at the cold ashes stage of the process. I doubt my heart will warm to the new place even when it is built. Mr Sheridan has turned my world into a wasteland so I will have to look somewhere else for a home.

You mustn't worry about me getting into more trouble. I'm not short of offers of help of a more attractive kind than that extended to me by Billy Shepherd. Your gift secured my freedom—though for a moment I thought it was also going to be the means to my end. If you do decide to do business with Shepherd (and I suppose it is useless for me to warn you against it?), watch your back.

273

My own business dealings are looking up. Mr Sheridan said that several publishers have been making discreet enquiries about my manuscripts, now recovered by his lawyer from the printer's safe. He was so pleased to see me back safe and sound without a political scandal attached to his name that he even gave me two guineas (!) for the letters I wrote that never reached him. He said it was the least he could do. Money from my famously tight-fisted patron, Mr Sheridan—what is the world coming to?

I will end here with just these few words to assure you all is well. I've two guineas in my pocket, friends, a roof over my head—and best of all, thanks to you, I'm free of Billy Shepherd. I can stay or go as I like—unlike your unfortunate monarch. Sometimes, it really is better to be one of the nobility of the gutter.

Your dance partner,
Cat Royal, daughter of the people.

Curtain falls.

CAT'S GLOSSARY

BEDFORD SQUARE—a once elegant part of town, recently gone downhill since a certain person moved in

COCKADE—a red, white and blue ribbon demonstrating support for the revolution (N.B. don't forget to wear one!)

CONCIERGE—a porter, someone in charge of a building; also the title of the person in charge of the Conciergerie prison

CONCIERGERIE—former palace, now a prison in Paris on the *Ile de la Cité*

CORPUS CHRISTI—Church holiday; it literally means 'Christ's body'

CRACKSMEN—burglars who 'crack' open a house

DAUPHIN—the French version of the Prince of Wales

DODGE—trick

EXEUNT OMNES—cue in play script for everyone to leave the stage

THE FANCY—boxing

FIACRE—French carriage

FLASH—showy

FLAT—gullible fool

FOP—a man who makes a study of being fashionable and nothing else

GADABOUT—pejorative term for someone who gets around a lot

GIVE SOMEONE THE EYE—look them up and down in an amorous way

HUSSY—woman of low reputation

IN LOCO PARENTIS—Latin for 'in place of the parent', an overused phrase in my opinion

LA FILLE MAL GARDÉE—a ballet, roughly translated as 'the badly guarded girl'

MAGSMAN—a street trickster

MANUMISSION—a slave's freedom

MINT OF MONEY—an awful lot of it

MOLL—female thief or one who associates with thieves, definitely not applicable to me

NAB—steal, catch

NOTRE DAME—twin-towered cathedral of Paris

PELISSE—cloak with sleeves

PISSING IN THE WIND—perhaps not one of my most elegant phrases but denotes something that will in the end backfire on you

POPINJAY—overdressed man aspiring to be a leader of the fashion, upstart

ROAST BEEF—French term for us English people

RUM DO—strange thing

ROOKERIES—poor area of London, also known as St Giles, best to be avoided

SAVE SOMEONE'S BACON—get someone out of trouble

SCRATCH—marked area in centre of boxing ring

THE SEASON—fashionable time of year to be in town, usually considered to be from the New Year to late Spring

SKIVVY—low status maid-of-all-work

SWEET AS A NUT—to do something completely right

TERPSICHORE—name of the Greek muse of dance

TUILERIES—Royal residence in Paris

YOUNG BLOODS—high-spirited, sporting gentlemen